T0114251

PRAISE FOR

Ann Beattie

"Beattie writes out of a wisdom and maturity that are timeless."
— *The New York Times Book Review*

"A remarkable talent."
— *Chicago Tribune*

"Beattie reminds us why she stands out among her many imitators."
— *Philadelphia Inquirer*

"Beattie evokes her characters with clarity and accuracy and creates a poignancy around them... the kind of powerful, haunting quality that we feel in *The Sun Also Rises* and *The Great Gatsby*."
— *Cleveland Plain Dealer*

"A mesmerizing, exalting, uncannily unsettling talent."

— *Washington Star*

"Ann Beattie's stories are the most perceptive since Salinger's. They are not just good writing, not just true to life; they have wonder in them and vision."
— Mary Lee Settle

"[Beattie's] ear is faultless, her eye as ruthless as a hawk's."
— *Washington Post Book World*

"A master chronicler of our life and times."
— *Newsday*

DISTORTIONS

DISTORTIONS

Ann Beattie

VINTAGE CONTEMPORARIES
VINTAGE BOOKS
A DIVISION OF RANDOM HOUSE, INC.
NEW YORK

All rights reserved under International and Pan-American Copyright
Conventions. Published in the United States by Vintage Books,
a division of Random House, Inc., New York, and distributed in Canada
by Random House of Canada Limited, Toronto. Originally published
in hardcover by Doubleday & Company, Inc., in 1976.

Grateful acknowledgment is made for the use of random lines of lyrics
from the following copyrighted material:
Promopub B.V.: "Angie," words and music by Mick Jagger and Keith
Richard. Copyright © 1973 Promopub B.V. Reprinted by permission.
Warner Bros. Music: "Just Like Tom Thumb's Blues" by Bob Dylan.
Copyright © 1965 Warner Bros. Inc. All Rights Reserved.
Used by permission.

The following stories appeared originally in *The New Yorker:*
"A Platonic Relationship," "Fancy Flights," and "Wolf Dreams,"
copyright © 1974 by The New Yorker Magazine, Inc.; "Dwarf House,"
"Snakes' Shoes," "Vermont," "Downhill," and "Wanda's,"
copyright © 1975 by The New Yorker Magzine, Inc.

Other stories in this book have been published as follows:
"Eric Clapton's Lover," in *The Virginia Quarterly Review*; "It's Just
Another Day in Big Bear City, California," in *Transatlantic Review*;
"Imagined Scenes," in *The Texas Quarterly*; "Victor Blue," in
The Atlantic Monthly, copyright © 1973 by The Atlantic Monthly
Company; and "Four Stories About Lovers," in *Bitches and Sad Ladies*,
Edited by Pat Rotter, Published by Harper's Magazine Press.

Library of Congress Cataloging-in-Publication Data
Beattie, Ann.
Distortions/Ann Beattie. —
p. cm. —(Vintage contemporaries)
ISBN 978-0-679-73235-8
I. Title.
[PS3552.E177D57 1991]
813'.54—dc20   90-39020
CIP

Manufactured in the United States of America
BVG   01

145038997

To David

CONTENTS

DISTORTIONS

Dwarf House

▪▪▪▪▪▪▪▪▪▪▪▪▪▪▪▪▪▪▪▪▪▪▪▪▪▪▪

■■■■■■■■■■■■■■■■■■■■■

"Are you happy?" MacDonald says. "Because if you're happy I'll leave you alone."

MacDonald is sitting in a small gray chair, patterned with grayer leaves, talking to his brother, who is standing in a blue chair. MacDonald's brother is four feet, six and three-quarter inches tall, and when he stands in a chair he can look down on MacDonald. MacDonald is twenty-eight years old. His brother, James, is thirty-eight. There was a brother between them, Clem, who died of a rare disease in Panama. There was a sister also, Amy, who flew to Panama to be with her dying brother. She died in the same hospital, one month later, of the same disease. None of the family went to the funeral. Today MacDonald, at his mother's request, is visiting James to find out if he is happy. Of course James is not, but standing on the chair helps, and the twenty-dollar bill that MacDonald slipped into his tiny hand helps too.

"What do you want to live in a dwarf house for?"

"There's a giant here."

"Well it must just depress the hell out of the giant."

"He's pretty happy."

"Are you?"

"I'm as happy as the giant."

"What do you do all day?"

"Use up the family's money."

"You know I'm not here to accuse you. I'm here to see what I can do."

"She sent you again, didn't she?"

"Yes."

"Is this your lunch hour?"

"Yes."

"Have you eaten? I've got some candy bars in my room."

"Thank you. I'm not hungry."

"Place make you lose your appetite?"

"I do feel nervous. Do you like living here?"

"I like it better than the giant does. He's lost twenty-five pounds. Nobody's supposed to know about that—the official word is fifteen—but I overheard the doctors talking. He's lost twenty-five pounds."

"Is the food bad?"

"Sure. Why else would he lose twenty-five pounds?"

"Do you mind . . . if we don't talk about the giant right now? I'd like to take back some reassurance to Mother."

"Tell her I'm as happy as she is."

"You know she's not happy."

"She knows I'm not, too. Why does she keep sending you?"

"She's concerned about you. She'd like you to live at home. She'd come herself . . ."

"I know. But she gets nervous around freaks."

"I was going to say that she hasn't been going out much. She sent me, though, to see if you wouldn't reconsider."

"I'm not coming home, MacDonald."

"Well, is there anything you'd like from home?"

"They let you have pets here. I'd like a parakeet."

"A bird? Seriously?"

"Yeah. A green parakeet."

"I've never seen a green one."

"Pet stores will dye them any color you ask for."

"Isn't that harmful to them?"

"You want to please the parakeet or me?"

*

"How did it go?" MacDonald's wife asks.

"That place is a zoo. Well, it's worse than a zoo—it's what it is: a dwarf house."

"Is he happy?"

"I don't know. I didn't really get an answer out of him. There's a giant there who's starving to death, and he says he's happier than the giant. Or maybe he said he was as happy. I can't remember. Have we run out of vermouth?"

"Yes. I forgot to go to the liquor store. I'm sorry."

"That's all right. I don't think a drink would have much effect anyway."

"It might. If I had remembered to go to the liquor store."

"I'm just going to call Mother and get it over with."

"What's that in your pocket?"

"Candy bars. James gave them to me. He felt sorry for me because I'd given up my lunch hour to visit him."

"Your brother is really a very nice person."

"Yeah. He's a dwarf."

"What?"

"I mean that I think of him primarily as a dwarf. I've had to take care of him all my life."

"Your mother took care of him until he moved out of the house."

"Yeah, well it looks like he found a replacement for her. But you might need a drink before I tell you about it."

"Oh, tell me."

"He's got a little sweetie. He's in love with a woman who lives in the dwarf house. He introduced me. She's three feet eleven. She stood there smiling at my knees."

"That's wonderful that he has a friend."

"Not a friend—a fiancée. He claims that as soon as he's got enough money saved up he's going to marry this other dwarf."

"He is?"

"Isn't there some liquor store that delivers? I've seen liquor trucks in this neighborhood, I think."

*

His mother lives in a high-ceilinged old house on Newfield Street, in a neighborhood that is gradually being taken over by Puerto Ricans. Her phone has been busy for almost two hours, and MacDonald fears that she, too, may have been taken over by Puerto Ricans. He drives to his mother's house and knocks on the door. It is opened by a Puerto Rican woman, Mrs. Esposito.

"Is my mother all right?" he asks.

"Yes. She's okay."

"May I come in?"

"Oh, I'm sorry."

She steps aside—not that it does much good, because she's so wide that there's still not much room for passage. Mrs. Esposito is wearing a dress that looks like a jungle: tall streaks of green grass going every which way, brown stumps near the hem, flashes of red around her breasts.

"Who were you talking to?" he asks his mother.

"Carlotta was on the phone with her brother, seeing if he'll take her in. Her husband put her out again."

Mrs. Esposito, hearing her husband spoken of, rubs her hands in anguish.

"It took two hours?" MacDonald says good-naturedly, feeling sorry for her. "What was the verdict?"

"He won't," Mrs. Esposito answers.

"I told her she could stay here, but when she told him she was going to do that he went wild and said he didn't want her living just two doors down."

"I don't think he meant it," MacDonald says. "He was probably just drinking again."

"He had joined Alcoholics Anonymous," Mrs. Esposito says. "He didn't drink for two weeks, and he went to every meeting, and one night he came home and said he wanted me out."

MacDonald sits down, nodding nervously. The chair he sits in has a child's chair facing it, which is used as a footstool. When James lived with his mother it was his chair. His mother still keeps his furniture around—a tiny child's glider, a mirror in the hall that is knee-high.

"Did you see James?" his mother asks.

"Yes. He said that he's very happy."

"I know he didn't say that. If I can't rely on you I'll have to go myself, and you know how I cry for days after I see him."

"He said he was pretty happy. He said he didn't think you were."

"Of course I'm not happy. He never calls."

"He likes the place he lives in. He's got other people to talk to now."

"Dwarfs, not people," his mother says. "He's hiding from the real world."

"He didn't have anybody but you to talk to when he lived at home. He's got a new part-time job that he likes better, too, working in a billing department."

"Sending unhappiness to people in the mail," his mother says.

"How are you doing?" he asks.

"As James says, I'm not happy."

"What can I do?" MacDonald asks.

"Go to see him tomorrow and tell him to come home."

"He won't leave. He's in love with somebody there."

"Who? Who does he say he's in love with? Not another social worker?"

"Some woman. I met her. She seems very nice."

"What's her name?"

"I don't remember."

"How tall is she?"

"She's a little shorter than James."

"Shorter than James?"

"Yes. A little shorter."

"What does she want with him?"

"He said they were in love."

"I heard you. I'm asking what she wants with him."

"I don't know. I really don't know. Is that sherry in that bottle? Do you mind . . ."

"I'll get it for you," Mrs. Esposito says.

"Well, who knows what anybody wants from anybody," his mother says. "Real love comes to naught. I loved your father and we had a dwarf."

"You shouldn't blame yourself," MacDonald says. He takes the glass of sherry from Mrs. Esposito.

"I shouldn't? I have to raise a dwarf and take care of him for thirty-eight years and then in my old age he leaves me. Who should I blame for that?"

"James," MacDonald says. "But he didn't mean to offend you."

"I should blame your father," his mother says, as if he hasn't spoken. "But he's dead. Who should I blame for his early death? God?"

His mother does not believe in God. She has not believed in God for thirty-eight years.

"I had to have a dwarf. I wanted grandchildren, and I know you won't give me any because you're afraid you'll produce a dwarf. Clem is dead, and Amy is dead. Bring me some of that sherry, too, Carlotta."

*

At five o'clock MacDonald calls his wife. "Honey," he says, "I'm going to be tied up in this meeting until seven. I should have called you before."

"That's all right," she says. "Have you eaten?"

"No. I'm in a meeting."

"We can eat when you come home."

"I think I'll grab a sandwich, though. Okay?"

"Okay. I got the parakeet."

"Good. Thank you."

"It's awful. I'll be glad to have it out of here."

"What's so awful about a parakeet?"

"I don't know. The man at the pet store gave me a ferris wheel with it, and a bell on a chain of seeds."

"Oh yeah? Free?"

"Of course. You don't think I'd buy junk like that, do you?"

"I wonder why he gave it to you."

"Oh, who knows. I got gin and vermouth today."

"Good," he says. "Fine. Talk to you later."

MacDonald takes off his tie and puts it in his pocket. At least once a week he goes to a run-down bar across town, telling his wife that he's in a meeting, putting his tie in his pocket. And once a week his wife remarks that she doesn't understand how he can get his tie wrinkled. He takes off his shoes and puts on sneakers, and takes an old brown corduroy jacket off a coat hook behind his desk. His secretary is still in her office. Usually she leaves before five, but whenever he leaves looking like a slob she seems to be there to say good-night to him.

"You wonder what's going on, don't you?" MacDonald says to his secretary.

She smiles. Her name is Betty, and she must be in her early thirties. All he really knows about his secretary is that she smiles a lot and that her name is Betty.

"Want to come along for some excitement?" he says.

"Where are you going?"

"I knew you were curious," he says.

Betty smiles.

"Want to come?" he says. "Like to see a little low life?"

"Sure," she says.

They go out to his car, a red Toyota. He hangs his jacket in the back and puts his shoes on the back seat.

"We're going to see a Japanese woman who beats people with figurines," he says.

Betty smiles. "Where are we really going?" she asks.

"You must know that businessmen are basically depraved," MacDonald says. "Don't you assume that I commit bizarre acts after hours?"

"No," Betty says.

"How old are you?" he asks.

"Thirty," she says.

"You're thirty years old and you're not a cynic yet?"

"How old are you?" she asks.

"Twenty-eight," MacDonald says.

"When you're thirty you'll be an optimist all the time," Betty says.

"What makes you optimistic?" he asks.

"I was just kidding. Actually, if I didn't take two kinds of pills, I couldn't smile every morning and evening for you. Remember the day I fell asleep at my desk? The day before I had had an abortion."

MacDonald's stomach feels strange—he wouldn't mind having a couple kinds of pills himself, to get rid of the strange feeling. Betty lights a cigarette, and the smoke doesn't help his stomach. But he had the strange feeling all day, even before Betty spoke. Maybe he has stomach cancer. Maybe he doesn't want to face James again. In the glove compartment there is a jar that Mrs. Esposito gave his mother and that his mother gave him to take to James. One of Mrs. Esposito's relatives sent it to her, at her request. It was made by a doctor in Puerto Rico. Supposedly, it can increase your height if rubbed regularly on the soles of the feet. He feels nervous, knowing that it's in the glove compartment. The way his wife must feel having the parakeet and the ferris wheel sitting around the house. The house. His wife. Betty.

They park in front of a bar with a blue neon sign in the window that says IDEAL CAFÉ. There is a larger neon sign above that that says SCHLITZ. He and Betty sit in a back booth. He orders a pitcher of beer and a double order of spiced shrimp. Tammy Wynette is singing "D-I-V-O-R-C-E" on the jukebox.

"Isn't this place awful?" he says. "But the spiced shrimp are great."

Betty smiles.

"If you don't feel like smiling, don't smile," he says.

"Then all the pills would be for nothing."

"Everything is for nothing," he says.

"If you weren't drinking you could take one of the pills," Betty says. "Then you wouldn't feel that way."

*

"Did you see *Esquire?*" James asks.

"No," MacDonald says. "Why?"

"Wait here," James says.

MacDonald waits. A dwarf comes into the room and looks under his chair. MacDonald raises his feet.

"Excuse me," the dwarf says. He turns cartwheels to leave the room.

"He used to be with the circus," James says, returning. "He leads us in exercises now."

MacDonald looks at *Esquire*. There has been a convention of dwarfs at the Oakland Hilton, and *Esquire* got pictures of it. Two male dwarfs are leading a delighted female dwarf down a runway. A baseball team of dwarfs. A group picture. Someone named Larry—MacDonald does not look back up at the picture to see which one he is—says, "I haven't had so much fun since I was born." MacDonald turns another page. An article on Daniel Ellsberg.

"Huh," MacDonald says.

"How come *Esquire* didn't know about our dwarf house?" James asks. "They could have come here."

"Listen," MacDonald says, "Mother asked me to bring this to you. I don't mean to insult you, but she made me promise I'd deliver it. You know she's very worried about you."

"What is it?" James asks.

MacDonald gives him the piece of paper that Mrs. Esposito wrote instructions on in English.

"Take it back," James says.

"No. Then I'll have to tell her you refused it."

"Tell her."

"No. She's miserable. I know it's crazy, but just keep it for her sake."

James turns and throws the jar. Bright yellow liquid runs down the wall.

"Tell her not to send you back here either," James says. Mac-

Donald thinks that if James were his size he would have hit him instead of only speaking.

"Come back and hit me if you want," MacDonald hollers. "Stand on the arm of this chair and hit me in the face."

James does not come back. A dwarf in the hallway says to Mac-Donald, as he is leaving, "It was a good idea to be sarcastic to him."

*

MacDonald and his wife and mother and Mrs. Esposito stand amid a cluster of dwarfs and one giant waiting for the wedding to begin. James and his bride are being married on the lawn outside the church. They are still inside with the minister. His mother is already weeping. "I wish I had never married your father," she says, and borrows Mrs. Esposito's handkerchief to dry her eyes. Mrs. Esposito is wearing her jungle dress again. On the way over she told MacDonald's wife that her husband had locked her out of the house and that she only had one dress. "It's lucky it was such a pretty one," his wife said, and Mrs. Esposito shyly protested that it wasn't very fancy, though.

The minister and James and his bride come out of the church onto the lawn. The minister is a hippie, or something like a hippie: a tall, white-faced man with stringy blond hair and black motorcycle boots. "Friends," the minister says, "before the happy marriage of these two people, we will release this bird from its cage, symbolic of the new freedom of marriage, and of the ascension of the spirit."

The minister is holding the cage with the parakeet in it.

"MacDonald," his wife whispers, "that's the parakeet. You can't release a pet into the wild."

His mother disapproves of all this. Perhaps her tears are partly disapproval, and not all hatred of his father.

The bird is released: it flies shakily into a tree and disappears into the new spring foliage.

The dwarfs clap and cheer. The minister wraps his arms around himself and spins. In a second the wedding ceremony begins, and just a few minutes later it is over. James kisses the bride, and the dwarfs swarm around them. MacDonald thinks of a piece of

Hershey bar he dropped in the woods once on a camping trip, and how the ants were all over it before he finished lacing his boot. He and his wife step forward, followed by his mother and Mrs. Esposito. MacDonald sees that the bride is smiling beautifully—a smile no pills could produce—and that the sun is shining on her hair so that it sparkles. She looks small, and bright, and so lovely that MacDonald, on his knees to kiss her, doesn't want to get up.

Snakes' Shoes

■■■■■■■■■■■■■■■■■■■■■■■

The little girl sat between her Uncle Sam's legs. Alice and Richard, her parents, sat next to them. They were divorced, and Alice had remarried. She was holding a ten-month-old baby. It had been Sam's idea that they all get together again, and now they were sitting on a big flat rock not far out into the pond.

"Look," the little girl said.

They turned and saw a very small snake coming out of a crack between two rocks on the shore.

"It's nothing," Richard said.

"It's a snake," Alice said. "You have to be careful of them. Never touch them."

"Excuse me," Richard said. "Always be careful of everything."

That was what the little girl wanted to hear, because she didn't like the way the snake looked.

"You know what snakes do?" Sam asked her.

"What?" she said.

"They can tuck their tail into their mouth and turn into a hoop."

"Why do they do that?" she asked.

"So they can roll down hills easily."

"Why don't they just walk?"

"They don't have feet. See?" Sam said.

The snake was still; it must have sensed their presence.

"Tell her the truth now," Alice said to Sam.

The little girl looked at her uncle.

"They have feet, but they shed them in the summer," Sam said. "If you ever see tiny shoes in the woods, they belong to the snakes."

"Tell her the truth," Alice said again.

"Imagination is better than reality," Sam said to the little girl.

The little girl patted the baby. She loved all the people who were sitting on the rock. Everybody was happy, except that in the back of their minds the grownups thought that their being together again was bizarre. Alice's husband had gone to Germany to look after his father, who was ill. When Sam learned about this, he called Richard, who was his brother. Richard did not think that it was a good idea for the three of them to get together again. Sam called the next day, and Richard told him to stop asking about it. But when Sam called again that night, Richard said sure, what the hell.

They sat on the rock looking at the pond. Earlier in the afternoon a game warden had come by and he let the little girl look at the crows in the trees through his binoculars. She was impressed. Now she said that she wanted a crow.

"I've got a good story about crows," Sam said to her. "I know how they got their name. You see, they all used to be sparrows, and they annoyed the king, so he ordered one of his servants to kill them. The servant didn't want to kill all the sparrows, so he went outside and looked at them and prayed, 'Grow. Grow.' And miraculously they did. The king could never kill anything as big and as grand as a crow, so the king and the birds and the servant were all happy."

"But why are they called crows?" the little girl said.

"Well," Sam said, "long, long ago, a historical linguist heard the story, but he misunderstood what he was told and thought that the servant had said 'crow,' instead of 'grow.' "

"Tell her the truth," Alice said.

"That's the truth," Sam said. "A lot of our vocabulary is twisted around."

"Is that true?" the little girl asked her father.

"Don't ask me," he said.

Back when Richard and Alice were engaged, Sam had tried to talk Richard out of it. He told him that he would be tied down; he said that if Richard hadn't got used to regimentation in the Air Force he wouldn't even consider marriage at twenty-four. He was so convinced that it was a bad idea that he cornered Alice at the engagement party (there were heart-shaped boxes of heart-shaped mints wrapped in paper printed with hearts for everybody to take home) and asked her to back down. At first Alice thought this was amusing. "You make me sound like a vicious dog," she said to Sam. "It's not going to work out," Sam said. "Don't do it." He showed her the little heart he was holding. "Look at these God-damned things," he said.

"They weren't my idea. They were your mother's," Alice said. She walked away. Sam watched her go. She had on a lacy beige dress. Her shoes sparkled. She was very pretty. He wished she would not marry his brother, who had been kicked around all his life—first by their mother, then by the Air Force ("Think of me as you fly into the blue," their mother had written Richard once. Christ!)—and now would be watched over by a wife.

The summer Richard and Alice married, they invited Sam to spend his vacation with them. It was nice that Alice didn't hold grudges. She also didn't hold a grudge against her husband, who burned a hole in an armchair and who tore the mainsail on their sailboat beyond repair by going out on the lake in a storm. She was a very patient woman. Sam found that he liked her. He liked the way she worried about Richard out in a boat in the middle of the storm. After that, Sam spent part of every summer vacation with them, and went to their house every Thanksgiving. Two years ago, just when Sam was convinced that everything was perfect, Richard told him that they were getting divorced. The next day, when Sam was alone with Alice after breakfast, he asked why.

"He burns up all the furniture," she said. "He acts like a madman with that boat. He's swamped her three times this year. I've been seeing someone else."

"Who have you been seeing?"

"No one you know."

"I'm curious, Alice. I just want to know his name."

"Hans."

"Hans. Is he a German?"

"Yes."

"Are you in love with this German?"

"I'm not going to talk about it. Why are you talking to me? Why don't you go sympathize with your brother?"

"He knows about this German?"

"His name is Hans."

"That's a German name," Sam said, and he went outside to find Richard and sympathize with him.

Richard was crouching beside his daughter's flower garden. His daughter was sitting on the grass across from him, talking to her flowers.

"You haven't been bothering Alice, have you?" Richard said.

"Richard, she's seeing a God-damned German," Sam said.

"What does that have to do with anything?"

"What are you talking about?" the little girl asked.

That silenced both of them. They stared at the bright-orange flowers.

"Do you still love her?" Sam asked after his second drink.

They were in a bar, off a boardwalk. After their conversation about the German, Richard had asked Sam to go for a drive. They had driven thirty or forty miles to this bar, which neither of them had seen before and neither of them liked, although Sam was fascinated by a conversation now taking place between two blond transvestites on the bar stools to his right. He wondered if Richard knew that they weren't really women, but he hadn't been able to think of a way to work it into the conversation, and he started talking about Alice instead.

"I don't know," Richard said. "I think you were right. The Air Force, Mother, marriage—"

"They're not real women," Sam said.

"What?"

Sam thought that Richard had been staring at the two people he had been watching. A mistake on his part; Richard had just been glancing around the bar.

"Those two blondes on the bar stools. They're men."

Richard studied them. "Are you sure?" he said.

"Of course I'm sure. I live in N.Y.C., you know."

"Maybe I'll come live with you. Can I do that?"

"You always said you'd rather die than live in New York."

"Well, are you telling me to kill myself, or is it O.K. if I move in with you?"

"If you want to," Sam said. He shrugged. "There's only one bedroom, you know."

"I've been to your apartment, Sam."

"I just wanted to remind you. You don't seem to be thinking too clearly."

"You're right," Richard said. "A God-damned German."

The barmaid picked up their empty glasses and looked at them. "This gentleman's wife is in love with another man," Sam said to her.

"I overheard," she said.

"What do you think of that?" Sam asked her.

"Maybe German men aren't as creepy as American men," she said. "Do you want refills?"

After Richard moved in with Sam he began bringing animals into the apartment. He brought back a dog, a cat that stayed through the winter, and a blue parakeet that had been in a very small cage that Richard could not persuade the pet-store owner to replace. The bird flew around the apartment. The cat was wild for it, and Sam was relieved when the cat eventually disappeared. Once, Sam saw a mouse in the kitchen and assumed that it was another of Richard's pets, until he realized that there was no cage for it in the apartment. When Richard came home he said that the mouse was not his. Sam called the exterminator, who refused to come in and spray the apartment because the dog had growled at him. Sam told this to his brother, to make him feel guilty for his irresponsibility. Instead, Richard brought another cat in. He said that it would get the mouse, but not for a while yet—it was only a kitten. Richard fed it cat food off the tip of a spoon.

Richard's daughter came to visit. She loved all the animals—the big mutt that let her brush him, the cat that slept in her lap, the bird that she followed from room to room, talking to it, trying to get it to land on the back of her hand. For Christmas, she gave her father a rabbit. It was a fat white rabbit with one brown ear, and it was kept in a cage on the night table when neither Sam nor Richard was in the apartment to watch it and keep it away from the cat and the dog. Sam said that the only vicious thing Alice ever did was giving her daughter the rabbit to give Richard for Christmas. Eventually the rabbit died of a fever. It cost Sam one hundred and sixty dollars to treat the rabbit's illness; Richard did not have a job, and could not pay anything. Sam kept a book of I.O.U.s. In it he wrote, "Death of rabbit—$160 to vet." When Richard did get a job, he looked over the debt book. "Why couldn't you just have written down the sum?" he asked Sam. "Why did you want to remind me about the rabbit?" He was so upset that he missed the second morning of his new job. "That was inhuman," he said to Sam. "'Death of rabbit—$160'" that was horrible. The poor rabbit. God damn you." He couldn't get control of himself.

A few weeks later, Sam and Richard's mother died. Alice wrote to Sam, saying that she was sorry. Alice had never liked their mother, but she was fascinated by the woman. She never got over her spending a hundred and twenty-five dollars on paper lanterns for the engagement party. After all these years, she was still thinking about it. "What do you think became of the lanterns after the party?" she wrote in her letter of condolence. It was an odd letter, and it didn't seem that Alice was very happy. Sam even forgave her for the rabbit. He wrote her a long letter, saying that they should all get together. He knew a motel out in the country where they could stay, perhaps for a whole weekend. She wrote back, saying that it sounded like a good idea. The only thing that upset her about it was that his secretary had typed his letter. In her letter to Sam, she pointed out several times that he could have written in longhand. Sam noticed that both Alice and Richard seemed to be raving. Maybe they would get back together.

Now they were all staying at the same motel, in different rooms. Alice and her daughter and the baby were in one room, and Richard and Sam had rooms down the hall. The little girl spent the nights with different people. When Sam bought two pounds of fudge, she said she was going to spend the night with him. The next night, Alice's son had colic, and when Sam looked out his window he saw Richard holding the baby, walking around and around the swimming pool. Alice was asleep. Sam knew this because the little girl left her mother's room when she fell asleep and came looking for him.

"Do you want to take me to the carnival?" she asked.

She was wearing a nightgown with blue bears upside down on it, headed for a crash at the hem.

"The carnival's closed," Sam said. "It's late, you know."

"Isn't anything open?"

"Maybe the doughnut shop. That's open all night. I suppose you want to go there?"

"I love doughnuts," she said.

She rode to the doughnut shop on Sam's shoulders, wrapped in his raincoat. He kept thinking, Ten years ago I would never have believed this. But he believed it now; there was a definite weight on his shoulders, and there were two legs hanging down his chest.

The next afternoon, they sat on the rock again, wrapped in towels after a swim. In the distance, two hippies and an Irish setter, all in bandannas, rowed toward shore from an island.

"I wish I had a dog," the little girl said.

"It just makes you sad when you have to go away from them," her father said.

"I wouldn't leave it."

"You're just a kid. You get dragged all over," her father said. "Did you ever think you'd be here today?"

"It's strange," Alice said.

"It was a good idea," Sam said. "I'm always right."

"You're not always right," the little girl said.

"When have I ever been wrong?"

"You tell stories," she said.

"Your uncle is *imaginative*," Sam corrected.

"Tell me another one," she said to him.

"I can't think of one right now."

"Tell the one about the snakes' shoes."

"Your uncle was kidding about the snakes, you know," Alice said.

"I know," she said. Then she said to Sam, "Are you going to tell another one?"

"I'm not telling stories to people who don't believe them," Sam said.

"Come on," she said.

Sam looked at her. She had bony knees, and her hair was brownish-blond. It didn't lighten in the sunshine like her mother's. She was not going to be as pretty as her mother. He rested his hand on the top of her head.

The clouds were rolling quickly across the sky, and when they moved a certain way it was possible for them to see the moon, full and faint in the sky. The crows were still in the treetops. A fish jumped near the rock, and someone said, "Look," and everyone did—late, but in time to see the circles widening where it had landed.

"What did you marry Hans for?" Richard asked.

"I don't know why I married either of you," Alice said.

"Where did you tell him you were going while he was away?" Richard asked.

"To see my sister."

"How is your sister?" he asked.

She laughed. "Fine, I guess."

"What's funny?" Richard asked.

"Our conversation," she said.

Sam was helping his niece off the rock. "We'll take a walk," he said to her. "I have a long story for you, but it will bore the rest of them."

The little girl's knees stuck out. Sam felt sorry for her. He lifted her on his shoulders and cupped his hands over her knees so he wouldn't have to look at them.

"What's the story?" she said.

"One time," Sam said, "I wrote a book about your mother."

"What was it about?" the little girl asked.

"It was about a little girl who met all sorts of interesting animals—a rabbit who kept showing her his pocket watch, who was very upset because he was late—"

"I know that book," she said. "You didn't write that."

"I did write it. But at the time I was very shy, and I didn't want to admit that I'd written it, so I signed another name to it."

"You're not shy," the little girl said.

Sam continued walking, ducking whenever a branch hung low.

"Do you think there are more snakes?" she asked.

"If there are, they're harmless. They won't hurt you."

"Do they ever hide in trees?"

"No snakes are going to get you," Sam said. "Where was I?"

"You were talking about *Alice in Wonderland.*"

"Don't you think I did a good job with that book?" Sam asked.

"You're silly," she said.

It was evening—cool enough for them to wish they had more

than two towels to wrap around themselves. The little girl was sitting between her father's legs. A minute before, he had said that she was cold and they should go, but she said that she wasn't and even managed to stop shivering. Alice's son was asleep, squinting. Small black insects clustered on the water in front of the rock. It was their last night there.

"Where will we go?" Richard said.

"How about a seafood restaurant? The motel owner said he could get a babysitter."

Richard shook his head.

"No?" Alice said, disappointed.

"Yes, that would be fine," Richard said. "I was thinking more existentially."

"What does that mean?" the little girl asked.

"It's a word your father made up," Sam said.

"Don't tease her," Alice said.

"I wish I could look through that man's glasses again," the little girl said.

"Here," Sam said, making two circles with the thumb and first finger of each hand. "Look through these."

She leaned over and looked up at the trees through Sam's fingers.

"Much clearer, huh?" Sam said.

"Yes," she said. She liked this game.

"Let me see," Richard said, leaning to look through his brother's fingers.

"Don't forget me," Alice said, and she leaned across Richard to peer through the circles. As she leaned across him, Richard kissed the back of her neck.

Fancy Flights

▪▪▪▪▪▪▪▪▪▪▪▪▪▪▪▪▪▪▪▪▪▪▪

▪▪▪▪▪▪▪▪▪▪▪▪▪▪▪▪▪▪▪▪▪▪▪

Silas is afraid of the vacuum cleaner. He stands, looking out the bedroom door, growling at it. He also growls when small children are around. The dog is afraid of them, and they are afraid of him because he growls. His growling always gets him in trouble; nobody thinks he is entitled to growl. The dog is also afraid of a lot of music. "One Little Story that the Crow Told Me" by the New Lost City Ramblers raises his hackles. Bob Dylan's "Positively Fourth Street" brings bared teeth and a drooping tail. Sometimes he keeps his teeth bared even through the quiet intervals. If the dog had his way, all small children would disappear, and a lot of musicians would sound their last notes. If the dog had his way, he would get Dylan by the leg in a dark alley. Maybe they could take a trip—Michael and the dog—to a recording studio or a concert hall, wherever Dylan was playing, and wait for him to come out. Then Silas could get him. Thoughts like these ("fancy flights," his foreman called them) were responsible for Michael's no longer having a job.

He had worked in a furniture factory in Ashford, Connecticut. Sometimes when his lathe was churning and grinding, he would start laughing. Everyone was aware of his laughter, but nobody did anything about it. He smoked hash in the parking lot in back of the factory during his break. Toward the end of his shift, he often had to choke back hysteria. One night, the foreman told him a Little Moron joke that was so funny Michael almost fell down laughing. After that, several people who worked there stopped by to tell him jokes, and every time he nearly laughed himself sick. Anybody there who spoke to him made him beam, and if they told a joke, or even if they said they had "a good one," he began to laugh right away. Every day he smoked as much hash as he could stand. He wore a hairnet—everyone had to wear a hairnet, after a woman had her face yanked down to within a fraction of an inch of a blade when a machine caught her hair—and half the time he forgot to take it off after he finished work. He'd find out he was still wearing it in the morning when he woke up. He thought that was pretty funny; he might be somebody's wife, with pink curlers under the net and a cigarette dangling out of his mouth.

He had already been somebody's husband, but he and his wife

were separated. He was also separated from his daughter, but she looked so much like his wife that he thought of them as one. Toward the end, he had sometimes got confused and talked baby talk to his wife and complained about his life to his four-and-a-half-year-old daughter. His wife wrote to his grandmother about the way he was acting, and the old woman sent him a hundred dollars and told him to "buy a psychiatrist," as if they were shirts. Instead, he bought his daughter a pink plastic bunny that held a bar of soap and floated in the bath. The bunny had blue eyebrows and a blue nose and an amazed look, probably because its stomach was soap. He had bought her the bunny because he was not ungenerous, and he spent the rest on fontina cheese for his wife and hash for himself. They had a nice family gathering—his daughter nose-to-nose with the bunny, his wife eating the cheese, he smoking hash. His wife said that his smoking had killed her red-veined maranta. "How can you keep smoking something that killed a plant?" she kept asking. Actually, he was glad to see the maranta dead. It was a creepy plant. It looked as if its veins had blood in them. Smoke hadn't killed the plant, though. A curse that his friend Carlos put on it at his request did it. It died in six days: the leaves turned brown at the tips and barely unfolded in the daytime, and soon it fell over the rim of the pot, where it hung until it turned completely brown.

Plant dead, wife gone, Michael still has his dog and his grandmother, and she can be counted on for words of encouragement, mail-order delicacies, and money. Now that they are alone together, he devotes most of his time to Silas, and takes better care of him than ever before. He gives Silas Milk-Bones so that his teeth will be clean. He always has good intentions, but before he knows it he has smoked some hash and put on "One Little Story that the Crow Told Me," and there is Silas listening to the music, with his clean, white teeth bared.

Michael is living in a house that belongs to some friends named Prudence and Richard. They have gone to Manila. Michael doesn't have to pay any rent—just the heat and electricity bills. Since he never turns a light on, the bill will be small. And on nights when he smokes hash he turns the heat down to fifty-five. He does this gradually—smoke for an hour, turn it from seventy to sixty-five; smoke another hour and put it down to fifty-five. Prudence, he discovers, is interested in acupuncture. There is a picture in one of her books of a man with his face contorted with agony, with a long, thin spike in his back. No. He must be imagining that. Usually Michael doesn't look at the books that are lying around. He goes through Prudence's and Richard's bureau drawers. Richard wears size thirty-two Jockey shorts. Prudence has a little blue barrette for her hair. Michael has even unwrapped some of the food in the freezer. Fish. He thinks about defrosting it and eating it, but then he forgets. He usually eats two cans of Campbell's Vegetarian Vegetable soup for lunch and four Chunky Pecan candy bars for dinner. If he is awake in time for breakfast, he smokes hash.

One evening, the phone rings. Silas gets there first, as usual, but he can't answer it. Poor old Silas. Michael lets him out the door before he answers the phone. He notices that Ray has come calling. Ray is a female German shepherd, named by the next-door neighbor's children. Silas tries to mount Ray.

"Richard?" says the voice on the telephone.

"Yeah. Hi," Michael says.

"Is this Richard?"

"Right."

"It doesn't sound like you, Richard."

"You sound funny, too. What's new?"

"What? You really sound screwed up tonight, Richard."

"Are you in a bad mood or something?" Michael counters.

"Well, I might be surprised that we haven't talked for months, and I call and you just mutter."

"It's the connection."

"Richard, this doesn't *sound* like you."

"This is Richard's mother. I forgot to say that."

"What are you so hostile about, Richard? Are you all right?"

"Of course I am."

"O.K. This is weird. I called to find out what Prudence was going to do about California."

"She's going to go," Michael says.

"You're kidding me."

"No."

"Oh—I guess I picked the wrong time to call. Why don't I call you back tomorrow?"

"O.K.," Michael says. "Bye."

Prudence left exact directions about how to take care of her plants. Michael has it down pretty well by now, but sometimes he just splashes some water on them. These plants moderately damp, those quite damp, some every third day—what does it matter? A few have died, but a few have new leaves. Sometimes Michael feels guilty and he hovers over them, wondering what you do for a plant that is supposed to be moderately dry but is soaking wet. In addition to watering the plants, he tries to do a few other things that will be appreciated. He has rubbed some oil into Prudence's big iron frying pan and has let it sit on the stove. Once, Silas went out and rolled in cow dung and then came in and rolled on the kitchen floor, and Michael was very conscientious about washing that. The same day, he found some chalk in the kitchen cabinet and drew a hopscotch court on the floor and jumped around a little bit. Sometimes he squirts Silas with some of Prudence's Réplique, just to make Silas mad. Silas is the kind of dog who would be offended if a homosexual approached him. Michael thinks of the dog as a displaced person. He is aware that he and the dog get into a lot of clichéd situations—man with dog curled at his side, sitting by fire; dog accepts food from man's hand, licks hand when food is gone. Prudence was reluctant to let the big dog stay in the house. Silas won her over, though. Making fine use of another cliché at the time, Silas curled around her feet and beat his tail on the rug.

"Where's Richard?" Sam asks.

"Richard and Prudence went to Manila."

"Manila? Who are you?"

"I lost my job. I'm watching the house for them."

"Lost your job—"

"Yeah. I don't mind. Who wants to spend his life watching out that his machine doesn't get him?"

"Where were you working?"

"Factory."

Sam doesn't have anything else to say. He was the man on the telephone, and he would like to know why Michael pretended to be Richard on the phone, but he sort of likes Michael and sees that it was a joke.

"That was pretty funny when we talked on the phone," he says. "At least I'm glad to hear she's not in California."

"It's not a bad place," Michael says.

"She has a husband in California. She's better off with Richard."

"I see."

"What do you do here?" Sam asks. "Just watch out for burglars?"

"Water the plants. Stuff like that."

"You really got me good on the phone," Sam says.

"Yeah. Not many people have called."

"You have anything to drink here?" Sam asks.

"I drank all their liquor."

"Like to go out for a beer?" Sam asks.

"Sure."

Sam and Michael go to a bar Michael knows called Happy Jack's. It's a strange place, with "Heat Wave" on the jukebox, along with Tammy Wynette's "Too Far Gone."

"I wouldn't mind passing an evening in the sweet arms of Tammy Wynette, even if she is a redneck," Sam says.

The barmaid puts their empty beer bottles on her tray and walks away.

"She's got big legs," Michael says.

"But she's got nice soft arms," Sam says. "Like Tammy Wynette."

As they talk, Tammy is singing about love and barrooms.

"What do you do?" Michael asks Sam.

"I'm a shoe salesman."

"That doesn't sound like much fun."

"You didn't ask me what I did for fun. You asked me what my job was."

"What do you do for fun?" Michael asks.

"Listen to Tammy Wynette records," Sam says.

"You think about Tammy Wynette a lot."

"I once went out with a girl who looked like Tammy Wynette," Sam says. "She wore a nice low-cut blouse, with white ruffles, and black high-heel shoes."

Michael rubs his hand across his mouth.

"She had downy arms. You know what I mean. They weren't really hairy," Sam says.

"Excuse me," Michael says.

In the bathroom, Michael hopes that Happy Jack isn't drunk anywhere in the bar. When he gets drunk he likes to go into the bathroom and start fights. After a customer has had his face bashed in by Happy Jack, his partners usually explain to the customer that he is crazy. Today, nobody is in the bathroom except an old guy at the washbasin, who isn't washing, though. He is standing there looking in the mirror. Then he sighs deeply.

Michael returns to their table. "What do you say we go back to the house?" he says to Sam.

"Have they got any Tammy Wynette records?"

"I don't know. They might," Michael says.

"O.K.," Sam says.

"How come you wanted to be a shoe salesman?" Michael asks him in the car.

"Are you out of your mind?" Sam says. "I didn't want to be a shoe salesman."

Michael calls his wife—a mistake. Mary Anne is having trouble in the day-care center. The child wants to quit and stay home and watch television. Since Michael isn't doing anything, his wife says, maybe he could stay home while she works and let Mary Anne have her way, since her maladjustment is obviously caused by Michael's walking out on them when he *knew* the child adored him.

"You just want me to move back," Michael says. "You still like me."

"I don't like you at all. I *never* make any attempt to get in touch with you, but if you call you'll have to hear what I have to say."

"I just called to say hello, and you started in."

"Well, what did you call for, Michael?"

"I was lonesome."

"I see. You walk out on your wife and daughter, then call because you're lonesome."

"Silas ran away."

"I certainly hope he comes back, since he means so much to you."

"He does," Michael says. "I really love that dog."

"What about Mary Anne?"

"I don't know. I'd like to care, but what you just said didn't make any impression on me."

"Are you in some sensitivity group, or something?"

"No."

"Well, before you hang up, could you think about the situation for a minute and advise me about how to handle it? If I leave her at the day-care center, she has a fit and I have to leave work and get her."

"If I had a car I could go get her."

"That isn't very practical, is it? You don't have a car."

"You wouldn't have one if your father hadn't given it to you."

"That seems a bit off the subject."

"I wouldn't drive a car if I had one. I'm through with machines."

"Michael, I guess I really don't feel like talking to you tonight."

"One thing you could do would be to give her calcium. It's a natural tranquilizer."

"O.K. Thanks very much for the advice. I hope it didn't tax you too much."

"You're very sarcastic to me. How do you expect me to be understanding when all I get is sarcasm?"

"I don't really *expect* it."

"You punch words when you talk."

"Are you stoned, Michael?"

"No, I'm just lonesome. Just sitting around."

"Where are you living?"

"In a house."

"How can you afford that? Your grandmother?"

"I don't want to talk about how I live. Can we change the subject?"

"Can we hang up instead, Michael?"

"Sure," Michael says. "Good-night, baby."

Sam and Carlos are visiting Michael. Carlos's father owns a plastics plant in Bridgeport. Carlos can roll a joint in fifteen seconds, which is admirable to Michael's way of thinking. But Carlos can be a drag, too. Right now he is talking to Michael about a job Michael could have in his father's plant.

"No more factories, Carlos," Michael says. "If everybody stopped working, the machines would stop, too."

"I don't see what's so bad about it," Carlos says. "You work the machines for a few hours, then you leave with your money."

"If I ask my grandmother for money she sends it."

"But will she *keep* sending money?" Sam asks.

"You think I'm going to ask her?"

"I'll bet you wouldn't mind working someplace in the South, where the women look like Tammy Wynette."

"North, South—what's the difference?"

"What do you mean, 'What's the difference?' Women in the South must look something like Tammy Wynette, and women up North look like mill rats."

Carlos always has very powerful grass, which Michael enjoys. Carlos claims that he puts a spell on the grass to make it stronger.

"Why don't you put a curse on your father's machines?" Michael says now.

"What for?" Carlos asks.

"Why don't you change all the machines into Tammy Wynettes?" Sam asks. "Everybody would wake up in the morning and there would be a hundred Tammy Wynettes."

Sam realizes that he has smoked too much. The next step, he thinks now, is to stop smoking.

"What do you do?" Carlos asks Sam.

"I sell shoes." Sam notices that he has answered very sanely. "Before that, I was a math major at Antioch."

"Put a curse on that factory, Carlos," Michael says.

Carlos sighs. Everybody smokes his grass and pays no attention to what he says and then they want him to put curses on things all the time.

"What if I put a curse on you?" Carlos asks.

"I'm already cursed," Michael says. "That's what my grandmother says in her letters—that I was such a blessing to the family, but I myself am cursed with ill luck."

"Change me into George Jones," Sam says.

Carlos stares at them as he rolls a joint. He isn't putting a curse on them, but he is considering it. He firmly believes that he is responsible for his godfather's getting intestinal cancer. But he isn't really a magician. He would like his curses to be reliable and perfect, like a machine.

Michael's grandmother has sent him a present—five pounds of shelled pecans. A booklet included with the package says that they are "Burstin' with wholesome Southern goodness." They're the first thing he has eaten for a day and a half, so he eats a lot of them. He thinks that he is eating in too much of a hurry, and he smokes some hash to calm down. Then he eats some more pecans. He listens to Albinoni. He picks out a seed from a pouch of grass that is lying under the couch and buries it in one of Prudence's plants. He will have to remember to have Carlos say a few words over it; Carlos is just humble when he says he can't bless things. He rummages through the grass and finds another seed, plants it in another pot. They'll never grow, he thinks sadly. Albinoni always depresses him. He turns the record off and then is depressed that there is no music playing. He looks over the records, trying to decide. It is hard to decide. He lights his pipe again. Finally, he decides—not on a record but what to eat: Chunky Pecans. He has no Chunky Pecans, but he can just walk down the road to the store and buy some. He counts his change: eighty cents, including the dime he found in Prudence's underwear drawer. He can buy five Chunky Pecans for that. He feels better when he realizes he can have the Chunky Pecans and he relaxes, lighting his pipe. All his clothes are dirty, so he has begun wearing things that Richard left behind. Today he has on a black shirt that is too tight for him, with a rhinestone-studded peacock on the front. He looks at his sparkling chest and dozes off. When he awakens, he decides to go look for Silas. He sprays deodorant under his arms without taking off the shirt and walks outside, carrying his pipe. A big mistake. If the police stopped to question him and found him with that . . . He goes back to the house, puts the pipe on a table, and goes out again. Thinking about Silas being lost makes him very sad. He knows it's not a good idea to go marching around town in a peacock shirt weeping, but he can't help it. He sees an old lady walking her dog.

"Hello, little dog," he says, stopping to stroke it.

"It's female," the old woman says. The old woman has on an incredible amount of makeup; her eyes are circled with blue— bright blue under the eyes, as well as on top.

"Hello, girl," he says, stroking the dog. "She's thirteen," the old woman says. "The vet says she won't live to see fourteen."

Michael thinks of Silas, who is four.

"He's right, I know," the old woman says.

Michael walks back around the corner and sees Silas on the front lawn. Silas charges him, jumps all over him, barking and running in circles. "Where have you been?" Michael asks the dog. Silas barks. "Hello, Silas. Where have you *been?*" Michael asks. Silas squirms on his back, panting. When Michael stoops to pat him, Silas lunges, pawing the rhinestone-studded shirt and breaking the threads. Rhinestones fall all over the lawn.

Inside, Silas sniffs the rug, runs in and out of rooms. "You old dog," Michael says. He feeds Silas a pecan. Panting, Silas curls up at his feet. Michael pulls the pouch of grass out from under the couch and stuffs a big wad in his pipe. "Good old Silas," Michael says, lighting his pipe. He gets happier and happier as he smokes, but at the height of his happiness he falls asleep. He sleeps until Silas's barking awakens him. Someone is at the door. His wife is standing there.

"Hello, Elsa," he says. She can't possibly hear him above Silas's barking. Michael leads the barking dog into the bedroom and closes the door. He walks back to the door. Elsa has come into the house and shut the door behind her.

"Hi, Elsa," he says.

"Hi. I've come for you."

"What do you mean?"

"May I come in? Is this your house? This can't be your house. Where did you get all the furniture?"

"I'm staying here while some friends are out of town."

"Did you break into somebody's house?"

"I'm watching the place for my friends."

"What's the matter with you? You look horrible."

"I'm not too clean. I forgot to take a shower."

"I don't mean that. I mean your face. What's wrong with you?"

"How did you find me?"

"Carlos."

"Carlos wouldn't talk."

"He did, Michael. But let's argue at home. I've come to get you and make you come home and share the responsibility for Mary Anne."

"I don't want to come home."

"I don't care. If you don't come home, we'll move in here."

"Silas will kill you."

"I know the dog doesn't like me, but he certainly won't kill me."

"I'm supposed to watch these people's house."

"You can come back and check on it."

"I don't want to come with you."

"You look sick, Michael. Have you been sick?"

"I'm not leaving with you, Elsa."

"O.K. We'll come back."

"What do you want me back for?"

"To help me take care of that child. She drives me crazy. Get the dog and come on."

Michael lets Silas out of the bedroom. He picks up his bag of grass and his pipe and what's left of the bag of pecans, and follows Elsa to the door.

"Pecans?" Elsa asks.

"My grandmother sent them to me."

"Isn't that nice. You don't look well, Michael. Do you have a job?"

"No. I don't have a job."

"Carlos can get you a job, you know."

"I'm not working in any factory."

"I'm not asking you to work right away. I just want you in the house during the day with Mary Anne."

"I don't want to hang around with her."

"Well, you can fake it. She's your daughter."

"I know. That doesn't make any impression on me."

"I realize that."

"Maybe she isn't mine," Michael says.

"Do you want to drive, or shall I?" Elsa asks.

Elsa drives. She turns on the radio.

"If you don't love me, why do you want me back?" Michael asks.

"Why do you keep talking about love? I explained to you that I couldn't take care of that child alone any more."

"You want me back because you love me. Mary Anne isn't that much trouble to you."

"I don't care what you think as long as you're there."

"I can just walk out again, you know."

"You've only walked out twice in seven years."

"The next time, I won't get in touch with Carlos."

"Carlos was trying to help."

"Carlos is evil. He goes around putting curses on things."

"Well, he's your friend, not mine."

"Then why did he talk?"

"I asked him where you were."

"I was on the verge of picking up a barmaid," Michael says.

"I don't know how I could help loving you," Elsa says.

"Where are we going, Daddy?"

"To water plants."

"Where are the plants?"

"Not far from here."

"Where's Mommy?"

"Getting her hair cut. She told you that."

"Why does she want her hair cut?"

"I can't figure her out. I don't understand your mother."

Elsa has gone with a friend to get her hair done. Michael has the car. He is tired of being cooped up watching daytime television with Mary Anne, so he's going to Prudence and Richard's even though he just watered the plants yesterday. Silas is with them, in the back seat. Michael looks at him lovingly in the rearview mirror.

"Where are we going?"

"We just started the ride. Try to enjoy it."

Mary Anne must have heard Elsa tell him not to take the car; she doesn't seem to be enjoying herself.

"What time is it?" Mary Anne asks.

"Three o'clock."

"That's what time school lets out."

"What about it?" Michael asks.

He shouldn't have snapped at her. She was just talking to talk. Since all talk is just a lot of garbage anyway, he shouldn't have discouraged her. He reaches over and pats her knee. She doesn't smile, as he hoped she would. She is sort of like her mother.

"Are you going to get a haircut, too?" she asks.

"Daddy doesn't have to get a haircut, because he isn't trying to get a job."

Mary Anne looks out the window.

"Your great-grandma sends Daddy enough money for him to stay alive. Daddy doesn't want to work."

"Mommy has a job," Mary Anne says. His wife is an apprentice bookbinder.

"And you don't have to get your hair cut, either," he says.

"I want it cut."

He reaches over to pat her knee again. "Don't you want long hair, like Daddy?"

"Yes," she says.

"You just said you wanted it cut."

Mary Anne looks out the window.

"Can you see all the plants through that window?" Michael says, pulling up in front of the house.

He is surprised when he opens the door to see Richard there.

"Richard! What are you doing here?"

"I'm so sick from the plane that I can't talk, man. Sit down. Who's this?"

"Did you and Prudence have a good time?"

"Prudence is still in Manila. She wouldn't come back. I just had enough of Manila, you know? But I don't know if the flight back was worth it. The flight back was really awful. Who's this?"

"This is my daughter, Mary Anne. I'm back with my wife now. I've been coming to water the plants."

"Jesus, am I sick," Richard says. "Do you know why I'd feel sick after I've been off the plane for half a day?"

"I want to water the plants," Mary Anne says.

"Go ahead, sweetheart," Richard says. "Jesus—all those damn plants. Manila is a jungle, did you know that? That's what she wants. She wants to be in the jungle. I don't know. I'm too sick to think."

"What can I do for you?"

"Is there any coffee?"

"I drank it all. I drank all your liquor, too."

"That's all right," Richard says. "Prudence thought you'd do worse than that. She thought you'd sell the furniture or burn the place down. She's crazy, over there in that rain jungle."

"His girlfriend is in Manila," Michael says to his daughter. "That's far away."

Mary Anne walks off to sniff a philodendron leaf.

Michael is watching a soap opera. A woman is weeping to another woman that when her gallbladder was taken out Tom was her doctor, and the nurse, who loved Tom, spread *rumors*, and
. . .

Mary Anne and a friend are pouring water out of a teapot into little plastic cups. They sip delicately.

"Daddy," Mary Anne says, "can't you make us real tea?"

"Your mother would get mad at me."

"She's not here."

"You'd tell her."

"No, we wouldn't."

"O.K. I'll make it if you promise not to drink it."

Michael goes into the kitchen. The girls are squealing delightedly and the woman on television is weeping hysterically. "Tom was in line for chief of surgery once Dr. Stan retired, but *Rita* said that he . . ."

The phone rings. "Hello?" Michael says.
"Hi," Carlos says. "Still mad?"
"Hi, Carlos," Michael says.
"Still mad?" Carlos asks.
"No."
"What have you been doing?"
"Nothing."
"That's what I figured. Interested in a job?"
"No."
"You mean you're just sitting around there all day?"
"At the moment, I'm giving a tea party."
"Sure," Carlos says. "Would you like to go out for a beer? I could come over after work."
"I don't care," Michael says.
"You sound pretty depressed."
"Why don't you cast a spell and make things better?" Michael says. "There goes the water. Maybe I'll see you later."
"You're not really drinking tea, are you?"
"Yes," Michael says. "Good-bye."
He takes the water into the living room and pours it into Mary Anne's teapot.
"Don't scald yourself," he says, "or we're both screwed."
"Where's the tea bag, Daddy?"
"Oh, yeah." He gets a tea bag from the kitchen and drops it into the pot. "You're young, you're supposed to use your imagination," he says. "But here it is."
"We need something to go with our tea, Daddy."
"You won't eat your dinner."
"Yes, I will."
He goes to the kitchen and gets a bag of M&Ms. "Don't eat too many of these," he says.
"I've got to get out of this town," the woman on television is saying. "You know I've got to go now, because of Tom's dependency on Rita."
Mary Anne carefully pours two tiny cups full of tea.
"We can drink this, can't we, Daddy?"
"I guess so. If it doesn't make you sick."
Michael looks at his daughter and her friend enjoying their tea

party. He goes into the bathroom and takes his pipe off the window ledge, closes the door and opens the window, and lights it. He sits on the bathroom floor with his legs crossed, listening to the woman weeping on television. He notices Mary Anne's bunny. Its eyebrows are raised with amazement at him. It is ridiculous to be sitting in the bathroom getting stoned while a tea party is going on and a woman shrieks in the background. "What else can I do?" he whispers to the bunny. He envies the bunny—the way it clutches the bar of soap to its chest. When he hears Elsa come in, he leaves the bathroom and goes into the hall and puts his arms around her, thinking about the bunny and the soap. Mick Jagger sings to him: "All the dreams we held so close seemed to all go up in smoke . . ."

"Elsa," he says, "what are your dreams?"

"That your dealer will die," she says.

"He won't. He's only twenty years old."

"Maybe Carlos will put a curse on him. Carlos killed his godfather, you know."

"Be serious. Tell me one real dream," Michael says.

"I told you."

Michael lets her go and walks into the living room. He looks out the window and sees Carlos's car pull up in front of the walk. He goes out and gets into Carlos's car. He stares down the street.

"Don't feel like saying hello, I take it," Carlos says.

Michael shakes his head.

"Hell," Carlos says, "I don't know what I keep coming around for you for."

Michael's mood is contagious. Carlos starts the car angrily and roars away, throwing a curse on a boxwood at the edge of the lawn.

Imagined Scenes

....

"I've unlaced my boots and I'm standing barefoot on a beach with very brown sand, ocean in front of me and mountains in the distance, and trees making a pretty green haze around them."

"Pretty," David says.

"Where would that be?"

"Greece?"

When she wakes from a dream, David is already awake. Or perhaps he only wakes when she stirs, whispers to him. He doesn't sound sleepy; he's alert, serious, as though he'd been waiting for a question. She remembers last year, the week before Christmas, when she and David had gone out separately to shop. She got back to the house first, her keys lost—or locked in the car. Before she could look for them, headlights lit up the snowy path. David jumped out of his car, excited about his purchases, reaching around her to put the key in the door. Now she expects him to wake up when she does, that they will arrive home simultaneously. But David still surprises her—at the end of summer he told her he wouldn't be working in the fall. He was going back to college to finish the work for his Ph.D.

He sits in a gray chair by the fireplace and reads; she brings coffee to the table by his chair, and he turns off the light and goes upstairs to bed when she is tired. By unspoken agreement, he has learned to like Roquefort dressing. He pokes the logs in the fireplace because the hot red coals frighten her.

"After I take orals in the spring we'll go to Greece to celebrate."

She wants to go to Spain. Couldn't the beach have been in Spain? No more questions—she should let him sleep. She shakes the thought out of her head.

"No?" he says. "We will. We'll go to Greece when I finish the orals."

The leaves of the plant look like worn velvet. The tops are purple, a shiny, fuzzy purple, and the underside is dark green. Suddenly the plant has begun to grow, sending up a narrow shoot not strong enough to support itself, so that it falls forward precariously, has to be staked. They agree it's strange that a plant should have such a spurt of growth in midwinter. David admires the plant, puts it in a window that gets the morning light and moves it into a side room late in the afternoon. Now when he waters the plant a little plant food is mixed in with the water. David is enthusiastic; he's started to feed the others to see if they'll grow. She comes home and finds him stretched by the fireplace, looking through a book about plants. Their plant isn't pictured, he tells her, but it may be mentioned in the text. She goes into the other room to look at the plant. The shoot appears to be taller. They bought the plant in a food store last winter—not very pretty then. It was in a small cracked pot, wrapped in plastic. They replanted it. In fact, David must have replanted it again.

She puts away the groceries and goes back to the living room. David is still on the rug reading the book. He's engrossed. The coffee would probably get cold if she brought it. She has to work that night. She goes upstairs to take a nap and sets the alarm. She rests, but can't fall asleep, listening to the quiet music downstairs. She pushes in the alarm button and goes back to the living room. David is in his chair, reading the book, drinking coffee.

"I spent the most terrible winter in my life in Berlin. I don't know why, but birds don't leave Berlin in the winter. They're big, strong birds. They nest in the public buildings. I think the winter just comes too suddenly in Berlin, no plans can be made. The birds turn gray, like snowbirds. I think snowbirds are gray."

The old man is looking out the window. He is her patient. His daughter and son-in-law are away for a week, and his sister stays with him in the day. She has been hired to stay with him at night. He is not very ill, but old and unsteady.

She drinks tea with him, tired because she didn't nap.

"I don't sleep well," he tells her. "I want to talk all the time. My daughter doesn't sleep either. In the day we fight, or I worry her, but at night I think she's glad to have someone to talk to."

The snowplow is passing the house, slowly, the lights blinking against the newly plowed snowpiles. The lights illuminate a snowman on the next lawn—crudely made, or perhaps it's just not lit up from the right angle. She remembers her first snowman; her mother broke off the broom handle to give her and helped push the handle through the snowman. Her mother was impetuous, al-

ways letting her stay home from school to enjoy the snow, and her
father had been surprised when he returned from work to see the
broom head on the kitchen table. "Well, we couldn't get out.
How could we go out in the snow to get anything?" her mother
had asked her father. The snowplow has passed. Except for the
wind, it is very quiet outside. In the room, the man is talking to
her. He wants to show her his postcards. She's surprised; she
hadn't realized she was being spoken to.

"Oh, not that kind of postcard. I'm an old man. Just pretty
postcards."

He has opened a night-table drawer. Inside there is a box of tissues, a comb and brush, an alarm clock. He sits on the side of the
bed, his feet not quite touching the floor, reaching into the
drawer without looking. He finds what he wants: an envelope. He
removes it and carefully pulls out the flap. He lets her look
through the postcards. There is a bird's nest full of cherubs, a picture of a lady elegantly dressed in a high, ruffled collar, curtseying
beneath a flowering tree, and one that she looks at longer than
the rest: a man in boots and a green jacket, carrying a rifle, is pictured walking down a path through the woods in the moonlight.
Stars shine in the sky and illuminate a path in front of him. Tiny
silver sparkles still adhere to the postcard. She holds it under the
lamp on the night table: the lining of his jacket is silver, the edges
of the rocks, a small area of the path. There is a caption: "Joseph
Jefferson as Rip Van Winkle." Beneath the caption is a message,
ornately written: "Not yet but soon. Pa."

"Did your father write the postcard?"

"That's just one I found in a store long ago. I could make up a
romantic story to tell you. I love to talk."

She waits, expecting the man's story. He leans back in bed, putting the envelope back in the drawer. His bedroom slippers fall to
the floor, and he puts his legs under the covers.

"People get old and they can't improve things," he says, "so
they lie all the time."

He waves his hand, dismissing something.

"I trust young people," he says. "I'd even tell you where my
money is: in the dresser drawer, in the back of a poetry book."

The snowplow has returned, driving up the other side of the

street. The lights cast patterns on the wall. He watches the shadows darken the wallpaper.

"I have real stories," he says, pointing to a photograph album on a table by the chair. "Look through and I can tell you some real stories if you want to know."

He is ready to sleep. She arranges the quilt at the bottom of the bed and starts to leave.

"The light doesn't bother me," he says, waving her toward the chair. "Look through my album. I'm old and cranky. I'm afraid for my pictures to leave the room."

It's early afternoon and no one is in the house. There are dishes on the dining-room table, records and record-album covers. There's a plate, a spoon, two bowls, three coffee cups. How many people have been here? There's no one to ask. There's some food on the counter top—things she doesn't remember buying. An apple pie. She goes into the living room and sits in a chair, looking out the window. More snow is predicted, but now the day is clear and bright, the fields shining in the sun. She goes into the kitchen again to look for the note he hasn't left. On her way to the bedroom to sleep, she looks out the window and sees David coming up the road, only a sweater and scarf on, holding a stick at his side that the dog is jumping for. On the floor by the chair the plant book is open, and several others, books he's studying for his exams. The front door is open. The dog runs into the living room, jumps on her.

"You should be asleep. You can't work at night if you're not going to sleep in the day."

"I thought I'd wait for you to come back."

"You shouldn't have waited. I could have been anywhere."

"Where would you go?"

He's chilled. His knuckles are bright pink, untying the scarf at his throat. He's putting another log on the fire, pushing the screen back into place.

"How's the old man?"

"He's no trouble. Last night I fixed his photograph album for him. Some of the pictures had come loose and I glued them in."

"You look like you need sleep."

"Looks like you've been working," she says, pointing to the books by the chair.

"I've had trouble concentrating. The snow was so beautiful last night. I took the dog out for long walks in the woods."

David is stroking the dog, who lies curled by the fire, panting in his sleep.

"Get some rest," he says, looking at his watch. "I met the people who moved in down the hill and told them I'd help put a sink in. He's very nice. Katherine and Larry Duane."

David kisses her on his way out. The dog wakes and wants to go with him, but at the front door he's told to stay. The dog whines when the door closes, then waits a minute longer before going back to the living room to sleep by the fireplace.

"It's awful. When you get old you expect things to be the same. Sometimes I think the cold air could clear my head. My neighbor is ten years younger than me and he jogs every day, even through snow."

"I'm leaving now," his sister says. She puts on a blue coat and a blue velvet cap that ties under the chin. Her hair is white and copper. She has small, dainty hands. She repeats that she's leaving and pats him on the shoulder, more to make sure he's listening than out of affection. "There are oranges in the bag on your bureau. Linus Pauling says that a sufficient intake of vitamin C will prevent colds."

"How would I get a cold? Every day is the same. I don't go out."

Her coat is buttoned, her hat tied securely. "That's like asking where dust comes from," she says, and disappears down the stairs.

"She's very good to come every day. I forget to thank her. I take it for granted. Fifteen years makes so much difference. She's able to do so much more, but her hands hurt her. She does embroidery so they don't go stiff."

He is looking through a book of Currier and Ives prints. "I suppose I'll have to eat her oranges. There'll be more from Florida when they get back."

She looks at a picture he holds up for her to see, offers to read him science-fiction stories.

"I don't think so. My sister read them this morning. I've had enough make-believe. No spaceships are coming to Earth today, only snow."

She looks at her watch to see if it's time for his medicine. Her watch isn't there. Did she forget to wear it? He asks for tea, and while the water is boiling in the kitchen she dials David, to see if the watch is on the night table. She hangs up and dials again, but there's still no answer. She looks out the window and sees that it has already begun to snow. Perhaps she lost the watch on the way in. The clasp was loose—she should have asked David to fix it. She turns off the burner and goes outside, looking quickly up and down the front walk before the snow begins to accumulate. She doesn't see it. The car? She looks, but it isn't there. She looks on the front steps and in the entranceway. No. It must be at home. She reheats the water, making tea, and carries the cup and saucer upstairs.

She puts it down quietly on the bureau. He's fallen asleep. She sits in a chair and watches the snow fall, and in a while she closes her eyes and begins imagining things: mountains, and blue, blue water, all the snow melted into water. This time the name of the country comes to her: Greece. She's been sent to Greece to find something on the beach, but she just stands there staring at the mountains in the distance, the water washing over her feet. Her feet are cold; she takes them out of the water, backing up onto the sandy beach. She's lifted her feet from the floor, waking up. She goes to the bureau and gets the tea, even though it's cold. The snow is falling heavily now. Everything is blanketed in whiteness; it clings to the trees, her car is covered with snow. She must have slept through the night. She hears his sister downstairs, closing the door behind her.

"I take her for granted," the old man says. "Like snow. Every day I expect more snow."

The plant is gone. She looks in all the rooms and can't find it. Her watch is on the bathroom sink, where she put it when she showered. She showers again and washes her hair, blows it dry. The bathroom is steamy; she can't see her face in the glass.

"David?"

She thought she heard something, but it was only a branch brushing against the bathroom window. She walks naked up to the bedroom and puts on jeans and one of David's sweaters. She notices that some of the books he's been studying have been replaced in the bookcase. Now she's sure she hears him. The dog runs into the house. The front door bangs shut.

"Hi," she calls.

"Hi." David is climbing the steps. "I'm not used to you working for a whole week. I never see you." His cheeks are so cold they sting when he kisses her. "I was down at the Duanes'. They had puppies born this morning."

"What kind?"

"Collies."

"Take me to see them," she says.

"They were going out when I left."

"We could go later in the afternoon."

"They'll think I live there," he laughs.

"It's good for you to be out. You've been working so hard."

"I haven't done any work for a couple of days."

"Yes you have. I saw pages of notes on the dining-room table."

"Larry left his notes behind. He brought them down to read me an article he's working on. He teaches at the university. Botany."

"Botany?" she says. "Is that what happened to the plant?"

"They liked it so much I gave it to them. It was such a freak thing, to grow that way in the winter."

She calls early in the morning: 4 A.M. The telephone rings, and there is no answer. The old man can tell that she's worried when he awakens.

"I tried to get my husband last night but there was no answer."

"Men are heavy sleepers."

"No," she says. "He'd wake up."

"All men are heavy sleepers. I can sleep when people are talking —I don't even hear the children talking on their way to school any more. I can sleep with the light on."

"I think school was canceled," she says, looking out the window.

It has snowed all night. It's still snowing.

"Call my sister and tell her not to come," he says. "If anything happens I can call."

She picks up the phone in the upstairs hallway and gives his sister the message, but the old lady is coming anyway. She has boots and an umbrella, and she's coming. He shakes his head.

"It's terrible to be old. You have no power."

He gets out of bed and opens a bureau drawer.

"Can I help you?"

"I'm putting on my things to go for a walk in the snow."

"You should stay inside. It's too cold today."

"I don't feel the cold any more. I can go out."

"Have breakfast first," she says.

"No. I want to go out before she comes."

She leaves the room while he dresses. He takes a long time. Maybe his sister will come early, before they go out. No. He opens the door and walks out without his cane, wearing a sweater and a silk scarf tucked into the neck.

"My jacket is in the hall closet," he says. "I need the air."

She helps him down the stairs. He doesn't weigh much. She asks if he'll take his cane, but he wants her arm instead. She gets his jacket and holds it for him to put on. She takes her own jacket out of the closet and zips it.

It's bright outside. They both stop, momentarily blinded by the glare. The snow is wet and deep.

"Just down the walk," she says.

"Yes. All right."

Children, off from school, are playing in the yards. Someone has already built a snowman. He likes it, wants a closer look. They go down the walk to the sidewalk. The children next door call hello. A little boy comes over to tell the old man about the snowman he's built. On another lawn some children are building a fort. Two little girls in snowsuits are carrying snow to the fort in buckets. She sees a big boy push a small boy into a snowbank. It's just fun. It's not just fun—he's kicking snow on him, kicking the little boy.

"Wait!" she says.

The big boy kicks snow in her face and runs. She pulls the younger boy out of the snow, brushing it out of his hair.

"What happened?" she asks him. He's crying, brushing himself and pointing to the boy who ran away at the same time. Now another boy is screaming. She turns and sees that the old man has slipped in the snow. She runs back. He's red in the face, but he's all right. He bent over to make a snowball and one of the children accidentally ran into him. She reaches down to help him up. He's light, but it's hard to get a good grip. The pavement is slippery, she's afraid she might slip. She sends one of the children home to get his mother. But a man walking down the sidewalk has already bent to help the old man up.

"What are you doing here?"

"I came to pick you up," David says. "Your car never would have made it up the hill. I had chains put on."

They help the old man into the house. In the hallway he brushes snow off his shoulders, embarrassed and angry. He thinks the child knocked him over on purpose. She hangs up his coat and David helps him upstairs. He goes up the stairs more quickly than he came down, talking about the boy who knocked into him. But he's forgotten about it by the time his sister arrives. He's telling David about Berlin in the winter, about the birds. He complains about his memory—Berlin must have been beautiful in the spring. When his sister arrives she's brought fruit for her, too, saying that she's a nurse, she must know about Dr. Pauling. It's her last day. The daughter and the husband will be coming home from Florida. But the sister comes every day, even when they're home—she has an umbrella and high boots. Wait. The old man has something for her: a postcard. He's giving her the postcard. The stars twinkle brightly in her hand.

The children are still playing when she goes outside with David. The big boy she spoke to earlier hides behind a car and tries to hit them with a snowball, but he misses. David's mad at her, mad that she took the old man out. He won't speak.

"We'll have to go back for my car," she says.

No answer.

"I called you last night and there was no answer."

He looks up. "You called?"

"Yes. You weren't there."

"I didn't know it was you. I was asleep. Why were you calling?"

The snow is very deep. He's driving slowly, concentrating so the car doesn't skid. On the radio, the weather forecast calls for more snow.

"I guess you were walking the dog in the woods," she says.

"I just told you," he says. "I was asleep."

She closes her eyes, imagines him sleeping, then imagines him with the dog, pulling a broken branch out of the snow, holding it high for the dog to jump up. The dog yelps, runs in circles, but the snow is too deep to jump out of. David is asleep, under the covers. He's walking up the hill, the dog barking, jumping for the stick. She tries to imagine more, but she's afraid that if she doesn't open her eyes she'll fall asleep in the car.

Back in the house, she closes her eyes again. He's drawn the curtains, and the room is a little less bright. She's very tried. The dog whines outside the door, wanting David. David takes his trumpet off the night table and puts it in the case. He must be practicing again.

David leaves, saying that he's going downstairs to clean up. He hears some noise: cups and saucers? and much later, ringing. She's calling David, but there's no answer. David is calling her at the foot of the stairs.

"What?"

"Someone on the phone for you."

She goes downstairs to answer the phone. She sits at a chair by the table. The table is clear. Everything has been cleared away.

"Hello?"

The voice is soft. She can hardly hear. It's the old man's sister. She's tired of the old man and his sister, tired of work. She had already dismissed the old man from her mind, like last week's dreams, but now the old man's sister has called. His sister is upset. She's talking about the snow. Apparently she's snowed in, the snow is deeper than her boots, she's been trying to reach her husband to tell him. The planes from Florida won't land. No planes are landing. The old lady is thanking her for taking care of her brother. Why is she whispering?

"I come every day. I have my umbrella and my high boots so I can do my duty. I always try to bring him things that will please him so he won't think I only do it because I have to. My niece has to get away. He's so demanding. He wants her attention all day and night."

She's still half asleep, squinting against the glare, straining to hear. His sister is at the phone outside his bedroom in the hallway. The plane is still in Florida; it hasn't left because it can't land. His sister is asking if there's any way she can come back.

As she talks, the runway is buried deeper in snow. They're trying to clear it, but the snow is heavy, the planes can't land. The planes from Greece won't land. Now no one is on the beach in Greece, or at home in the United States; they're up in the air, up above the snow. She's sitting in a chair by the table. The table is clear. What was on the table when she came in? David has cleaned the room.

"You're so lucky," the woman whispers. "You can come and go. You don't know what it's like to be caught."

Wally Whistles
Dixie

▪▪▪▪▪▪▪▪▪▪▪▪▪▪▪▪▪▪▪▪▪▪▪▪▪

■■■■■■■■■■■■■■■■■■■■■

What an amazing life David has had: born in the Sierras, completely unexpected, his mother in labor only two hours, two and a half months premature, weighing four pounds even. Not much larger than two trout in a pan, his father was fond of saying, staring at his extended flat palm. Given up for dead in India at age ten, he then gained weight, his heart beat normally again, the fever vanished overnight. Married at sixteen—an elopement—in Reno, Nevada, to a thirty-year-old ballerina. But these are facts, and the trivia is more interesting: he can find a mosquito in a room even when it's not humming, go straight to its hiding place and catch it. Once he lifted his car by the back bumper—not in a moment of terror, nothing pinned under it, just to see . . . and he did it! He has memorized pages of Fitzgerald's notebooks: descriptions of pretty girls, F's thoughts on poetry, things F. will write etc. But he has read no F. novels! A lot of men cook, but David has published a cookbook that was translated into Japanese. The dedication is to the doctor who pronounced him doomed in India. David once played the oboe on a Scott Silver record, and before that time he had only played the violin. He practiced for a couple of days, and bleup bleuuuu buhloo. His wife, Sheila, is interesting too. There aren't many forty-five-year-old ballerinas who are still with it. She still flies from the floor like a bouncer on a trampoline. She proposed to her husband on impulse, in a place called The Silver Slipper Café in Reno, telling him that he might spend years looking and she might spend years looking, and that they could end all the looking, what the hell. He insisted that they wait twenty-four hours, secretly suspecting that she was drunk. She was a little insulted, and the wait just gave her more time to look, but when he realized that she was and had been sober he took her to The Wedding Chapel by the Pool. After a brief ceremony, witnessed by a drunken fat woman and a weeping thin woman with a Doberman held on a leash that wrapped around her legs, Sheila and David exited the chapel swinging their arms and smiling. Sheila did a dance that ended with her diving into the pool and splashing another couple on their way into the chapel. So graceful! He didn't know until then that she danced. They became servants for rich people on Long Island, and after five years—timed perfectly because Sheila was pregnant—the daughter of the rich people died, leaving a lot of money to her secret love, David. They left Long Island and went to Vermont, where they opened a restaurant. David wrote his cookbook and Sheila danced through their basement with paper flowers in her hair, followed by young children who looked like they were limping. The restaurant was a success, sushi being then very hard to find in that part of Vermont. He told the patrons about F's ideas. Her class gave after-dinner performances, throwing their paper flowers to the customers at the end of the show. They made rhubarb wine. He sewed his own shirts, from material shipped to him from Hong Kong. She shaved her eyebrows and penciled thin arcs above her blue-gray eyes when it was outré. They had lawn furniture in their house, covered by fur rugs of nonendangered species during the winter. It was suspected that they were serious dopers. Not so. They drank the rhubarb wine, lounged on the fur, and tried to contend with their baby, Wally. At first it wasn't bad—a small, pinkish, naked thing that lay on its back on a fur rug and played with wine-bottle corks laced together on a string by David. Wally liked the way they smelled. His mother's pirouettes, the regular creaking of the floor, lulled him to sleep. He learned to speak at an early age, calling the mess he made in his pants "poopy"—which he also called the puppy. They meant to think of a name for the puppy, but nothing seemed appropriate. Wally was named for a male nurse who took care of Sheila after the baby's birth. "Not really!" the nurse kept saying. Apparently it is untrue that babies are often named for doctors and nurses. The male nurse was extremely flattered and gave Sheila two bed baths a day when other women went to the showers. When Wally was a year old he got a strange look in his eye; he looked pissed off, to tell the truth. He and the puppy would be lying on their backs side by side, and Wally would straighten up and look very pissed off. Heredity? His mother was a bit cynical, but should this influence a one-year-old? Did he somehow sense that Sheila pounded her calves at night, telling them not to bulge? Did he sense an air of dissatisfaction in the house? They took him to a young doctor whom they felt they could speak frankly to, about vibrations . . . that the baby might be picking up bad vibrations. The doctor was shocked. They found an older man who was indifferent to the idea of vibrations, and stuck with him. David liked the way the doctor shrugged when he asked if bad vibrations could be getting to Wally. The first doctor had said, "You don't beat this child, do you?"

When he was two, Wally began to wander off. A free spirit, Sheila felt. David thought he would fall off a cliff or drown. He *was* more practical; after all, he hadn't proposed to her in The Silver Slipper Café. "You hold my love against me!" Sheila said, aghast. Wally took the aghast facial expression from his mother and combined it with a very distressed downturned mouth and ran away. You might also say that his eyes were very large and he pouted. It is a little difficult to describe his expression, but it was strange, and Sheila thought so too, although she didn't say that to David. When he was three, Wally jumped off a table and broke his leg. While he was laid up, he colored to pass the time. Wally's doctor paid a house call—amazing things happened to these amazing people—and pronounced Wally "just fine." "But his expression," David said to the doctor as the doctor was leaving. "You wouldn't look so happy if you were a three-year-old with a broken leg," the doctor assured him.

A vacationing photographer and his wife, who had stopped to eat at the restaurant, noticed Wally's pictures hung in back of the cash register and wanted to buy them. David wouldn't part with them, but he let the photographer take pictures. David didn't think much of it. About a month later, though, the photographer was back, this time with another man. They wanted to write an article about Wally for a magazine; Wally's art would appear with it. Sheila was delighted. She told the men that her son was artistic, like her. David felt that they should think about it; what if he developed a terrific ego? "He's already strange," Sheila said. The photographer took pictures of Wally at his fourth birthday party. There was also a birthday interview, during which Wally echoed everything the interviewer asked:

"Do you like to draw a lot, Wally?"

"Do you like to draw a lot, Wally?"

"Ha! You're a nice kid. And a good artist."

"Ha! You're a nice kid. And a good artist."

"Do you know any famous artists, Wally?"

"Do you know any famous artists, Wally?"

"Have you ever heard of the Mona Lisa?"

"Have you ever heard of the Mona Lisa?"

"Sure, I have. Have you ever seen it?"

"Sure, I have. Have you ever seen it?"

"You don't feel like talking today, do you?" the photographer asked.

Wally pulled up his top lip, showing his two big front teeth. "You don't feel like talking today, do you?" he repeated.

"Nope. I'll just take some pictures," the photographer said.

A little girl from Wally's party stood on her head for the photographer. The photographer noted with interest that Carters still manufactured white pants with yellow roses on them.

Wally's fourth birthday party was immortalized on a magazine cover. There was a picture of Wally's head, and above it, in little balloons as if he were imagining them, reproductions of his drawings. The magazine sold a lot of copies, tourists came to the restaurant, Sheila agreed to part with a few drawings—to museums only—and Wally jumped off the roof of David's station wagon and broke his right arm five days after the cast was removed from his left leg.

Sheila consulted a child psychologist, who had written them to say how interested he was in Wally. She wrote that Wally jumped off of cars and tables and broke his bones. What was she to do? The psychologist appeared in person! Perhaps it was related in some way to her being a ballerina. After that, she beat her legs much harder at night, danced in private, locked the basement door to Wally when she gave lessons. The psychologist, in answer to David's question about why Wally repeated what was said to him, suggested that it might be related to David's memorization and quotation of F. Aha! From then on he thought F. He said nothing. Wally didn't break any more bones. During the year he gave up repeating things. He also gave up art. In fact, when he had to color maps in the first grade, he did it sloppily. "What is your new interest?" David asked Wally optimistically. "Nothing," Wally said.

In the second grade Wally had a girlfriend, who was in the fifth grade: Susan Leigh. They played the harmonica to each other.

When his romance with Susan Leigh ended he took a leap—again from the car top—crushing the harmonica with his fall. Sheila wrote to the child psychologist, saying that Wally was no longer interested in doing anything. After a long time she got a letter. The doctor had retired and was living in the Bahamas. There was a check for eight dollars with the letter. The doctor asked her if she would buy a best-seller he had read about and send it to him, as it was unavailable on his island. She had trouble finding *Murderous Midnight*, and about a month later she received an angry note from the doctor, asking why she had failed him.

In the fifth grade, Wally was expelled from school, along with another boy; the two had forced a younger boy to pick up a stick and peel off the bark and eat it. Two years later, when he began junior high school, he told his father he wanted permission to marry another thirteen-year-old. "Where would you live?" David asked. "In a tent," Wally said. "Where would you live in the winter?" David asked. David won his point, but Wally did not speak to him for two months. Then he asked again for David to sign the necessary papers, and for David to give him enough money to live in an apartment during the winter with his bride. "You owe it to me for exploiting me," Wally said. "I never exploited you," David told him. Again, Wally did not speak for a long time. His silence was now as predictable as his mimicry when he was younger. Apparently he also refused to speak in school, and a new teacher thought that he was deaf. They would not allow him to continue school until a doctor had tested his hearing. This made Sheila and David angry, and they told Wally that he was being ridiculous. He ran away. He lived in a tent not far from home. He was dirty. He said he wanted to take a trip to New York when David went to the tent to talk to him. "Here, take it," David said, giving him the money. "I'm sick of all this." Wally went to New York, then returned to the tent. He never returned to school.

There was a family meeting when Wally dropped out of school. It was the second family meeting they had ever had; the first— when his mother felt that they were drifting apart because of their separate interests, shortly before Wally left for the tent— had not been very successful. Wally explained how to pitch a tent, and his father talked about the virtues of homemade pasta, and after his mother insisted that store-bought pasta tasted exactly the same and that when you bought it in a store you didn't have to spend half a day scraping crap out of a pasta machine, she did a plié. One plié. Then, no more energy left, sat down. That night she slept in the same chair, and the following day she clawed the upholstery on the chair arm before she left it.

"We did not get to the essence of Wally's problem," David said to Sheila as they cleaned up the restaurant.

"He doesn't have any real problem. He's just a selfish son of a bitch like you," she said.

"Why do you say he's selfish?"

"I'm not going to clean that pasta machine tonight or any other night as long as I live," Sheila screamed, and ran ungracefully from the restaurant.

David began keeping a journal. Mostly it was criticism of Sheila or worries about Wally, and when David realized this he made an effort to say more about his own feelings and life. His feelings were so clichéd that he couldn't go on with them, though: "I am a nothing," "Nobody loves me," "Some days I wonder why I'm alive." So after a while the book began to fill up with receipts, bills he still had to pay, snapshots, even letters from Wally's former child psychologist, who was now a severely disturbed man.

"What is that thing?" Sheila asked.

"Unpaid bills," David said.

"Then why don't you pay them?" she asked.

Wally began seeing the sister of his second-grade sweetheart, Susan Leigh. They ate out of cans in Wally's tent. She hung an Escher print in the tent and told Wally he should paint and draw again. Her name was Dianna Leigh. Susan visited the tent once or twice, when she was in town. She was appearing sporadically in off-off-Broadway plays and living with another woman who was in the process of being changed surgically into a man. The woman-man liked the Escher print. Susan declined an offer of Spam on a roll. "Aren't you vegetarians?" the woman-man asked.

"No. Are you?" Dianna Leigh asked.

"I'm going to become a vegetarian when I become a man," the woman-man said.

"Why are you waiting until then?" Wally asked.

"She's going through enough hell now," Susan Leigh said.

One night Wally walked through the woods to his parents' place. His father was lying on his back on the front lawn. "You'll get mosquito bites," Wally said, and David screamed because he had not heard him approaching. Wally took a small can out of his shirt pocket and sprayed David.

"I want to know how it all began," Wally said.

David thought that it was a variation of the questions about sex that he had answered when Wally was five and that he had talked about again when Wally was seven because Wally had forgotten it all.

"In Las Vegas," Wally said. "Wasn't that where you met my mother?"

"Oh. You mean how all *that* began. I thought you were talking about the beginning of life. I told you: I was hitching around the country and I ended up in Reno. It was Reno, not Las Vegas. I was sitting in a place called The Silver Slipper Café. Your mother sat down next to me. She said that she didn't think that anything in the place was worth eating. I don't know where the conversation went from there, but she ended up proposing."

Wally was silent.

"Why don't you go back to school?" David asked Wally.

"Why don't we go to Reno?"

"What for?"

"Sort of like a second honeymoon or . . . getting back in touch."

"You want us to take you on our second honeymoon?"

"A family vacation, then. I don't care what you call it."

"Reno is a sleazy place. I don't want to spend money to get back there. And anyway—your mother isn't here."

"Where is she?"

"Visiting her sister."

"Why do you sound so depressed?"

"I'm not in a very good mood, Wally. And I don't really like to be reminded of how your mother picked me up in Reno, Nevada."

"Do you think there's something awful about it?"

"I just don't like to think about it."
"Do you want me to go?"
"I don't care what you do, Wally. It's your mother who calls the family meetings and who gets all emotional and walks out on both of us. I just want to lie here in the grass."
"Well, keep this with you," Wally said, dropping the insect repellent next to David. Wally walked off. David watched the beam of Wally's flashlight shining in the woods.

                                    *

"You're really an amazing family," Dianna Leigh says to Wally. "Like a Salinger family."
"Who's that?" Wally asks.
"Didn't you ever hear of J. D. Salinger? The Glass family?"
"No."
"They were this crazy family. My mother gave me the book. She says that Salinger is nuts, too. He runs away if anybody approaches him on the street."
"Where does he live? Manhattan?"
"I don't think so . . ."
"I've been thinking," Wally says. "I don't think my parents were unhappy until they had me. Because I was a prodigy and all."

"That's not your fault."
"I'm going to write her a letter. I think that if they went back to Reno they could recapture something."
"That's romantic."
"There's nothing wrong with romanticism."
"I didn't mean that there was anything wrong with romance."
Dianna Leigh pouts; she and Wally have not been getting along well in the tent lately.

                                    *

David remembers: "Imagine that you turn on a hose. Imagine your penis as a hose. And the water that sprays out is sperm, those things I just told you about. And the water shoots all over the lawn. Imagine the woman as a lawn. That's what sex is like, more or less—watering the lawn." Even at the time, he realized that he had botched it.

*

Wally's namesake: On vacation, he falls into the Grand Canyon!!!!!!!!! Every year people slip, fall down mountains, into gorges, stumble into snake-infested pools. Well, Wally's namesake, on a vacation with his wife, twin sons, and his wife's father, taking a picture, leaning a bit, supporting himself on a fragile tree, falls!!!!!!!!!!!!!!!SzzzzzzzzzzWAAAAAAAAAYAAAAA-AA!!!!right into the Grand Canyon.

*

Wally talks to Dianna Leigh in the tent: "It all comes to nothing. That must be the way she feels about her dancing. My father is the only one left who's creative, and I think that she complains so much about the pasta machine because he creates the pasta—you know, putting a little spinach and some brains into the linguini . . . and I can't think of anything to paint any more. Even my father, and he's creative, lies on the ground, letting the mosquitoes eat him alive. I guess we are a messed-up family. What happened to that writer's family?"

"I don't really remember. I think that they were religious, though."

*

And now, here's what will happen to David and Sheila and Wally:

☞ Other people like them for having only one child and not adding to the world's overpopulation problem.

☞ The restaurant gets a glowing recommendation from the AAA; they say that "the pasta is cooked divinely *al dente.*"

☞ Wally and Dianna Leigh separate. In Provincetown, years later, he sees a copy of *The Catcher in the Rye* and buys it. It confirms his suspicion that she was full of shit, because there is no Glass family in the book.

☞ Sheila has one breast cut off, then the other. It becomes her new excuse for not dancing. If you don't believe that this is at all logical, try taking a few leaps without your breasts and see how hard it is to keep your balance.

*

Background information on the trip to Reno, Nevada: If she can't be a great dancer, at least she can be a good mother, and if Wally wants to go to Nevada, that isn't much to ask. He's a good boy. He may live in a tent with that girl, but he hasn't gotten her pregnant. And perhaps he doesn't draw because he's frustrated, the way she is. And David doesn't feel that he should be so quick to say that what Wally wants to do is nuts. Grinding internal organs into pasta is pretty nutty, as though a customer can tell the difference when it's smothered in tomato sauce. What the hell—it'll be a good test for the new car.

*

At The Silver Slipper Café: Two men walk into The Silver Slipper Café. One of the men—a pasty-white, tall man in a shirt with palm trees on it—has a black cat sitting on his shoulder. The other man, also tall, but with a good tan and bloodshot eyes, takes a knife from his friend's shirtpocket and cuts the phone off from the cord. The waitress notices and starts for the other end of the counter, but both men mouth, "No," and she freezes.

"Hello, family," the first man says. The cat looks down at them.

"Hello," David says.

"What are you enjoying there, family?" the man asks.

"Apple pie," David says.

"Don't pick up that hot coffee," the second man says to the waitress.

She doesn't. The second man hands Sheila the phone. "I'm gonna call you on this telephone," he says. "I'm gonna ask you a question. You be Betty Crocker, okay?"

Sheila looks at David, about to cry.

"Sure she will," David says. "Go ahead, honey."

"And just so the young fellow won't be bored, he can whistle 'Dixie,' " the first man says, tapping Wally's shoulder.

"Hello, Betty?" the second man says.

"Yes," Sheila says.

"What ingredients go into an apple pie, Betty?"

"Apples. And sugar and flour."

"Don't you put in anything else, Betty?"

"Yes. Lemon juice. Sometimes raisins . . ."

"What else, Betty?"

"Uh—cinnamon. That's all, I think."

"But what accounts for the special goodness of your pies, Betty?"

"Nutmeg. I use . . . cinnamon and nutmeg."

"Thanks, Betty. I'll be ringing off now."

The other man is standing in back of Wally, who is loudly whistling "Dixie."

"Out!" he screams, and the two run from The Silver Slipper Café. The waitress screams. The police are called. Sometime during the confusion the cat wanders in.

"That was their cat!" the waitress says, pointing.

"Oh yeah?" one of the cops says. "I don't think we've got anything on it, though."

"You're real comedians," the waitress says angrily.

"This town just puts you in a good mood all the time," the cop says. "You folks here for a little vacation in vacationland?"

"I don't know what we're here for," David says, trying to comfort Sheila.

"Well, don't lose what you already got," the other cop says. He finishes writing something on a piece of paper, rolls up the paper, and holds the door open for his partner.

Marshall's Dog

▪▪▪▪▪▪▪▪▪▪▪▪▪▪▪▪▪▪▪▪▪▪

######## ●●●●●●●●●●●●●●●●●●●●●●● ########

She was eighty-two when she died. She had the usual old-lady fears—Democratic Presidents, broken bones. When the spaghetti was snapped in half and dropped into the boiling water she heard the sound of her own bones cracking. She loved spaghetti. They had to eat so much spaghetti. She wouldn't eat the sauce. She had butter with her spaghetti. She used to knit for her son, Marshall. She loved her son, she knitted all the time. Once she knitted him a bathrobe and he broke out in a rash all over, an allergy to wool. She cooked for Edna. She made alphabet soup. Edna remembers fishing out letters, saying, "Let's see what Mom wants to tell us this time." Fish. Fawn. Up. Dollar. She wouldn't be left alone. When Edna went to work at the sporting-goods store she was there. At the store snowmobiles are sold, and wool hats, helmets, boots. Edna rode to work on her snowmobile; Marshall brought his mother in the car. She sat in a comfortable chair behind the counter and waited for Edna to finish work. She watched television. When customers came in, she turned up the volume. When the reception was bad, she listened to the radio instead. Marshall is talking to Edna. Edna has held the door open too long—the house is getting cold. Where is the dog? Didn't she call the dog in? Edna closes the door. But then it's open again—Edna and Marshall go out for a walk in the snow.

*

The boy at the table behind Mary is singing to her. He is no longer at the table behind her, he is at her table, and Kathy, her girlfriend, has gone to the bathroom. Now there is laughter in addition to the music. His friends are going crazy. They looked drunk when Mary and Kathy walked in an hour ago. One of the boy's friends has a harmonica that he is blowing.

"Can you see?"

The boy has pulled the neck of his shirt down. Across his chest is a scattering of moles, a brown blur of them.

"It looks like the Milky Way galaxy," he says. He waves his arm, motioning his friend to stop playing the harmonica. The music is replaced by *a cappella* singing. Kathy comes out of the bathroom and looks the situation over. She orders a Coke at the bar and returns to the table. Two summers ago, Mary danced for the boy and his friend. They paid her two dollars. Since then the boy's friend lost a finger that got infected after he caught it in a mattress spring. He used to play electric guitar.

The waitress is at the table. Beverly tonight. Beverly has bright-blue eyes and wears blue eyeshadow. Her sister Miriam is on weekends. Miriam has green eyes and wears green eyeshadow.

"Miriam comin' in Saturday night?"

Beverly puts the boy's drink down.

"Rest of you want anything?" she says.

"Bring her a hamburger," the boy says, nodding to Mary.

"Who's paying for it?" Mary asks.

"I already paid," the boy's friend hollers. "They're tradin' hamburgers for fingers tonight. Tomorrow night there's a spaghetti special."

Laughter. An explosion of music. A dog has wandered into the bar. The dog is confused, running everywhere. Two women in a booth across the bar meow. Finally Sam sees the dog.

"It's Marshall's dog," he says to Beverly. "Want to call him?"

"Take my toes," the boy's friend calls to Beverly. "I want a hot dog."

"I'll come back for your orders," Beverly says over her shoulder.

"I'm leavin'!"

One of the boys is yelling. He has gotten up from the table. The dog has wandered over to their table. Mary recognizes the dog—her uncle's. She reaches out to pat the dog, but the boy has grabbed the dog up into his arms. He starts to run.

"Did he pay?" Beverly hollers.

One of the boy's friends holds up a wad of dollar bills.

"Well, what about the dog?" Beverly asks Sam.

"I told you," Sam says. "Call Marshall."

"He took it."

"Tell Marshall."

Beverly lifts the phone and dials.

*

"It's Marshall, George. Things aren't very good over here."

"No? Is Mom's cold still hanging on?"

"Yes and no. Edna took her to the doctor a week ago, and the medicine he gave her has helped. She gets around better. She's depressed, though. Really, Edna wanted me to call you . . ."

"George," Edna says, "she says that at night her heart stops, and if she's very still it starts again. I know that isn't true, but she's very depressed. She's cleaning out her drawers and gave me things to give you."

George is speaking to Marshall again.

"The doctor recommends a cardiologist, but she says she won't go. I think she'll pay attention to you, George."

"Anna and I'll come over tomorrow night after work."

"It's no emergency. We wanted you to know." Marshall lowers his voice. "Can you hear that?"

"Yeah. What is it?"

"The television and radio. She's got them both going . . . stays right with them."

"Wouldn't the doctor give her sleeping pills?"

"She won't take them." Marshall hesitates. "What Edna told you about."

*

Mrs. Anna Wright. She signs her name to a note she has written Mary's homeroom teacher—an excuse for Mary's absence from school on Monday and Tuesday. She writes so many notes. She feels obliged to offer details now. In this note she mentions a specific drug given to Mary by the doctor: penicillin. Rainy, cold weather, a sore throat, a tendency toward strep, penicillin. Her husband has told her to stop writing notes, but what is she supposed to do? Mary is overweight and embarrassed to go to school. The only place she socializes with boys is at Sam's . . . they never ask her out. It is the week of the dance. If Mary isn't in school, she can say that's why she wasn't invited. On Tuesday she made Mary dress for school. But she was crying; she couldn't send her out of the house crying.

Now it is Wednesday. She didn't think Mary would go to school, but she is dressed, sitting at the breakfast table. She cooks Mary a big breakfast—she doesn't want to spoil her mood. George tells her to serve Mary only small portions, but he isn't home when Mary eats, he doesn't have to hear her complaints or watch the way she stalks out of the house, deliberately leaving her books behind on the hall table. Last week she had a big scene with Mary —not about breakfast or school, about the Parents' Association. Mary said the Association was no good, that they spent their time thinking about parties and dances and that the guidance counselor was no good. Why couldn't they do something about the guidance counselor? She had been surprised—what did Mary want to talk to a guidance counselor about? Mary had argued with her, saying that she didn't understand anything, that it wasn't only her —they all needed a good guidance counselor so they'd be able to get into college.

"Did you write a note?" Mary says.

"I left it on the table for you."

"What did you say?"

"I said you had a sore throat."

"She always has something to say about your notes."

"What do you mean? What has she said?"

"When I put it on her desk she reads it right away."

"That's her job, Mary."

"As soon as she reads it she says something to me. The last time she came over to my desk and asked me if my cold was gone."

Mrs. Wright is turning eggs. What Mary says must be true. Once she forgot to write a note when Mary had been sick, and the homeroom teacher had called at home that night. Another time the guidance counselor called to say that he was disturbed by the number of absences. What is she supposed to say to these people? She tells them that it was her mistake not to have sent a note promptly, that it's better to nip things in the bud so Mary doesn't miss a whole week of school, that Mary has a good academic average.

Mary is eating her breakfast. But it is late—eight-thirty—and she should hurry. It makes people sick to hurry, it gives them indigestion. She sits down across from Mary.

"You uncle Marshall called last night. Grandma isn't feeling well, and your father wants us to visit her tonight."

"What's wrong with her?"

"She had a cold . . . she has trouble sleeping."

"She just wants to stay up late and watch television."

82 *Distortions*

"No, she doesn't," she says angrily. "Edna took her to a doctor and he had to give her medication."

Mary does not look up.

"Do you think you're dressed warmly enough?"

Mary will not continue the conversation. Eventually she gets up, her napkin carefully folded beside her plate. It is eight forty-five. Mary will be late to school, and there is no excuse for tardiness in the note.

"I'll drive you," she says.

Mrs. Wright looks at the car through the frosty window.

*

It is cold in the house. She is making soup and baking a roast for dinner. The dog barks and jumps. Marshall is home from work. He and Edna are talking in the living room. Soon they will go out to ride their snowmobiles; she'll hear them making a circle around the house, will look out the window, cupping her hands so she can see clearly the tracks in the snow. She had been for a ride on the snowmobile with Marshall. She wore scarves on her head, afraid to put on the helmet. There is talk about outlawing snowmobiles. Edna and Marshall are always upset about it. On the television they said people died on snowmobiles, riding them through barbed-wire fences. She rubs her throat, thinking about barbed wire piercing the skin.

"Are you all right, Mom? Sore throat hasn't come back?"

"No, Marshall."

"We're going to take a ride for a few minutes. I'm looking for some bread to feed the birds."

Marshall has opened the breadbox. Marshall explains everything. The other night when he was fixing a kitchen cabinet she came in for a drink of water and he explained to her how an electric drill worked. He wanted her to hold it. Edna came in. She told Marshall it was too heavy, it vibrated too much. She got the drink of water and left.

One of the women in town, Beverly Brent, helped her husband build a house. She knew Beverly when she was young. The Brents built a big house. But when the house was built she lost twenty pounds and went to New York to become a model. Beverly got sick in New York—she had an appendectomy and returned to the house. She gained weight. Not long ago she came into the store and asked if they needed any saleswomen. Most of the women in town disliked Beverly—the men too. Beverly was never very popular. People liked her sister Miriam. She can remember when they were little girls, fighting on the sidewalk outside the drugstore. Girls fighting! No matter what flavor ice-cream cone Miriam got, Beverly wanted it. Beverly would throw her own ice cream on the sidewalk. Marshall buys her little white bottles of niacin to improve her memory. But she could remember all the things before she took the pills. Edna doesn't think she needs to take the pills either, but she does it to please Marshall. Marshall takes vitamins every day. He never has a cold. Edna gets sick and can't go to work. She herself feels pains in her chest and can't sleep at night because she hears her heart beat and stop, beat and stop.

She is a little surprised that Marshall doesn't say that he is shutting the door when he shuts the door. She stops stirring the soup and looks at them on their snowmobiles. Marshall looks up and sees her. He points to the snowmobile and smiles. Just as he said, he is going to take a ride on the snowmobile. It is snowing lightly outside. She watches until the snowmobiles are out of sight. She fears they can't see in the snow, that they'll run into barbed wire. She goes to the closet and looks on the top shelf. Their goggles are there. She takes them down and puts them on; everything turns bright yellow. She goes back and pours a bag of alphabet letters into the soup. She forgets that she has the goggles on until they begin to steam up. She quickly puts them back on the top shelf so Edna and Marshall won't see her in them. She goes into the bedroom and empties the niacin pills in the trash and replaces them with aspirin from the medicine cabinet. But she takes too long. She hears Marshall and Edna in the kitchen, realizes that they are calling her. The dog is barking. The soup is boiling over.

*

"What a mess."

"Your mother'll kill you."

It is summer. Mary and Kathy are fifteen. They are in Sam's, with several boys, and Mary has pizza down her shirt. The boy who caused the accident has spilled his beer on her too. He is twenty-one, the oldest one at the table. Sam saw what happened and is coming over. Mary stands and screams at the boy; he stands too. He is drunk. Mary swings at him—to push, really, not to hit. Sam grabs the boy's arms.

"It was an accident," he hollers in Sam's face.

"Go throw some water on your face," Sam says.

Kathy is wiping pizza off Mary's shirt. The pizza sticks to Kathy's hands, cold and greasy.

"Give her a towel," Sam says to Beverly.

"Never mind," Mary says, "I'm going."

"Let me *get* it," Kathy says.

One of the other boys is handing Kathy napkins.

"It's not doing any good," Mary says. "I can feel it through my shirt."

"I'll give you a ride home," the boy says.

"It's got to come off," Mary says. "She'll find out I was here."

"So what? You can't smell anything on you."

"I'm just not supposed to be here," Mary says.

"Okay. I got an idea."

Mary and Kathy leave Sam's with the two boys. All four are in the front seat. Sam has come out; he is still trying to give them a towel. Mary thanks Sam and takes it. She puts it in her blouse so she can't feel the cold pizza against her chest. They are going down a narrow road. The car windows are rolled up because it has started to get cold at night. Nobody talks until they turn into a driveway.

"Go wash your blouse in the bathroom. We can iron it dry."

"Where are we?"

"My parents' house."

"Well, where are they?"

"Out."

They are going up the front walk. Mary even has pizza in her hair. Everything is sticky. Kathy laughs at her.

"Thanks a lot," Mary says.

"It'll come off," Kathy says.

The boy turns on a light. His friend sits down in the living room. A white cat rubs against his legs, rolls on its back and grabs his pants leg. The boy shakes his leg.

"Where's the bathroom?"

"Over here."

Mary and Kathy are in the bathroom. Running water in the sink. Mary starts combing her hair, but it is matted. She scoops some water out of the sink and wets it. She wets it again, then reaches for a comb on the windowsill. She yanks a little and the comb goes through her hair. She pushes her hair behind her ears. Kathy has her blouse. She is dipping it in the water. She soaps it, kneading the material into a tight ball. Mary dries her chest with a towel. It leaves pink stains on the towel. She refolds the towel so the stains are on the inside, and hangs it up again. Kathy is running fresh water in the sink. Someone is knocking on the door. Kathy opens it! Mary steps in back of Kathy.

"Here," the boy says. He has opened two bottles of beer.

Kathy's hands are wet and soapy. Mary stands in back of Kathy.

He puts the bottles down. "I'm going to get you the iron," he says.

Kathy and Mary go out of the bathroom. Mary has a towel around her.

"I'll do it," Kathy says.

Mary is left standing next to the boy. She stands there a minute, then goes back into the bathroom and gets the bottles of beer the boy left on the windowsill. She leans against the wall and drinks some beer.

"It came out pretty good," Kathy says. "It's awfully wet to iron."

Kathy takes a sip of beer.

"I was gonna ask you to dance," the boy says to Mary, "before you got all that crap on you."

"We dance all the time."

"I'll give you two dollars if you'll dance now."

Mary considers. "What records have you got?"

"Without records."

"All right," she says. "Come on."

"Without me."

"Just dance by myself?"

He nods. Kathy laughs.

Mary shrugs. She turns toward the boy and starts dancing. Her wet hair swings in front of her face. The other boy has left the liv-

ing room. He is stroking the cat in his arms, watching. Kathy has
stopped ironing and is watching too.

"Are you going to give me two dollars to dance?" Kathy asks
the other boy.

He shakes his head. His friend grabs the front of Mary's towel
and pulls.

*

Edna pulls the cord. The engine starts. She rides her Arctic Cat
over the grave in the snow. Edna goes to the store early, before
the customers arrive. She turns on the television and the radio.
There is no picture on the television, only bright streaks rolling
down the picture tube. She turns up the volume on the radio. It
has been so quiet at home since she died. Marshall and George
and Anna speak in whispers. It is so quiet you can hear the snow
in the wind. She sits in the chair and shakes the radio, then
throws it hard against the door of the shop. The television pushes
over easily. It is snowing hard—there will be a lot of people on
the weekend, but unless the snow lets up, few people will come
into the shop today. The broken glass is only in back of the
counter. No danger to the customers.

*

"It's not going away."

Beverly is talking to George in a bar in New York.

"You're very pale," George says. "Do you feel any better?"

Didn't he hear her? Maybe she didn't say anything. It hurts to
talk. She feels drowsy, but at the same time she is in pain. Her
hands are on her ribs. No—his hands are on her ribs.

"Let me get a cab outside. Did this just happen suddenly?"

He nods. She must be answering him. Suddenly there is no
more pain. She is talking to more than one man, several men, or a
nurse and a man, in a hospital. Then there is pain again. She is on
a bed. The man is not with her any more. The doctor sees her
looking around.

"Your husband is in the waiting room. He has your things."

"He comes to New York. He's my lover. Someone else's husband."

New York was a crazy idea. Seeing George in New York was a

crazy idea. The pain has come back; it makes her feel like she's going crazy. The doctor is still talking. She is having trouble hearing. They have given her an injection. His hand is out to pay the cab driver. His hand is out putting a needle in her arm. The nurse's hand is on top of her hand. They are holding hands in a bar. Someone's hands are on her ribs. Someone's hands remove her appendix.

*

He takes them out carefully, throwing the crumbs low so the wind doesn't take them away after he crumbles the bread in his hand. Edna watches. He is so methodical, so thorough. She imagines that just for him there will be one bird that otherwise might have starved that will find these breadcrumbs. But the sky is empty, except for snow.

"There aren't any birds, Marshall."

"There are animals."

"I'm surprised you don't scatter vitamin pills in the snow."

Edna's helmet sparkles. Marshall has scattered all the crumbs. He looks satisfied. Usually she tries to disturb him when he looks satisfied. She laughed at his vitamin pills when he first took them. She decides that, yes, there will be one bird—just as God punished her with a cold because she ridiculed Marshall's vitamin pills. Marshall does not seem to notice when she tries to disturb him. The only way she can disturb him is by being a martyr about his mother, and even then Marshall can offer no response: Edna is with the old lady all day; Edna drives her to doctors; Edna sits up with her at night when Marshall is asleep. They both know that she is dying. Edna sits on her snowmobile and watches. He has carefully put the empty bread bag in his pocket.

"Want to go back?" Marshall asks.

There is snow all over Marshall's coat and hair.

"You told her we'd be right back," Edna says.

She is cold and doesn't want to ride any more. But Marshall understands something else. There is nothing he can say.

*

Mary picks up the phone, but the boy doesn't say anything. He can see her at Sam's—he doesn't have to ask her to the dance.

*

"I don't know what to say, Marshall. You don't think it was deliberate, do you? I thought he came back in when I was holding the door open. I thought I saw him."

*

Why say anything to the cardiologist? He is a young man, his office is filled with books. Would he believe that her heart stops and starts again? That she knows when her heart is going to stop?

*

It's awkward; they run into each other in town. There is a boutique, painted white and yellow, where the card shop used to be: a post office, a drugstore, beauty salon, movie house, sporting-goods store. They both hate the town—no need to say anything about that. When they walk through town they think of New York. Neither of them understands what happened in New York. When she got well she came home. They can't think of anything to say.

*

The snow continues to fall, three nights after the funeral. Mary and Kathy are sitting in Sam's. The boys are sitting with them. Kathy is already at the jukebox, putting money in, and Beverly has come to the table to offer condolences. A cold night. There aren't many people in Sam's. Beverly sits down a minute, rearranging her hair. She complains that her car acted funny earlier and decides to call her sister to pick her up after work.

"I'm staying until closing if Miriam's coming," the boy says.

Kathy is dancing with his friend.

"Christ, look," Beverly says. "I couldn't move my feet that much. They're so painful now that I'd like to cut them off."

"That's what I did," a boy tells Beverly, looking at her through the gap in his hand where his middle finger is missing.

"You get crazy when you're drunk," Beverly says. "I remember the night you almost hauled off and hit Mary."

Beverly leaves the table. She makes a phone call, then waits on two women at a table on the other side of the bar. Mary is listening to the boys at the table in back of her, singing along with tho jukebox. She can't tell what they're singing because the jukebox is turned up full blast. Mary takes a bite of the hamburger. One of the boys ordered it for her. They order food for her without telling her, then Mary has to argue with them about who pays for it. Tonight she doesn't care, though. Her father gave her some money and told her to go have a good time. It's depressing at Edna and Marshall's house night after night. It's worse than school. Edna is very upset, but she doesn't talk about the death. She says things that make no sense—that she's going to sell her snowmobile and never ride again. Her mother and father go to her aunt and uncle's every night; Edna sits in the rocking chair by the window and rocks back and forth, holding her knees, asking what they're going to do. One of the boys is smiling at Mary. He's the one who ordered the hamburger.

"Who's paying for it?" Mary asks automatically.

He makes a crude joke. There is loud music; it gets so loud that she blocks it out. Two people come in in raincoats. Wind blows across the floor; the wind is blowing so hard that they have to force the door shut behind them. Mary is glad when the door is closed. She is tired of looking at snow. The four stained-glass squares in the top of the door shine brightly. The street light outside illuminates them. Mary is listening to the music, looking at the colors. There aren't many people. Sam tells Beverly to go home early. Beverly makes another phone call, comes back to the table for last orders. The people in the raincoats are telling some other people that it's not their dog. There is a large brown-and-white dog in Sam's; it is wet, confused, stopping to shake itself, then running forward to sniff under a table. Mary recognizes the dog—it belongs to her uncle. But the dog doesn't recognize Mary. It runs forward to sniff under another table. Beverly goes after the dog, intending to lead it outside. One of the boys watches what's going on through the space in his hand, then goes after Beverly with his arms out, grabs her from behind, lets her go. Then the boy grabs the dog. Sam is talking to Beverly.

"I told you," he says. "It's Marshall's dog. Call Marshall."

"The boy took it."

"Tell Marshall."

Beverly shrugs. Sam can be as unreasonable as a drunk. Years ago she was going to get away from all this. She looks up Marshall's number. She stares at the last name. Then she dials him. The phone rings and rings, no answer. Later, when Marshall does answer the phone, they'll tell him his dog is dead.

*

The boy runs out of the restaurant, into the snow. He hadn't realized how warm it was in Sam's. He left his jacket behind. He is shivering. The dog is shivering, trying to jump out of his arms. He sees the streetlight; the light is higher and higher above him. He has fallen. The dog is gone. There is a noise, a thump, the noise he makes falling into the snow, the noise the dog makes running into the car. There is someone else outside Sam's with him. Miriam. Miriam is just walking in the snow. He smiles at her—he waited all night to see Miriam, and now she's here, walking in the snow. There are more lights—car headlights as well as the streetlight. Miriam's car is stopped in the middle of the street. Miriam is kneeling in front of it, then walking back and forth, shaking him, lying there in the snow. It's noisy—as noisy as it was inside, but it's all Miriam! She's calling Beverly, but Beverly's already there, and she doesn't have a jacket either. The door opens and closes. More snow blows into Sam's. There is cold snow all around him.

"He took it."

"Tell Marshall."

Beverly shudders. She runs into the restaurant.

"Forget it," Sam calls after her. "I'll call him."

"What about the boy?" Miriam whispers to Sam.

Sam knocks some snow off the heel of his boot.

"Snow'll sober him up."

Downhill

■■■■■■■■■■■■■■■■■■■■■

Walking the dog at 7:30 A.M., I sit on the wet grass by the side of the road, directly across from the beaver pond and diagonally across from the graveyard. In back of me is a grapevine that I snitch from. The grapes are bitter. The dog lifts a leg on the gravestone, rolls in dead squirrel in the road, comes to my side finally—thank God none of the commuters ran over him—and licks my wrist. The wet wrist feels awful. I rub it along his back, passing it off as a stroke. I do it several times. "Please don't leave me," I say to the dog, who cocks his head and settles in the space between my legs on the grass.

*

My mother writes Jon this letter:

"Oh, John, we are so happy that September marks the beginning of your last year in law school. My husband said to me Saturday (we were at the Turkish restaurant we took you and Maria to when she was recuperating—the one you both liked so much) that now when he gets mad he can say, 'I'll sue!' and mean it. It has been uphill for so long, and now it will be downhill."

Curiously, that week an old friend of Jon's sent us a toy—a small bent-kneed skier who, when placed at the top of a slanting board, would glide to the bottom. I tried to foul up the toy every which way. I even tried making it ski on sandpaper, and it still worked. I tacked the sandpaper to a board, and down it went. The friend had bought it in Switzerland, where he and his wife were vacationing. So said the note in the package that was addressed to Jon, which I tore open because of the unfamiliar handwriting, thinking it might be evidence.

*

Why do I think Jon is unfaithful? Because it would be logical for him to be unfaithful. Some days I don't even comb my hair. He must leave the house and see women with their hair clean and brushed back from their faces, and he must desire them and then tell them. It is only logical that if he admires the beauty of all the women with neatly arranged hair, one of them will want him to mess it up. It is only logical that she will invite him home. That smile, that suggestion from a woman would lure him as surely as a spring rain makes the earthworms twist out of the ground. It is even hard to blame him; he has a lawyer's logical mind. He remembers things. He would not forget to comb his hair. He would certainly not hack his hair off with manicuring scissors. If he cut his own hair, he would do it neatly, with the correct scissors.

"What have you done?" Jon whispered. Illogical, too, for me to have cut it in the living room—to leave the clumps of curls fallen on the rug. "What have you done?" His hands on my head, feeling my bones, the bones in my skull, looking into my eyes. "You've cut off your hair," he said. He will be such a good lawyer. He understands everything.

*

The dog enjoys a fire. I cook beef bones for him, and when he is tired of pawing and chewing I light a fire, throwing in several gift pinecones that send off green and blue and orange sparks, and I brush him with Jon's French hairbrush until his coat glows in the firelight. The first few nights I lit the fire and brushed him, I washed the brush afterward, so Jon wouldn't find out. The doctors would tell me that was unreasonable: Jon said he would be gone a week. A logical woman, I no longer bother with washing the brush.

*

I have a scotch-and-milk before bed. The fire is still roaring, so I bring my pillow to the hearth and stretch out on the bricks. My eyelids get very warm and damp—the way they always did when I cried all the time, which I don't do any more. After all, this is the fifth night. As the doctors say, one must be adaptable. The dog tires of all the attention and chooses to sleep under the desk in the study. I have to call him twice—the second time firmly—before he comes back to settle in the living room. And when my eyes have been closed for five minutes he walks quietly away, back to the kneehole in the desk. At one time, Jon decided the desk was not big enough. He bought a door and two filing cabinets and made a new desk. The dog, a lover of small, cramped spaces, wandered unhappily from corner to corner, no longer able to settle anywhere. Jon brought the old desk back. A very kind man.

*

Like Columbus' crew, I begin to panic. It has been so long since I've seen Jon. Without him to check on me, I could wander alone in the house and then disappear forever—just vanish while rounding a corner, or by slipping down, down into the bathwater or up into the draft the fire creates. Couldn't that pull me with it —couldn't I go, with the cold air, up the chimney, arms outstretched, with my cupped hands making a parasol? Or while sitting in Jon's chair I might become smaller—become a speck, an ash. The dog would sniff and sniff, and then jump into the chair and settle down upon me and close his eyes.

To calm myself, I make tea. Earl Grey, an imported tea. Imported means coming to; exported means going away. I feel in my bones (my shinbones) that Jon will not come home. But perhaps I am just cold, since the fire is not yet lit. I sip the Earl Grey tea —results will be conclusive.

*

He said he was going to his brother's house for a week. He said that after caring for me he, also, had to recuperate. I have no hold on him. Even our marriage is common-law—if four years and four months make it common-law. He said he was going to his brother's. But how do I know where he's calling from? And why has he written no letters? In his absence, I talk to the dog. I pretend that I am Jon, that I am logical and reassuring. I tell the dog that Jon needed this rest and will soon be back. The dog grows anxious, sniffs Jon's clothes closet, and hangs close to the security of the kneehole. It *has* been a long time.

*

Celebrated my birthday in solitude. Took the phone off the hook so I wouldn't have to "put Jon on" when my parents called. Does the dog know that today is a special day? No day is special without beef bones, but I have forgotten to buy them to create a celebration. I go to the kneehole and stroke his neck in sorrow.

It occurs to me that this is a story of a woman whose man went away. Billie Holiday could have done a lot with it.

*

I put on a blue dress and go out to a job interview. I order a half cord of wood; there will be money when the man delivers it on Saturday. I splurge on canned horsemeat for the dog. "You'll never leave, will you?" I say as the dog eats, stabbing his mouth into the bowl of food. I think, giddily, that a dog is better than a hog. Hogs are only raised for slaughter; dogs are raised to love. Although I know this is true, I would be hesitant to voice this observation. The doctor (glasses sliding down nose, lower lip pressed to the upper) would say, "Might not *some* people love hogs?"

I dream that Jon has come back, that we do an exotic dance in the living room. Is it, perhaps, the tango? As he leads he tilts me back, and suddenly I can't feel the weight of his arms any more. My body is very heavy and my neck stretches farther and farther back until my body seems to stretch out of the room, passing painlessly through the floor into blackness.

Once when the electricity went off, Jon went to the kitchen to get candles, and I crawled under the bed, loving the darkness and wanting to stay in it. The dog came and curled beside me, at the side of the bed. Jon came back quickly, his hand cupped in front of the white candle. "Maria?" he said. "Maria?" When he left the room again, I slid forward a little to peek and saw him walking down the hallway. He walked so quickly that the candle blew out. He stopped to relight it and called my name louder—so loudly that he frightened me. I stayed there, shivering, thinking him as terrible as the Gestapo, praying that the lights wouldn't come on so he wouldn't find me. Even hiding and not answering was better than that. I put my hands together and blew into them, because I wanted to scream. When the lights came back on and he found me, he pulled me out by my hands, and the scream my hands had blocked came out.

*

After the hot grape jelly is poured equally into a dozen glasses, the fun begins. Melted wax is dropped in to seal them. As the white wax drips, I think, If there were anything down in there but jelly it would be smothered. I had laid in no cheesecloth, so I pulled a pair of lacy white underpants over a big yellow bowl, poured the jelly mixture through that.

In the morning Jon is back. He walks through the house to see if anything is amiss. Our clothes are still in the closets; all unnecessary lights have been turned off. He goes into the kitchen and then is annoyed because I have not gone grocery shopping. He has some toast with the grape jelly. He spoons more jelly from the glass to his mouth when the bread is gone.

"Talk to me, Maria. Don't shut me out," he says, licking the jelly from his upper lip. He is like a child, but one who orders me to do and feel things.

"Feel this arm," he says. It is tight from his chopping wood at his brother's camp.

I met his brother once. Jon and his brother are twins, but very dissimilar. His brother is always tan—wide and short, with broad shoulders. Asleep, he looks like the logs that he chops. When Jon and I were first dating we went to his brother's camp, and the three of us slept in a tent because the house was not yet built. Jon's brother snored all night. "I hate it here," I whispered to Jon, shivering against him. He tried to soothe me, but he wouldn't make love to me there. "I hate your brother," I said, in a normal tone of voice, because his brother was snoring so loudly he'd never hear me. Jon put his hand over my mouth. "Sh-h-h," he said. "Please." Naturally, Jon did not invite me on this trip to see him. I explain all this to the dog now, and he is hypnotized. He closes his eyes and listens to the drone of my voice. He appreciates my hand stroking in tempo with my sentences. Jon pushes the jelly away and stares at me. "Stop talking about something that happened years ago," he says, and stalks out of the room.

*

The wood arrives. The firewood man has a limp; he's missing a toe. I asked, and he told me. He's a good woodman—the toe was lost canoeing. Jon helps him stack the logs in the shed. I peek in and see that there was already a lot more wood than I thought.

Jon comes into the house when the man leaves. His face is heavy and ugly.

"Why did you order more wood?" Jon says.

"To keep warm. I have to keep warm."

*

I fix a beef stew for dinner, but feed it to the dog. He is transfixed; the steam warns him it is too hot to eat, yet the smell is delicious. He laps tentatively at the rim of the bowl, like an epicure sucking in a single egg of caviar. Finally, he eats it all. And then there is the bone, which he carries quickly to his private place under the desk. Jon is furious; I have prepared something for the dog but not for us.

"This has got to stop," he whispers in my face, his hand tight around my wrist.

*

The dog and I climb to the top of the hill and watch the commuters going to work in their cars. I sit on a little canvas stool—the kind fishermen use—instead of the muddy ground. It is September—mud everywhere. The sun is setting. Wide white clouds hang in the air, seem to cluster over this very hilltop. And then Jon's face is glowing in the clouds—not a vision, the real Jon. He is on the hilltop, clouds rolling over his head, saying to me that we have reached the end. Mutiny on the Santa Maria! But I only sit and wait, staring straight ahead. How curious that this is the end. He sits in the mud, calls the dog to him. Did he really just say that to me? I repeat it: "We have reached the end."

"I know," he says.

*

The dog walks into the room. Jon is at the desk. The kneehole is occupied, so the dog curls in the corner. He did not always circle before lying down. Habits are acquired, however late. Like the furniture, the plants, the cats left to us by the dead, they take us in. We think we are taking them in, but they take us in, demand attention.

I demand attention from Jon, at his desk at work, his legs now up in the lotus position on his chair to offer the dog his fine resting place.

"Jon, Jon!" I say, and dance across the room. I posture and prance. What a good lawyer he will be; he shows polite interest.

"I'll set us on fire," I say.

That is going too far. He shakes his head to deny what I have said. He leads me by my wrist to bed, pulls the covers up tightly. If I were a foot lower down in the bed I would smother if he kept his hands on those covers. Like grape jelly.

"Will there be eggs and bacon, and grape jelly on toast, for breakfast?" I ask.

There will be. He cooks for us now.

*

I am so surprised. When he brings the breakfast tray I find out that *today* is my birthday. There are snapdragons and roses. He kisses my hands, lowers the tray gently to my lap. The tea steams. The phone rings. I have been hired for the job. His hand covers the mouthpiece. Did I go for a job? He tells them there was a mistake, and hangs up and walks away, as if from something dirty. He walks out of the room and I am left with the hot tea. Tea is boiled so it can cool. Jon leaves so he can come back. Certain of this, I call and they both come—Jon and the dog—to settle down with me. We have come to the end, yet we are safe. I move to the center of the bed to make room for Jon; tea sloshes from the cup. His hand goes out to steady it. There's no harm done—the saucer contains it. He smiles, approvingly, and as he sits down his hand slides across the sheet like a rudder through still waters.

Hale Hardy
and the Amazing
Animal Woman

....

Hale Hardy went to college because he couldn't think of anything better to do, and he quit because he couldn't see any reason to stay. He lasted one and a half years. He did not exactly quit; he was thrown out. When that happened he went to visit his sister Mary, who was living with another girl, Paula, who was being supported by some dude. Hale didn't know the dude's name, or why he was supporting her, or why his sister was living there. He just went.

The sunsets he saw from the dining-room window knocked him out. It got so he'd pull a chair up to the window and wait for them, starting about one in the afternoon. He had a long wait, so he read. Sometime during the winter his former English teacher sent him *Lolita* in care of his parents, and they sent it on. That book put women in his mind. He thought it might be a good idea to pick up some woman and drive across the country with her— take some woman to the Grand Canyon. Eat ice cream with some woman, peering into the Grand Canyon. If they sold ice cream there. They probably did. They sold ice cream at the Alamo.

He couldn't keep one thought straight in his mind: first he'd be thinking about scoring some woman, then he'd be thinking about how good ice cream tasted, especially his favorite, French vanilla. Then he'd get up and eat—there was never ice cream in the place his sister was living, but there was a lot of other stuff—and then he'd sit down and wait for the sunset, trying to get through that long book, bogging down every few pages. He thought about writing his teacher. She couldn't have been much older than he was. He always thought she liked him. She called everybody by their last name, but she called him Hale. She had big blue eyes. Nothing else about her was big. Would his skinny teacher be pleased to get a note from him? If he didn't write, would he ever hear from her again? Yes; a postcard during the summer, from Seattle, Washington, saying that she was sailing around in a boat, which sure beat teaching. His mother forwarded that postcard with a comment: "If these are the people who are supposed to guide you, no wonder!!!" His mother put three exclamation points after everything; how much they were paying for heat, who was getting married, how many stray cats there were in New York City. Mary had nothing to do with their mother. Mary did not even refer to her by name; it was always "that wasted life." He agreed that his mother's life had been wasted, but he didn't hate her for that the way Mary did. He just didn't know what to do about it. He couldn't understand why such a sensible woman would name him Hale Hardy, though. And that was his mother's idea, not his father's, because he had checked. Why didn't she go through with the joke and give him N for a middle initial? What was she thinking of? His mother said that she had no way of knowing that Harold would get turned into Hale. That was partly Mary's fault, because when she was little she had trouble pronouncing Harold; it came out "Hal," got changed to Hale.

He was not very hale and hearty, probably his body's rebellion against such a nickname. He spent a lot of time reading Adelle Davis, trying to get together. Adelle never said what everybody was supposed to get together for, though. *Let's Stay Healthy for Our Trip to the Grand Canyon.*

There was a woman who came to clean whose name was Gloria Moratto. She was a woman in her thirties, hired by Paula's husband (turned out he was letting Paula use the house willed to him by an uncle). He told Paula that Gloria was pitiful. He felt sorry for her. Paula said that when her husband didn't know what to make of women he just gave in to them. Hale couldn't understand why she needed the job. She always had so much money. Money was stuffed in her purse, which she carried unfastened, and money fell out of her big apron as she cleaned, and she stuffed it back in the pockets the way people stuff used tissues away, hoping no one will notice. But it was easy to see why Paula's husband took pity on her: Gloria Moratto was indeed a sorrowful creature. Her large body was carried by small, narrow feet, and it rose up precariously, like a funnel. Her shoulders were very wide; on a man they would have been comforting. The most amazing thing about her was her head. It was big, accentuated by curly black hair bushing around it. Her eyes were big. Her mouth. But you could hardly see either because of the curly black hair. One time when Gloria came she had streaked her hair; the white and black was astonishing, like a skunk. He thought of her, then, as an animal, and watched with fascination as she did her work.

He imagined that this huge, strangely shaped woman would be capable of building a beaver dam. She vacuumed, polished, scrubbed, dusted, carried away trash, put things in their proper places, washed dishes, did the laundry. This amazing animal woman came every Friday and worked all day.

*

Hale wanted very much to see the Grand Canyon. When he was a child he had begged ceaselessly to see the Alamo until his mother told his father that either Hale would go to the Alamo or she was leaving forever. His father went with him to Texas, bought him an Alamo comb and two ice-cream cones. They stayed overnight, ate breakfast in a restaurant that looked like the inside of a barn, then went home. He treasured his Alamo comb. They bought an Alamo pin for Mary, which Hale could tell she didn't like. His father said that was to be expected; it was just nice to bring his sister a remembrance. Hale learned: you can give people things they don't like, and that's still nice. Hale was nuts about his comb. When his hair didn't need to be combed he'd stick it in his cowlick and just leave it there. What happened to that comb? Were there Grand Canyon combs?

Hale wanted to go to the Grand Canyon, but not alone. He would need someone to go along to verify that it was really happening, to take pictures of him standing on the rim of the Grand Canyon. His sister was not about to budge; it seemed that she loved Paula's ex-husband, who made regular visits, ostensibly to check up on Gloria's housekeeping. During his visits Paula left the house and so did Hale. Actually, he was kicked out. They didn't want Paula's ex-husband to know there was a man living there, so he and Paula would go into town and wait it out. One night Hale asked if she would like to go to the Grand Canyon. She had already seen it, when she was thirteen, and again when she was sixteen. He asked if there were a lot of stands that sold tourist crap. Yes; all along the road. She sighed. The landscape was being ruined. He sighed. She did not want to go with him.

That left Gloria, who was the only other person he knew in Connecticut. And what were the chances that the amazing animal woman, that woman of perseverance and strength, was going to pick up and go to the Grand Canyon with him? They were slim. Especially since she avoided talking to him. At least they were slim until he found out about her weakness. Her weakness was cats, and she loved to talk about how independent and smart and cute they were. She owned five cats. Hale found out about it from Paula, who found it out from Mary, who got the word from Paula's ex-husband. Why any of them bothered to talk about it was something else. He went to the Humane Society and got another one for her, a cat that came with a blue collar that matched its blue eyes. "La la la," Gloria sang, and the cat responded by turning his head to listen instead of jumping out of her arms. She gave it a dollar bill to play with, money wrinkled and twisted from being carried a long time in that deep apron pocket. The cat pounced on it, stuck his nose under it. Gloria had a new cat. His friendship with Gloria was beginning. From the living-room window a red-and-violet sunset flashed upon the sky.

*

Hale daydreams of Gloria, her paw-feet, her cat-eyes, only big, b-i-i-i-i-g. She is so competent; she will share the driving; her hand will be steady around the camera. Later, they would have lots of little kittens. It would be their house she took care of. No more exploitation of Gloria; let Paula and Mary keep house for themselves. On her birthday a little Siamese kitten; for Christmas an Angora. The pitter-patter of little paws. Cats, too: regal, willful, splendid cats. To broach the subject . . .

*

She might be willing to go to the Grand Canyon, but she would never marry him. She harbors a secret love? She says not. She says all her sisters are married and unhappy. One sister goes to a clinic for unhappiness. One brother-in-law, not married to that sister, also goes to unhappiness meetings.

"Group therapy, Gloria?"

"Yes. That's what I'm saying."

"The Grand Canyon is in the opposite direction from Niagara Falls."

She is not convinced.

"Paula and Mary and their dirty, dirty house. They exploit you."

"What's that?"

"They don't keep their own house clean."

"That's right. I have to clean for them."

"They exploit you. There's no reason they can't do it themselves. Paula and Mary are strong, aren't they?"

"Paula is divorced. Not strong."

"Paula is not too weak to take care of herself. We're talking about dust, Gloria. Getting rid of dust. Isn't it easy to clean up dust?"

Gloria dusts and listens.

"My sisters all got married and they are all unhappy."

"Not getting married. Just taking a trip."

"Immoral."

"A trip is immoral?"

"Sex."

"You don't have to sleep with me on the trip."

"I would sleep with you if you loved me. I don't think you're in love with me."

"I am, Gloria. I am."

"I'll think about it."

She pouts with her big lips.

"At least sleep with me here, Gloria."

She says she is willing to do that. Hale and Gloria go upstairs and lie down on the bed she has made earlier in the day. He gets on top of her big body. Over her head there is a window. The sky has begun to pale, a romantic pink. Gloria's body is pink. The sky gets pinker and pinker. How beautiful the sunsets must be over the Grand Canyon. Hale is looking at George Washington. A dollar fell out of some of Gloria's clothing. Gloria brushes her hair out of her eyes and says she wants to take Hale home with her. Why? "To think about going to the Grand Canyon with you." "I want to come home with you, Gloria, but how will my being there help you think?" "I will see you and think of you." "You're going to go to the Grand Canyon with me, aren't you?" Hale clutches Gloria's thigh. "Come home and let me think about it."

Paula and Mary do not speak to Gloria and Hale when they come downstairs. Hale senses that he is no longer welcome in the house—good he has somewhere to go. He wonders if there will be sunsets out Gloria's window. Gloria sings a happy tune, swinging her arms at her side, stubbornly refusing to hold hands: "La la la dum dum la la la."

*

There are cats all over Gloria's house. She loves them all, calls them to her, spoon-feeds her kitten. The cats walk across the table, superior, aggressive. He knows a few of the names: Mister Tom, Lucky, Antonio, Prince. Some are the offspring of others. She explains the lineages and he forgets as fast as she speaks. Her newest, the cat he gave her, has been named Blue Boy. It is the Superman of cats, that jumps suddenly into action, leaping from chair to table to floor. Hale watches the cats and they watch him. At night one of them mews; Prince, they think. He has never really felt a fondness for cats, and he does not like them better now that he lives with them. He thinks about getting rid of one of them; Prince, he thinks.

He asks Gloria when they can leave. She wants to know if there is a best time to go West. He tells her now, now is the best time, and she says she is thinking hard. She sits and looks puzzled. Her sisters call all the time, whining with unhappiness. Gloria strokes a passing cat, shakes her head, picks cat hair out of her slacks when things get tense.

"What do your sisters have to do with your taking a trip? I've already said it doesn't mean marriage. Can't we take a trip?"

One of her sisters took a trip, then married the man. Gloria sulks. A cat rubs against Hale's legs. He has to feed the cats. From a dark corner, small green eyes stare.

*

"You don't really love me. Why do you want to take this trip?"

"I love you. I really love you. I can't go on a trip and leave you."

"What would I do with my cats?"

"We can take them. We'll just put them in the car."

"Some of them won't ride."

"What do you mean they won't ride?"

"They're scared. They meow and walk all around the car."

"We'll put them in a box."

"Cruel."

"Gloria, it's cats. Just cats."

"I want to tell you something, then. I wasn't going to tell. Once I was a cat. You have to know that I am reincarnated."

That's the biggest word he's ever heard her use. He questions her to find out if she knows what she just said.

"I went to a fortune teller, and she said what I thought was right. Once I was a cat, and I think I lived somewhere very, very cold. I don't remember too much."

"You really think you were a cat?"

"I know I was a cat."

"Well, what does that have to do with our going across country?"

"I can't put a cat in a box. What if somebody put me in a box? How would I like it?"

"We'll leave it out of the box."

"Two would have to be in boxes."

"You conducted experiments with these cats or something?"

"I've tried to ride with them. Two won't ride."

"When they get to the Grand Canyon they'll love it. How many cats get taken to see the wonders of the world?"

"Why don't we go see my sister and then she wouldn't be so unhappy? It would only take eight hours of driving to see my sister."

"Your sister isn't one of the wonders of the world."

The plans for driving to the Grand Canyon are going badly.

*

He gives her a new kitten, hoping that now she will love him enough to take the trip. Instead, she loves the cat. She tries out names, strokes it, shields it from the other cats' curiosity.

She tells Hale that once she was a cat who sat on a velvet cushion in some cold room, maybe in Russia the fortune teller said, and was tended by some beautiful woman, maybe a princess, who wished she would become human. And now that she has, she imagines that the beautiful woman is dead, or that this all happened in some far country that she will never find again. The story puts her to sleep as she tells it, night after night, her own personal fairy tale. He shudders to think that before he came to live with her she probably told the story to the cats. He knows it. But there is something about Gloria that reminds him of an animal. When he thought of her as a skunk maybe he was close to seeing her as a cat. He doesn't believe or disbelieve the idea of reincarnation. He just wants to go to the Grand Canyon.

In the afternoon, while Gloria is out looking for a job, he drives to Paula's house to see if there is any mail for him. There is a letter from his mother and an advertisement from a record club. He fills out the record-club form with Paula's name, checks the "Country Favorites" category, checks "please bill me," does not check that he wants the free calendar he is entitled to. Wait until Paula opens that box and sees Country Charlie Pride grinning at her. He puts the blank in Paula's mailbox to be picked up. He opens the letter from his mother. It contains many exclamation points regarding his unwillingness to write, his unwillingness to take advantage of the educational opportunities his father etc. etc., and the news that a girl he went to high school with just got married to a man with leukemia and she *knew* it!!! He pockets the twenty dollars that is in the letter. He buys a postcard on the way to Gloria's and writes: "What a surprise to get your treat. Thank you!!!" and drops it in a mailbox. With the money he buys a cage. He drives home. Gloria is still out looking for a job. He rounds up as many cats as he can and tries to lure them into the cage. They will not walk into it, so he puts them in, closes the door, and peers in. They don't like it. He wants to go to the Grand Canyon.

Gloria comes home. She has found a job working in a department store. He tells her she must get away from such jobs, stop being taken advantage of, go West with him. She asks how people looking for thread and buttons exploit her. She sees the cage. She hates it. She does not want to go to the Grand Canyon. Go alone! He doesn't even love her. She is going to sell buttons to people.

He can leave her anytime he wants. Her eyes are larger, imagining her abandonment. Wasn't that what her sisters' husbands were always doing?

He tells her that the cats will get used to the cage, and at night they can be free in the car. He thinks the trip could be accomplished in two weeks, allowing them time to really see the Grand Canyon. She puts her hands over her ears, complaining that she can't stand any more talk about the Grand Canyon. In bed, she huddles on her side. It is strange that anything that big can huddle. She weighs the mattress down on her side, pulls the covers over her head to get away from him. Hale thinks that she may put him out. He doesn't want that. He wants them both out together, on their way West. He thinks about what he could do that would be nice for her, reaches over to stroke her arm. She squirms. All right, then. He will get her another cat.

*

He goes to a house where kittens are being given away. The house is near the university, and several hippies look at him long and hard before they even show him the kittens. The kittens are in a box of rags. The girl lifts them out gently. He says he would like all of them. "Wow," she says, "there's only one more we want to get rid of." She gives him a funny look. She also gives him a kitten. He buys a ribbon for its neck and takes it to Gloria's house and drops it on the sofa. Hale is depressed; soon summer will be over, the best time to see the Grand Canyon will have passed, the kitten will have grown into a cat, and here he will be, still waiting.

Gloria sees that he is sad when she comes home from work. Good. She begins to feel guilty because she won't go along with his plans. Good. She says that she has been thinking it over and that soon she will have reached a decision about the trip. As she talks, she sees the new addition. "Pretty little baby," she exclaims, and mothers the kitten, who has been sleeping on the sofa. She thanks Hale, says that she loves the little thing. He decides to turn the tables on her. She loves the kitten, but she doesn't love him. This makes her mad. She does love him. She sits on his lap —she is incredibly heavy—swaying her feet like a petulant little daddy's sweetheart, getting her way. She just needs a little more time to think, because her sisters all did things that were crazy and they were so unhappy, and she does not want to have to go to unhappiness meetings at night and let everyone know how unhappy she is. She kisses his neck, promising that tomorrow night she will tell him. Right now she is going to fix him a nice dinner, to show him that she loves him. She goes into the kitchen. One of the cats follows her, and as it passes his chair he gives it a shove with his foot. The cat runs after her. That's it! He's been doing this all wrong. He should be getting rid of the cats instead of bringing them home. He should round up all the damn animals and get rid of them, and then in her grief she would agree to do things his way. Hale decides to give Gloria one last chance to come through, and then he is going to start doing in her cats.

*

Gloria sits on his lap again. She says that she thought all day long while she was selling buttons, and as she looked at the customers she thought that those women were all loved and that she wasn't. She just couldn't agree to a trip with a man she felt didn't love her. Desperate, he assures her that her feelings are wrong. And when she leaves the room he grabs a cat to strangle, but realizes that she'll know he killed it—it has to be more subtle.

The next day he puts several cats in the car and drives to a farm far from the highway, and lets them out. He drives away, smirking. One of the cats has the last laugh, though. Several days later it finds its way back to Gloria's house. She has mourned for the cats, and now God is answering her prayers and has sent back a messenger. This messenger is going to tell her something about the other cats, but of course her cooing brings no response; the usual rubbing against her leg, a little more milk lapping than usual because of its long journey. So the piece of shit found its way home. He decides he will poison it.

*

They die like flies. The veterinarian doesn't know what happened to the first cat. Would she like an autopsy done? Sacrilege! No. No autopsy. And when she goes back with a dead kitten he says, at first, that sometimes this just happens with little kittens, gives her a tissue to dry her eyes, sends them away. He is afraid to let her see this veterinarian again, though, because eventually the man will suspect poisoning. So when the next cat is found dead, by a neighbor, in the neighbor's yard, Hale tells Gloria that their former veterinarian was no good—he didn't even know why her poor cats died. They have to find another veterinarian. In fact, this is too traumatic for her. *He* will take the corpse to the veterinarian and report to her. She thanks him, weeping, and pulls money out of her pocket. And he gets in the car with the cat wrapped in a towel on the seat beside him and heads for the imaginary veterinarian, parking the car off the highway and running up a slope to put the bundle beside a big tree. Two to go, and then it will be just the two of them.

Driving home, he stops at the Golden Arches, eats a victory cheeseburger, french fries and a Coke. The Golden Arches are a rainbow, and at the end of it lies the Grand Canyon.

*

He puts the kitten in the cage. He puts the cage in his car. He drives to the Humane Society. They want a donation. He says that he doesn't have the three dollars. The truth; but what a look the woman gives him. She accepts the animal wordlessly. Three dollars would make her say "Thank you" to exonerate him from guilt; for nothing, she just looks away.

Hale bides his time. In another week he can take the last kitten to the Humane Society, but he can't take it away from Gloria yet. She has been clinging to it, at night, sitting up in the dark house, certain that there is a curse on it that she must try to ward off. The kitten has a sleek coat, bright eyes, it plays with a ball of yarn. But she is right in knowing that its health is no protection. She pities the dead cats because she thinks God is punishing her through them, and that's not fair. He tells her that a vindictive God is nonsense. Maybe it was some virus that went through them . . . Gloria hangs on his words. She is so upset that he thinks about sparing Lucky, but he must have Gloria to himself, she must turn all her attention toward him so that their trip West will be wonderful. She must want to take pictures of him standing mighty on the edge of the Grand Canyon, instead of snapping

cute little kitten pictures for her photograph album, already filled
with pictures of the dead.

His sister calls, saying that she and Paula want his junk out of
their house. He drives over that afternoon, taking a big laundry
basket with him. He loads his clothing into it, and his book.

"I don't know why you decided that of all the women in the
world you had to take that poor broken-down maid," Paula says.

"We love each other," he says.

"You don't. You never used to speak. Paula and I were afraid
she was going to quit because there were bad feelings," Mary says.

"Then you should be happy now."

"I'm not happy. Are you doing this as a joke?"

"I'm in love with her."

"Are you going to marry her?"

"She doesn't want to get married. Her family is all fucked up.
She has a lot of sisters who are getting divorced or just sitting
around suffering. I don't know."

"She's piggy," Paula tells him.

"I know. But I love her."

"That's nice," Paula says.

"It's not nice. It's a sick joke," Mary says.

"We're going to take a trip to the Grand Canyon," Hale tells
them.

That afternoon he decides that Lucky's time is up. He puts
Lucky in the car. Trapped, Lucky raises his paws to the window
and looks out. The cat looks out the window until it gets where
it's going: the same farm where its friends disappeared, only
Lucky has the extra good luck to be discharged in front of two
children, who stare at Hale's car as if they expect something. You
should, little ones, he thinks, for I have brought you another kitty.
Lucky is dropped out the window. The children stare. They will
no doubt tell the story to their parents, exactly as it happened,
and if their parents do not let them keep Lucky they will think
their parents are cruel and they will hate them. The parents know
that! Lucky Lucky.

*

Because of all the horrible things that have been happening,
Gloria hasn't spoken about the trip yet. That night, as he rocks

her in his arms, he says that she must rest from this ordeal. They
will go West, forget. Just the two of them. He puts his head on
her big shoulder, lets it sink to her breast. A crackling noise;
money in her brassiere. Yes, she says. She supposes.

*

On the second day of the trip, Gloria is in good spirits. They
stop for lunch, and after lunch they sing. They were taught a lot
of the same songs when they were children. He can't talk to her
about politics because she knows so little and he gets bored trying
to fill her in, and she doesn't like the music he likes on the radio,
so usually they just hold hands or sing. He doesn't even let go of
her hand to shift gears. He smiles at her often, marveling at
those tiny feet, crossed so demurely, and at her large body. It's
good she has money and a car in good condition, because they
have to stop often for food—she's always hungry—and he
couldn't afford the highway prices, and his car never would have
made it.

They stop at a motel with a pool, and she is as excited as a
child. She hurries to get undressed and races out of the room
while he's still putting on his bathing trunks, and when he walks
across the parking lot to the pool he sees Gloria at the top of the
blue ladder, her hips spread over the sides; he is in time to see her
splash into the pool. He takes a picture of her with his Instamatic
as she surfaces, her thick hair untamed by the water.

They sit on chairs by the pool, sipping Coke from a can. The
water dries on the tops of her huge breasts and is replaced by
sweat. She drinks two Cokes and he drinks one. It is her idea to
ask the owner of the motel the name of a good restaurant, and
she goes to the desk while he's showering. He sings in the shower.
A delicious dinner! The Grand Canyon! Tum-de-dum, he sings, a
little tune he learned from her. He steps out of the shower, wraps
a towel around himself, and hears faintly, above the air conditioning, crying.

Gloria is crying. She has her arms crossed in front of her, protecting herself, sitting in front of the air conditioner and crying.
Hale rushes to her, and she puts her head on his shoulder—he is
freezing in front of the damn air conditioner—and speaks a single

word: "Cat." She has decided that the man she just talked to was one of her cats, reincarnated. She says this because he looked so much like Mister Tom. Really he did; he had Mister Tom's eyes. The way Mister Tom had one weak eye that went out of focus . . . and the man said, after he told her about restaurants, that she looked familiar. Hale said that people who ran places like motels were always thinking they saw familiar faces just because they saw so many people, that of course it was not Mister Tom. She told him to go talk to the man, to watch his eyes grow weak, drift away. But that's not uncommon! She won't accept it; the motel owner is Mister Tom, her own Mister Tom, and fate has guided them to this particular motel. She weeps.

"What if it is your cat? Why are you crying?"

"I don't know. I want to know if Mister Tom is happy."

"He's happy. He's got a nice business, this is a good location. He's doing fine."

"You don't believe in reincarnation," she wails. "You talk to me like I'm a child, instead of the woman you love. You don't love me. Why did you bring me on this trip?"

He does love her, he reassures her, and sings, "It Had To Be You."

"But now I'm so sad," she tells him. "I saw Mister Tom again, and I want him to be with me."

Gloria makes no sense. He tells her that the motel owner is blissfully happy. He points out that the motel owner is making a lot of money and that he can sit in the sunshine by his pool in the day if he wants. She dries her eyes, wanting to believe him.

*

Gloria has a nightmare and wakes up Hale with her screaming. She saw Blue Boy, and he told her something evil was happening in the world. Under the covers, she shudders. Hale tells her that the air conditioning is blowing right on them and gets out of bed to adjust the flow of air. His legs are shaking.

*

In North Platte, Nebraska, Hale gets a little drunk with Gloria in a bar. She can drink more than he can, because she's fatter, probably. He tells her about the people who made fun of his name in school, about all the boys who wanted to fight him because of his name, and how he always lost. He is morose. He becomes more morose when she tells him that she agrees with Blue Boy that the world is an evil place. He asks her what she means, exactly, and she can't say. She just senses something.

*

A panhandler comes up to them at a diner in Fort Defiance, New Mexico. Hale says he has no money. Gloria gives him a dollar. "It was Prince," she tells Hale, "but I must be brave."

"It wasn't Prince," he says angrily. "It was a Goddamn old bum."

"I know it was Prince," she shrieks.

"Okay, okay." He thinks she might really flip out.

*

Hale thinks about getting away from her, so he won't have to be responsible for committing her when she flips out. He thinks about ditching her somewhere, but it's her car, and she might get the police on him. He thinks about calling his parents collect and having them send him enough money to get a plane home. But what is he supposed to do—wait around Fort Defiance, New Mexico? Arizona is only a day away. If she would just be quiet and not fantasize all the time, he could even feel exalted about seeing the Grand Canyon. She has a faraway look on her face that she isn't willing to talk about. When she's not crying for no reason she's talking about all the cats and kittens she had not long ago, as though important people were dead. She's having trouble holding herself together. There are no more songs. She listens to the radio —he guesses she's listening—and to the songs he likes, because he doesn't care if he pleases her or not any more.

Riding into Arizona, she says, "Do you think that maybe the reason you want to see the Grand Canyon is because you had something to do with it in your former life?"

"I didn't have a former life."

"You don't remember it," she says.

"That reincarnation crap is all silly. There's nothing after

death. Nothing happens to change you. You get put in the
ground and you rot."

"I knew you didn't believe," she says.

"It's all a lot of crap."

"Then how come I can remember being on a big cushion in a
cold house somewhere? A castle, maybe."

"You made it up. It's all in your head. A story you tell yourself."

"I remember it," she says, and looks out the window with that
funny expression again.

*

A cat runs in front of the car and Hale hits the brakes. It
looked like one of Gloria's cats, the fat orange one, and Hale
knows what he's in for. Gloria sucks in her breath. "Antonio," she
whispers. "What is he doing on a road out here in the wilder-
ness?"

"Somebody's pet," Hale says.

"You almost killed him."

"It's okay. I saw it in the rearview mirror."

"Poor Antonio. He was trying to tell me something."

"What are you crying about now, for Christ's sake?"

"He risked his life. There was something he wanted me to
know."

"Oh for Christ's sake. Somebody's damn pet."

"You don't even like cats, do you?" Gloria asks. She is squinting
hard, much harder than the setting sun requires.

"Why should I care about cats?" he says.

"They all died," she says, as though he's unbelievably stupid.

"That's right. They died. They're gone. They aren't coming
back as motel owners or as messengers in the night, and they
aren't running in front of your car to attract your attention,
Gloria."

"Let me out."

"What are you talking about?"

"I want to get out of the car."

She has her hand on the door handle. As she turns to lift the
lock, Hale reaches around her.

"For Christ's sake. Don't be so dramatic."

"Just let me out."

"I'm not putting you out on some highway in Arizona."

"Let me out and pick up some pretty hitchhiker. Why don't you pick up some hitchhiker? You can have my car. Just let me out."

Hale notices that her body is not as large as it was when they began the trip. But she still seems larger than life, with her wide, big eyes and her big mouth, her lips more prominent because they're chapped. She's been biting her lips. If he did let her out, no one would ever pick her up.

"Come on, Gloria. Calm down. In a few minutes we'll be at the Grand Canyon."

"You think it's silly for me to think about my cats, but you don't think you're silly to always talk about the Grand Canyon. My sisters' husbands are all like that. Anything my sisters want is silly. But *they*'re never silly. At least I'm not married to you."

Gloria hates him now. But Hale doesn't hate Gloria. He is so used to her, to this big woman who sits complaining and crying day after day. He almost wishes she could be happy again.

"Just sit still and relax," Hale says. He is still covering the lock with his hand.

*

Gloria refuses to get out of the car when she has her chance, when it is parked at the Grand Canyon. Like a big, sulking child she sits inside with the doors locked, looking at Hale looking into the Grand Canyon. She has figured out the message the cats meant to give her. She weeps for her cats, her soft little kittens. She also cries a little because for the first two days of the trip she thought she might really be starting to love Hale, that it wouldn't be just another romance that ended sadly, like all her sisters' marriages.

Hale knows that he is locked out of the car. He stares into the Grand Canyon knowing that, and stands for a long time thinking before he goes to a refreshment stand. It is a little cooler under the red, white and blue striped awning. He buys two vanilla ice-cream cones and goes back to the car. He taps on the window.

She puts down the map she is fanning herself with and rolls it down a crack. "More," he says. "This is for you." She rolls down the window enough to take the ice-cream cone from him. The first lick is so cold that she shivers. She wipes her forehead on her arm, shifts in the seat to unstick her legs. He puts his hand through the window and strokes her hair.

"We could rent horses and ride down into the Canyon," Hale says. "Wouldn't that be fun?"

"No," she says. She has started to cry again.

"Maybe your cats would all be there waiting for you."

"Do you think I'm a fool? That I think my cats are in the Grand Canyon?"

"There's a mysterious elephant burial ground in Africa, isn't there?"

"So what? What does that have to do with me?"

"Come on, Gloria. Get out of the car."

"No," she says, but Hale can tell that she's wavering. It must be very hot in the car. Gloria looks terrible, sweating and crying. Her ice-cream cone is melting and running down her wrist.

"When you get out we can freshen up over there, by the refreshment stand. And you can buy us a couple of hot dogs for dinner."

"You think I'm going to get out now and buy you dinner?"

"Come on, Gloria," he says, trying to pull the door open as if it's unlocked. She moves away from the door.

"Then leave," Hale says. "You've got the keys. Go home."

"And then what would happen to you? I'd drive away and leave you here, and some pretty girl would give you a ride, and soon I'd see you again. You'd come after me."

"Of course I would, Gloria. I love you."

"No!" she cries. "I don't think you love me at all."

He tries the door again, but of course it does not open. Gloria has moved into the driver's seat now, but she makes no attempt to start the car. She is crying too hard to drive, anyway. Figuring that the car won't be going anywhere, he climbs on the hood and mournfully, chewing the last of his ice-cream cone, gazes into the vast pit of the canyon.

Four Stories About Lovers

▪▪▪▪▪▪▪▪▪▪▪▪▪▪▪▪▪▪▪▪▪

I

His wife is a very sick woman, because she thinks these things through very thoroughly. He wouldn't be surprised to find out that she likes the big white house so much not because it's big or white, but because the post office is across the street. She is very sick, and she mails letters to him from the post office. She gets up at night, and while other wives might read or do housework with their insomnia, she writes him a letter—usually a brief note, actually—and pulls the raincoat over her nightgown and crosses the street to the post office. Some nights when he too has insomnia, he raises himself to one elbow and parts the curtains to watch her. She is a pretty wife, and he'll be glad when she's come back to bed.

The matter of reading the letters, the matter of reading the letters. He is never sure what is best to do. He very rarely throws them out, though. He can't tell what reaction she wants—it seems to be neither extreme nor anything that he's tried yet in the in-between range. For example: one morning, reading a note detailing what hotel she went to at what hour with her lover (she doesn't let his name slip), he screamed with frustration, banged his hands on the breakfast table. She sipped coffee, shrugged. Another time he handed the note back to her saying, "So what?" She smiled, shrugged. There was also the time he asked her if she wanted to see a psychiatrist, and she said they hadn't helped anyone she knew, or the time he telephoned her mother and her mother said she didn't want to get involved. Sometimes he dreams that the messages will stop coming, that the mail will bring only blessed bills. Sometimes when he looks out the window to see her crossing the road at night a thought goes through his head: it's not for you. It's for someone else. That's no consolation, though, because if it's to someone else, chances are it's to her lover. He accepts her getting out of bed to do something related to him—mail him a letter—but what of her awakening to jot a fond message to someone else?

She said that she wanted a big house so the baby could run and play. They have one daughter, Elizabeth, who is five. He liked the house, but wasn't it too close to the road? She *watched* the baby, unlike other mothers, so what did it matter? Besides, it was the size of the house that mattered. The house had so many possibilities. When they first moved in she spent so much time redoing the house that she couldn't have had time for a lover. The messages were few and far between at that time. But in the fall Elizabeth went to kindergarten and most of the rooms were finished, and then he began to get the messages daily, and sometimes there were two a day. From the first he never thought they were a joke, and maybe that was where he bungled—if he had only scoffed at them she might have seen that he genuinely didn't believe it. There had been an envelope addressed to him in his wife's handwriting and she had brought it to him while he was having breakfast, and he had smiled, expecting some kind of joke, and of course he had been doubly let down. If only he hadn't recognized the handwriting.

The notes are different now. The first notes, the fall notes, were brief, specific, and often personally insulting. The winter notes were longer, less specific, more . . . what might be called mystical. She felt that she was becoming a part of something large, large and important. In the spring there were rhymes, or little drawings, sometimes a combination: a sketch of a little animal—groundhog?—with a verse: "We went to the zoo/The sky was so blue/The sky was so blue/Then what did we do?/Then what did we do?" Now the notes are questioning—no easy clues as in the spring notes: "There is something vast and warm as summer, and at times I am as warm as summer, but other times I am cold and pull up the blanket in my sleep. How, exactly, does the mind let you know you are cold? What signal makes me move when I intend not to move?"

One night he says her name out loud, whispers "Janet" in his sleep. Either asleep or awake she puts her arm out to stroke his side. He knows why he woke up, though—not her touch, but what he was thinking. What signaled him? What will happen now?

As a joke, almost, he writes her a message when he gets to work and has his secretary mail it. All day he thinks, Do I need a psychiatrist? Answered by, Who have they helped? Should I speak to her mother again? Answered by, Didn't she already tell you to leave her alone? He goes home, has dinner, plays with Elizabeth, does a little work, and goes to bed. For hours he turns in the bed, wondering what will happen. More than that, though, he is lonesome and wishes Janet would wake up. He thinks of pretending to be asleep and rolling over on her, or of calling her name—no whispering, right out loud. A cheap trick. He kicks the covers off and looks at whatever objects he can see in the room in spite of the dark and in spite of his limited perspective. And then she stirs too—for covers? No—she's quietly getting out of bed.

"A message?" he whispers.

"Yes."

This is the first time they have ever discussed the messages when she's in the process of writing them.

"Coffee?" he asks.

"All right."

She sits sleepily across from him at the kitchen table, and for a while as she drinks the coffee he thinks she's forgotten about the notes she intended to write. Almost mechanically she scrawls a few words on a pad and puts a piece of paper in an envelope, then drops the envelope on the counter and walks beside him down the hall to bed. It's a humid night and the sheets feel sticky. He has trouble going to sleep. Finally he stops trying and throws his legs over the side of the bed.

"Getting up?" she says.

"Yes."

"It's so humid it's hard to sleep."

He gets up and walks across the floor.

"Mail the letter while you're up," she says.

"No," he says. "I refuse."

The room is silent, and then she laughs. He goes back to the bed. She's half on his side of the bed and makes no attempt to move. He lies down anyway. She begins to whisper—about something vast that surrounds them. Doesn't he feel its presence? What can they do? He rests an arm across her stomach. He can't answer the question when she whispers to him any better than he can when she writes it. He takes his arm away and pounds the bed.

"Yes," she says. "There."

It is a humid night, so it will be difficult to sleep. In the morning she will get his note, and that will be inadequate too, because it doesn't contain any answers.

II

The lover thinks that he is compared unfavorably to other lovers. In fact he is no longer her lover, but he remembers when he was, and that depresses him because he never intended to become her lover and he never intended to stop being her lover. She left because he got nasty. One time they argued—well, a lot of times they argued—but one particular time they argued walking into the house and he bent to make a snowball, then another, and another. He threw them all at her, and instead of running into the house she ran around the house and, of course, finally fell. He didn't realize that she had really been frightened until he put out his hand to help her up and she tried to scramble backward with that strange expression on her face. Then, of course, the martyrdom: he could save his energy by just kicking snow over her instead of pulling her up. Go on, go on . . . He wasn't opposed to kicking a little snow? She was afraid of him sometimes, but she still fought with him.

Pulling up in front of the house where she lives now, he tries to remember pleasant things. How they had watched the snow falling in the morning. The morning of the day he threw snowballs at her. The morning of the day she turned her ankle. He didn't turn the ignition off. One of the girls she lived with looked at his car from where she stood on the front lawn. She must have been surprised when he took off again. She must have wanted to get a good look at him because no doubt she had heard stories about the girl's lover.

"Heard any stories about me?" he asks pleasantly when he returns to the house.

The girl has. She looks at him without speaking. She must be a little afraid of him, though, because she gives a half nod. The girl has brown braids and wears a backless summer dress. He toys with the idea of asking if she wants a lover.

"It's your lover," he calls through the screen door.

She comes to the door smiling. One of the things she likes

about him is his sense of humor. What does she think is funny about his having been her lover?

She shows him around. She says she is happy in the house. She points out a table she likes. This house is furnished. They had very little furniture in the other house, although that too was "furnished." He tries to remember the inside of the other house and ends up remembering being her lover. He says nothing about the table she shows him. She asks if he has eaten dinner. Does he want to go out, then, or just listen to some music? Go out. Where will they go? It was always her fault—she was always so quick to be cynical. He thinks about telling her they can go out and throw snowballs so he can watch her face change—so he can notice something familiar about her face. This doesn't even look like her face. He remembers that she shares the house with three other girls. What do they look like? Maybe one of *them* was his lover.

When he drove away from this house the first time he came, he went to a liquor store and bought some bourbon and drank it. She must have guessed that. She once thought he had been drinking when she smelled Lysol in the house. Lysol! If she's as uncomfortable as he thinks she is, maybe she'll drink some. She drank, too, but she always had something to say about his drinking.

The girl with the brown braids calls to them: "Have a good time."

She doesn't approve. He goes across the lawn to where the girl is digging in the garden. He picks up a handful of moist dirt, shapes it into a ball and throws it at the front of her dress.

"Whose lover am I?" he hollers.

The girl scrambles, regains her balance and tears off, calling, "You're her Goddamn lover!"

Exactly right. He raises his eyebrows questioningly to his lover.

"You won't scare me this time," she says.

She turns and walks to the car, pulls open the door, and sits down. She leaves the door open for him to close. He does: click. The proper little date.

"Did you do that to scare me?" she asks. "You won't scare me any more."

"You feel you understand me well enough now to be my lover?" he asks.

"What is there to understand?" she asks.

She's trying very hard to act self-assured. The speeding and changing-lanes trick always gets her. She wants to give in. Why else would she have agreed to see him? He looks at her questioningly again. That unnerves her a little; she repeats her question.

III

She suspects her husband, so instead of accomplishing anything, in spite of all the books and articles telling her how she can accomplish everything, she takes a bus downtown and sits in the park across from his office. She once went to a Christmas party at his office. They rode to the top floor. Does he work on the top floor, or is that only where they have parties? It seems as good a place as any to look, because she could not really see him *in* the building anyway. Sun glints off the glass, so she doesn't look for too long. She looks up high, then at the door. She does this for about two hours. She doesn't see her husband. She intends not to do anything so foolish again, but the next day she finds that she has no more work to do, so she drives her car to the bus stop and parks it and gets on a bus. She doesn't like the downtown traffic. He says she is spoiled, living in the suburbs. He drives downtown every day at rush hour. The park is crowded today, so she goes looking for his car. Foolish, really, because it's probably in a garage. But she walks up and down several blocks and doesn't stop doing it until she thinks she might get lost. She doesn't know her way around the business district well. When she returns to the park it is nearly noon, and she finds a seat next to a man eating his lunch from a bag. He smiles at her. She returns his smile. She wonders if he works with her husband. Was he at the Christmas party? Probably not. She watches the door and once she thinks she sees him, walking next to a short man in a pale-blue suit, but it isn't him after all when she rises off the bench and can see more clearly. What time does he go to lunch? That night as they eat dinner she asks what time he eats lunch. He says that he never eats lunch at the same time. Today he ate around two.

"Why do you ask?" he says.

"That's why you're not very hungry," she says.

He has eaten almost everything on his plate.

She skips a day and feels good all day, thinking that she will never do it again. But the next day something tells her that she will see him, so she drives downtown without realizing that she hasn't stopped at the bus stop, as she usually does. She's downtown in the traffic before she realizes what she's done. She's nervous and twice she gets in the wrong lane and has to wait while everyone makes a left turn, but she finally makes it safely to a parking garage. She's just nervous, so she goes into a drugstore and drinks a cup of coffee. Then she goes, as usual, to the bench. She thinks that she may not see him after all, because she spent a lot of time tied up in traffic, and then more time at the drugstore. She only waits for an hour, then gives up because he must have already been to lunch. So many people pour out of his building that she might not see him anyway. She goes back to the parking garage and finds that she's lost the ticket. The attendant calls the manager, who comes out to talk to her. He asks her to describe her car and she's very upset and can't think well—she almost describes her husband's car before she realizes her mistake. "Well, decide what you'd like best, lady," the manager says, laughing. He thinks it's funny. He asks how long she's been and she says two hours. He tells the attendant to charge her for three and walks back into his glass cubicle. She thinks about trying to hit him, but she wouldn't want to be hit back. If he has a sense of humor like that he might hit a woman. She doesn't want to make any excuses to her husband. She even tips the attendant.

She sits on the bench the next day from about ten o'clock— only an hour after her husband has left the house—until four o'clock. She stops at a store on the way to the bus stop and buys a pretty blouse. She has to stand on the bus all the way to her car. She's tired when she gets home. Her husband is already there. He asks where she's been.

"Shopping."

"That's why you look so tired," he says.

Her husband never has much energy himself, but she has nothing to accuse him with. She will. The next day she plans to stand outside the building, to be there when work lets out, right on the side of the street with the building so she won't miss him.

The next day she arrives early—three-thirty. He doesn't get out until six. She looks through some stores and looks idly for his car, without much hope of seeing it. She goes to the drugstore again and has a cup of coffee and sits in the park when she gets tired of walking. At five o'clock she gets up and crosses the street and leans against the building. To pass the time she examines the chapped spots on the backs of her hands and twirls her wedding band. She reaches in her purse for her comb to comb her hair and feels for the parking ticket. It isn't there. She searches thoroughly, even bending down to take things out of her purse. She can't find it. Thinking that she might have dropped it she retraces her path, but it's not on the ground. She hurries to the garage. There is a crowd of men—mostly men—waiting for their cars to be brought down. She tells the girl in the cashier's booth that she's lost her parking ticket. She talks a little too loudly—the girl leans back on her stool to get away from her voice, and several of the men stare at her. The girl calls the manager.

"Didn't this happen to you yesterday?"

"I'm very sorry, but I have to have my car back."

"What does your car look like today?"

She describes her car. It is a blue car. Blue. Yes, the roof is blue, too. A four-door blue car, and she can't remember the make. A Chevrolet. Blue. About three hours ago.

"Four hours ago," the manager says.

Tears spring into her eyes.

"Three," she says.

He shrugs. What is he going to do? He calls an attendant over and tells him to get a blue Chevy. She stands in front of the men, looking up the ramp.

"Move back," the manager hollers.

She backs into a group of men who quickly spread out to make room for her. She waits while six cars are brought. Seven. Eight. Then hers. She gets in without tipping the attendant and heads home, driving much too fast. She's home before she realizes that yet another day is ruined, and that she'll have to go the next day.

"Where were you?" her husband says.

She's been crying. She never did find time to comb her hair.

She's empty-handed, so she hasn't been shopping. What's the point of it? She'll never catch him.

"Where have you been?" she says.

IV

He calls this woman, who is not his mother, "Mother." It is her mother. She has come to stay with them not because of poor health or lack of money, but because she is lonely. She makes no trouble, except for the one annoying thing she does, and doesn't interfere with their life because she is always in her room. His wife thinks it's abnormal that she shuts her door after breakfast and does not reappear until dinner. Their son loves his grandmother and spends a lot of time in her room, talking to her, drawing pictures for her, and eating her candy when he gets home from school until dinner. There is no good reason for disliking her, except that he does not believe she has come to live with them because she is lonely. If that were true, why would she stay in her room? But he can't talk to his wife about it. It makes her think he wants her mother out of the house, and that upsets her. He suspects that it upsets her because her mother is necessary— she takes care of their son after school so his wife does not have to be home at three o'clock. In fact, he has called later in the afternoon several times and Mother has told him she isn't there. He called yesterday at four o'clock and she wasn't there, and that was the second time this week. He suspects that she is seeing her lover again. At any rate, he has started seeing his lover again. One of the things that nags at him is that his wife has seen his lover and knows she is rather plain and not very young, but he has never seen his wife's lover. Perhaps the lover used to come to the house when he was gone, but no longer comes because her mother is there. Perhaps things have not worked out so well for his wife after all.

He has decided to go home early, to be there when his wife walks in, just to make her uneasy. He takes the afternoon off and buys things at a sporting-goods store he'll need for his vacation. Then he stops in a gift shop and buys his wife a pretty little enamel box—a gift, to make her uneasy if she's seen her lover today.

The saleslady is all smiles, asks if she should wrap it. He tells her it will have just as much impact in the bag. She frowns a little, in sympathy for the woman whose pretty present will just be handed to her in a bag. She wraps the little box carefully in pink tissue paper. As an afterthought, he stops at the florist's and picks out a bouquet of assorted flowers for his wife's mother. Just in case it's a conspiracy. He goes into a phone booth at the corner and calls his lover to say that he'll take her to dinner Friday. Not until then? Impossible. She's a little angry, but she won't leave him. She has been his lover for years and years. He goes back to the florist's and sends her a bouquet of assorted flowers. The florist looks at him strangely. The man could at least make a joke of it—instead, he takes it personally that he has come back, that he didn't complete his business the first time. He decides to find another florist in the future.

As he thought, she isn't home. He knocks on her mother's door. She is surprised to see him and asks if he's sick. No—just home early. He's put the flowers in a vase for her, and she seems very pleased. She tells him where to put them. She doesn't know where his wife is and acts surprised that she's not in the house. His son? He must be with her. He goes downstairs and waits. He looks at the day's mail and reads the paper. The house is quiet and very empty; the cars that pass are monotonous. He can understand why his wife wouldn't want to spend much time in the house. It's depressing in late afternoon. He doesn't blame her for not being there, but he blames her for her lover. The bag with the enamel box is at his side.

She comes in at five o'clock. His son is with her. She's surprised to see him. His son is happy to see him. His son has a balloon.

"Where did that come from?" he asks his son.

"A man in the park gave it to me."

"You're not sick?" his wife asks.

"Just home early," he says. He gives her the bag. "For you."

She loves the little box. He can't tell if she's excited because he might know, or just surprised to see him, happy with the present. She goes into the kitchen.

"Did you ever see the man in the park before?" he asks his son.

"No."

"How come you got a free balloon?"

"The man had it." His son shrugs.

Late that night the phone rings. As usual, her mother has it on the first ring. She pounces on the phone—no chance for them to get to it first. And, as usual, whoever it is hangs up. That makes her mother nervous. She always opens her door and calls down the stairs that someone called and hung up. He feels like telling her that it was either her daughter's lover or his own. Neither of them says anything, and the door closes. He has already asked his lover if she calls and hangs up and she has denied it. He suspects her anyway—everyone lies to him. He tells his wife he has run out of cigarettes. Does she need anything from the drugstore? He puts his clothes back on and drives to the drugstore, where there is a phone booth. His lover is angry: she tells him he thinks she is a fool. She has better things to do than call his house. She tells him *he* is bothering *her*. So it was his wife's lover. He buys a carton of cigarettes and drives home. His wife is in her mother's room; the door is open, but they aren't talking. Or at least they're not talking now that he's coming up the stairs. He's tired. His mother-in-law must be tired of the calls. His wife must be tired of the depressing house.

"I was telling her what pretty flowers you brought me," his mother-in-law says.

"Who do you think was on the phone?" he asks.

"Who?" his wife says.

"That's right," he says. "Who?"

"I don't know," his mother-in-law says.

"Yes, you do," he says.

She looks startled. His wife looks at him blankly.

"You know," he says.

"Be quiet," his wife says. "You'll awaken Stevie."

"He already knows, too."

Whether his mother-in-law really knows or not, her expression, looking back and forth between them, makes him think she won't be staying there much longer. There is, of course, the slim chance that his lover was lying.

A Platonic Relationship

▪▪▪▪▪▪▪▪▪▪▪▪▪▪▪▪▪▪▪▪▪▪▪

■■■■■■■■■■■■■■■■■■■■■■■■

When Ellen was told that she would be hired as a music teacher at the high school, she decided that it did not mean that she would have to look like the other people on the faculty. She would tuck her hair neatly behind her ears, instead of letting it fall free, schoolgirlishly. She had met some of the teachers when she went for her interview, and they all seemed to look like what she was trying to get away from—suburbanites at a shopping center. Casual and airy, the fashion magazines would call it. At least, that's what they would have called it back when she still read them, when she lived in Chevy Chase and wore her hair long, falling free, the way it had fallen in her high-school graduation picture. "Your lovely face," her mother used to say, "and all covered by hair." Her graduation picture was still on display in her parents' house, next to a picture of her on her first birthday.

It didn't matter how Ellen looked now; the students laughed at her behind her back. They laughed behind all the teachers' backs. They don't like me, Ellen thought, and she didn't want to go to school. She forced herself to go, because she needed the job. She had worked hard to get away from her lawyer husband and almost-paid-for house. She had doggedly taken night classes at Georgetown University for two years, leaving the dishes after dinner and always expecting a fight. Her husband loaded them into the dishwasher—no fight. Finally, when she was ready to leave, she had to start the fight herself. There is a better world, she told him. "Teaching at the high school?" he asked. In the end, though, he had helped her find a place to live—an older house, on a side street off Florida Avenue, with splintery floors that had to be covered with rugs, and walls that needed to be repapered but that she never repapered. He hadn't made trouble for her. Instead, he made her look silly. He made her say that teaching high school was a better world. She saw the foolishness of her statement, however, and after she left him she began to read great numbers of newspapers and magazines, and then more and more radical newspapers and magazines. She had dinner with her husband several months after she had left him, at their old house. During dinner, she stated several ideas of importance, without citing her source. He listened carefully, crossing his knees and nodding attentively—the pose he always assumed with his clients.

The only time during the evening she had thought he might start a fight was when she told him she was living with a man—a student, twelve years younger than she. An odd expression came across his face. In retrospect, she realized that he must have been truly puzzled. She quickly told him that the relationship was platonic.

What Ellen told him was the truth. The man, Sam, was a junior at George Washington University. He had been rooming with her sister and brother-in-law, but friction had developed between the two men. Her sister must have expected it. Her sister's husband was very athletic, a pro-football fan who wore a Redskins T-shirt to bed instead of a pajama top, and who had a football autographed by Billy Kilmer on their mantel. Sam was not frail, but one sensed at once that he would always be gentle. He had long brown hair and brown eyes—nothing that would set him apart from a lot of other people. It was his calmness that did that. She invited him to move in after her sister explained the situation; he could help a bit with her rent. Also, although she did not want her husband to know it, she had discovered that she was a little afraid of being alone at night.

When Sam moved in in September, she almost sympathized with her brother-in-law. Sam wasn't obnoxious, but he was strange. She had to pay attention to him, whether she wanted to or not. He was so quiet that she was always conscious of his presence; he never went out, so she felt obliged to offer him coffee or dinner, although he almost always refused. He was also eccentric. Her husband had been eccentric. Often in the evenings he had polished the brass snaps of his briefcase, rubbing them to a high shine, then triumphantly opening and closing them, and then rubbing a little more to remove his thumbprints. Then he would drop the filthy cloth on the sofa, which was upholstered with pale French linen that he himself had selected.

Sam's strange ways were different. Once, he got up in the night to investigate a noise, and Ellen, lying in her room, suddenly realized that he was walking all over the house in the dark, without turning on any lights. It was just mice, he finally announced outside her door, saying it so matter-of-factly that she wasn't even upset by the news. He kept cases of beer in his room. He bought more cases than he drank—more than most people would ever consider drinking over quite a long period. When he did have a beer, he would take one bottle from the case and put it in the refrigerator and wait for it to get cold, and then drink it. If he wanted more, he would go and get another bottle, put it in the refrigerator, wait another hour, and then drink that. One night, Sam asked her if she would like a beer. To be polite, she said yes. He went to his room and took out a bottle and put it in the refrigerator. "It will be cold in a while," he said quietly. Then he sat in a chair across from her and drank his beer and read a magazine. She felt obliged to wait there in the living room until the beer was cold.

One night, her husband came to the house to talk about their divorce—or so he said. Sam was there and offered him a beer. "It will be cold in a while," he said as he put it in the refrigerator. Sam made no move to leave the living room. Her husband seemed incapacitated by Sam's silent presence. Sam acted as if they were his guests, as if he owned the house. He wasn't authoritarian—in fact, he usually didn't speak unless he was spoken to—but he was more comfortable than they were, and that night his offer of cigarettes and beer seemed calculated to put them at ease. As soon as her husband found out that Sam planned to become a lawyer, he seemed to take an interest in him. She liked Sam because she had convinced herself that his ways were more tolerable than her husband's. It became a pleasant evening. Sam brought cashews from his room to go with the beer. They discussed politics. She and her husband told Sam that they were going to get divorced. Sam nodded. Her husband had her to dinner once more before the divorce was final, and he invited Sam, too. Sam came along. They had a pleasant evening.

Things began to go smoothly at her house because of Sam. By Christmas, they were good friends. Sometimes she thought back to the early days of her marriage and remembered how disillusioned she had felt. Her husband had thrown his socks on the bedroom floor at night, and left his pajamas on the bathroom floor in the morning. Sam was like that sometimes. She found clothes scattered on the floor when she cleaned his room—socks and shirts, usually. She noticed that he did not sleep in pajamas. Things bother you less as you get older, she thought.

Ellen cleaned Sam's room because she knew he was studying hard to get into law school; he didn't have time to be fussy. She hadn't intended to pick up after a man again, but it was different this time. Sam was very appreciative when she cleaned. The first time she did it, he brought her flowers the next day, and he thanked her several times, saying that she didn't have to do it. That was it—she knew she didn't have to. But when he thanked her she became more enthusiastic about it, and after a while she began to wax his room as well as dust it; she Windexed the windows, and picked up the little pieces of lint the vacuum had missed. And, in spite of being so busy, Sam did nice things for her. On her birthday, he surprised her with a blue bathrobe. When she was depressed, he cheered her up by saying that any student would like a teacher as pretty as she. She was flattered that he thought her pretty. She began to lighten her hair a little.

He helped her organize her school programs. He had a good ear and he seemed to care about music. Before the Christmas concert for the parents, he suggested that the Hallelujah Chorus be followed by Dunstable's "Sancta Maria." The Christmas program was a triumph; Sam was there, third row center, and he applauded loudly. He believed she could do anything. After the concert, there was a picture in the newspaper of her conducting the singers. She was wearing a long dress that Sam had told her was particularly becoming to her. Sam cut out the picture and tucked it in his mirror. She carefully removed it whenever she cleaned the glass, and then replaced it in the same spot.

As time went on, Sam began to put a six-pack of beer in the refrigerator instead of a bottle at a time. They stayed up late at night on the weekends, talking. He wore the pajamas she had given him; she wore her blue bathrobe. He told her that her hair looked more becoming around her face; she should let it fall free. She protested; she was too old. "How old are you?" he asked, and she told him she was thirty-two. She rearranged her hair. She bought him a sweater-vest to keep him warm. But the colors were too wild, he said, laughing, when he opened the box. No, she insisted—he looked good in bright colors, and anyway the predominant color was navy blue. He wore the sweater-vest so long that finally she had to remind him that it needed to be dry-cleaned. She took it with her one morning when she dropped off her clothes.

Then they began talking almost every night, until very late. She got up in the mornings without enough rest, and rubbed one finger across the dark, puffy circles under her eyes. She asked him how his studies were coming; she was worried that he was not paying enough attention to his schoolwork. He told her everything was all right. "I'm way ahead of the game," he said. But she knew something was wrong. She offered to have his professor to dinner —the one who would write him a recommendation to law school —but Sam refused. It wouldn't be any trouble, she told him. No, he didn't want to impose on her. When she said again that she wanted to do it, he told her to forget it; he didn't care about law school any more. That night, they stayed up even later. The next day, when she tried to lead the Junior Chorus, she could hardly get out more than a few phrases of "The Impossible Dream" without yawning. The class laughed, and because she hadn't had enough sleep she became angry with them. That night, she told Sam how embarrassed she was about losing her temper, and he reassured her. They drank several beers. She expected Sam to go into his room and get another six-pack, but he didn't rise. "I'm not happy," Sam said to her. She said that he had been working too hard. He waved the thought away. Then perhaps the textbooks were at fault, or his professors weren't communicating their enthusiasm to the class. He shook his head. He told her he hadn't looked at a book for weeks. She became upset. Didn't he want to become a lawyer? Didn't he want to help people? He reminded her that most of the newspapers and magazines she subscribed to pointed out that the country was so messed up that no one could help. They were right, he said. It was useless. The important thing was to know when to give up.

Ellen was restless that night and slept very little. When she left in the morning, she saw that his door was closed. He was not even going through the pretense of going to classes. She would have to do something to help him. He should stay in school. Why should he quit now? Ellen had trouble concentrating that day. Everything the students did irritated her—even the usual requests for pop favorites. She kept control of herself, though. It was not right to yell at them. She let one of the students in Junior Chorus—a girl named Alison, who was taking piano lessons—play the piano, while she sat on her stool, looking out over the blur of faces, joining without enthusiasm in the singing of "Swanee River." Teaching had become meaningless to her. Let her husband vacuum those pastel rugs in their old house; let someone else teach these students. She knew that "Swanee River" was a trivial, silly song, and she wanted three o'clock to come as badly as the students did. When the bell finally rang, she left at once. She bought pastries at a delicatessen, selecting cherry tarts and eclairs. She planned to have a good dinner, and then a discussion in which she would be firm with Sam. She must make him care again. But when she got home Sam wasn't there. He didn't come home until ten o'clock, after she had eaten. She was very relieved when he came in.

"I was at your husband's," he said.

Was this a joke?

"No. He called when you were teaching. He wanted to ask you about some paper. We started talking about law school. He was disappointed that I'd decided not to go. He asked me to come over."

Had he been talked into going to law school?

"No. But your husband is a very nice man. He offered to write me a recommendation."

"Take it!" she said.

"No, it's not worth the hassle. It's not worth all those years of study, competing with punks. What for?"

What was there better to do?

"See the country."

"See the country!" she repeated.

"Get a motorcycle. Go out to the Coast. It's warm there. I'm sick of the cold."

There was nothing she could say. She decided that she was like a mother whose son has just told her he wants to design clothes. Couldn't he do something *serious?* Couldn't he be an architect? But she couldn't say this to him. If he had to go West, couldn't he at least buy a car? He told her it had to be a motorcycle. He wanted to feel the handlebars get warm as he got farther west. She went into the kitchen and got the box of pastries. On the way back to the living room, she clicked the thermostat up two degrees. They drank coffee and ate the eclairs and little tarts. It was a celebration; he was going to do what he was going to do. She said she would go with him on the weekend to look for a motorcycle.

On Monday he left. Just like that, he was gone. He left all his things in his room. After a few days, she realized that it would be practical to store his things in the attic and use his room for a study, but she couldn't touch anything. She continued to take care of the room, but not every day. Sometimes when she felt lonely, she would go in there and look at all his books in the bookcase. Other times, she would clean the house thoroughly at night, with a burst of energy, as if to make ready for his return. One night after she cleaned, she took some bottles of beer to put in the refrigerator, so they would be cool when she came home from work. She did not lose her temper any more, but her programs were no longer innovative. Alison's piano playing guided the Junior Chorus through the world, sad and weary, through the winter and into the spring.

One night, her husband called (he was her ex-husband now). He was still trying to track down the safe-deposit box where his mother had placed her jewelry. Quite a lot of old pieces were there; there were a few diamonds and some good jade. His mother was old; he didn't want to disturb her, or make her think of dying, and he was embarrassed to let her know he'd misplaced her instructions. She said she would look for the paper and call him back, and he asked if he could come and look with her. She said that would be all right. He came that night, and she offered him a beer. They looked through her file and found nothing. "The paper has to be somewhere," he said, full of professional assurance. "It has to be somewhere." She gestured hopelessly at the rooms of the house; it wasn't in the bathroom or the kitchen or the living room, and it certainly wasn't in Sam's room. He asked how Sam was doing, and she told him she hadn't heard from him. Every day she expected some word from him, but none had come. She didn't tell him that just that she hadn't heard. She drank several beers, as she did every night. They sat together in the living room, drinking beer. She asked if he would like something to eat, and fixed sandwiches. He said he would go, so she could get up in the morning. She gestured at the rooms of the house. He stayed, and slept in her bed.

In the morning, Ellen called the school and said she had a cold. "Everybody is sick," the switchboard operator told her. "It's the change in the weather." She and her husband took a drive and went to a nice restaurant for lunch. After lunch, they went to his house and hunted for the paper. They couldn't find it. He fixed her dinner, and she stayed at his house that night. In the morning, he dropped her off at school on his way to work.

A girl in Junior Chorus came up to talk to her after class. Shyly, the girl told her she played the piano. Could she also play the piano for the chorus sometime? Alison played very well, the girl said quickly; she didn't want Alison to stop playing, but could she try sometime, too? She could read music well, and she knew some classics and some Gilbert and Sullivan and a lot of popular songs, too. She mentioned some of them. Ellen watched the girl leave, blushing with nervousness at having spoken to the teacher and proud that she would be allowed to play the piano at the next meeting. She was a tall girl, with brown hair that had been cut too short; her glasses, which were harlequin-shape, looked more like something the girl's mother would wear. Ellen wondered if Sam had a girlfriend. If the girlfriend had brown hair, did it get tangled in the wind on the motorcycle? Sam would have been proud of her—the way she put the new pianist at ease, feigning interest in the girl's talent, thanking her for volunteering. The next afternoon, she thought of Sam again. He would have found it funny that the brown-haired girl also chose to play "Swanee River."

Her husband came to her house after work, and they had dinner. She had a postcard from Sam. She showed it to him—a picture of the Santa Monica Freeway, clogged with cars. The message read, "The small speck between the red and the yellow car is me, doing 110. Love, Sam." There were no specks between cars, which were themselves only specks in the picture, but Ellen looked and smiled anyway.

The next week there was another postcard—a scowling Indian —which had been mailed to her husband. Sam thanked him for the talk they had before he left. He closed with some advice: "Come West. It's warm and it's beautiful. How do you know until you try? Peace, Sam."

Later that week, while they were on their way to buy groceries, a couple on a motorcycle came out of nowhere and swerved in front of their car, going much too fast.

"Crazy son of a bitch!" her husband said, hitting the brakes.

The girl on the motorcycle looked back, probably to assure herself that they really had got through safely. The girl was smiling. Actually, the girl was too far away for Ellen to see her expression clearly, but she was certain that she saw a smile.

"Crazy son of a bitch," her husband was saying. Ellen closed her eyes and remembered being in the motorcycle shop with Sam, looking at the machines.

"I want one that will do a hundred with no sweat," Sam had said to the salesman.

"All of these will do a hundred easy," the salesman said, smiling at them.

"This one, then," Sam told him, tapping the handlebars of the one he stood by.

He paid for most of it with cash. She hadn't taken any rent money from him for a long time, so he had a lot of cash. He wrote a check to cover the rest of it. The salesman was surprised, counting the bills.

"Do you have streamers?" Sam had asked.

"Streamers?"

"Isn't that what they're called? The things kids have on their bikes?"

The salesman smiled. "We don't carry them. Guess you'd have to go to a bicycle shop."

"I guess I will," Sam said. "I've got to go in style."

Ellen looked at her husband. How can I be so unsympathetic to him, she wondered. She was angry. She should have asked Sam why she felt that way toward her husband sometimes. He would have explained it all to her, patiently, in a late-night talk. There had been no return address on the postcards. Someday he would send his address, and she could still ask him. She could tell him about the new girl who could have played anything she wanted and who selected "Swanee River." In the car, with her eyes closed, she smiled, and ahead of them—miles ahead of them now —so did the girl on the motorcycle.

Eric Clapton's
Lover

▪▪▪▪▪▪▪▪▪▪▪▪▪▪▪▪▪▪▪▪▪▪

■■■■■■■■■■■■■■■■■■■■■■

Franklin Fisher and his wife, Beth, were born on the same day of March, two years apart. Franklin was thirty-nine years old, and Beth was forty-one. Beth liked *chiles relenos*, Bass ale, gazpacho; Franklin liked mild foods: soufflés, quiche, pea soup. How could she drink Bass ale? And it was beginning to show on her figure. It wasn't just beginning to show—it was showing in more places, bulging actually, so that now she had big, fat hips and strong-man arms. Her disposition had changed, too; as she got larger, she got more vehement, less willing to compromise. Now she cooked two dinners and ate spicy lamb shish-kebob, smacking her lips, shaking on more salt, while Franklin, across from her, lifted a forkful of unseasoned spinach soufflé.

Things got worse between Franklin and Beth after Franklin Junior ("Linny" to his mother) got married and moved to San Bernardino. Their son's bride was "learning to drive a rig." She demonstrated how to turn a truck wheel coming down an incline by leaning forward on their sofa, spreading her legs, and moving her arms in what seemed to be two separate circles. Neither Franklin nor Beth knew what to talk to her about. Franklin Junior said, "Yes, sir!" as his bride-to-be simulated steering the truck. She talked about her rig, drank a shot of scotch, declining water or an ice cube, and left after half an hour.

"You're sorry they're moving so far away, aren't you?" Franklin said to Beth.

"No," Beth said. "She gives me the creeps."

"Maybe she was putting us on," Franklin said.

"What for?" Beth asked.

"Maybe she was high."

" 'High,' Franklin?"

"It could be," Franklin said.

"You don't understand anything," Beth said.

"What do you think it meant?" Franklin asked.

"She was learning to drive a truck."

"Why would she want to be a truck driver?" Franklin asked.

"It's better than being a mother," Beth said. "Then your kids grow up and marry truck drivers."

"There's nothing really *wrong* with driving a truck," Franklin said.

"You don't understand anything," Beth said.

It was one of the last times Beth spoke to him at any length. The following morning she turned her head on the pillow to face him and said, "I must have a day of silence," and wouldn't talk all day. He tried a lot of questions, but nothing provoked a reaction. "Did you know that a silver teaspoon inserted in a bottle of Coke will keep it fizzy for two days after it's opened?" he asked. Nothing.

The next morning she turned her head and said, "Another day of it."

"Want to hear why Avon is losing business?" he asked at breakfast.

"Interested in Nixon's phlebitis?" he called from the TV room.

"Would you like to adopt a Vietnamese child?" he whispered just before she dropped off.

On Monday Franklin went to work. He had worked on a magazine called *Canning Quarterly* and had just been promoted to editor of this magazine and another, *Horizontal World*, when his secretary said, "Congratulations, Mr. Fisher." He smiled, then realized that there was nothing to smile about. Her first and last official duty was to type his letter of resignation. Now he had a new job, selling tickets at the movies. It was always very quiet on the job, people filing past with puckered lips: "Two, two, two . . . ," the tickets snapping through the metal slot on the countertop. When the movie started, Franklin got an orangeade and sat on his stool reading "Dear Abby," hoping that she would deal with a problem similar to his own. She did not. She helped a daughter-in-law whose mother-in-law's seeing-eye dog snapped at her ankles, a teen-ager who wanted to know how to peel her own face to get rid of acne, and a waiter whose restaurant did not take BankAmericard. There was also a "confidential" to T.S. in Portland, Oregon, saying that, yes, many unwanted babies were eventually loved.

Franklin usually called Beth after the second show began, just to say hello, but tonight he kept flipping through the paper, looking for guidance: a picture of Teddy Kennedy behind a podium, his cheeks stuffed with nuts that he intended to store for the winter; a picture of a cat—Mr. Tom Cat—and below that, "Please Save Me"; a warning about contaminated canned lima beans; two

packs of pencils for the price of one. A teen-age girl came up to
the counter. She wanted a Coke.

"The girl will be right back," Franklin said.

Franklin smiled as the girl returned and got the teen-ager the
Coke. The week before, when he was there early in the morning
to look for his lost watch, he had seen the exterminators laughing
at a mouse that was swimming inside the Coke tank.

Franklin hopped off the stool and lifted the phone off the hook.
He expected at least a hello from Beth, but the phone rang once
and then there was silence.

"Beth?" he said.

"I can hardly wait to get home to you, darling," he said.

"Do you miss your beloved?" he asked.

He put the phone back on the hook. The girl behind the candy
counter looked away just before their eyes met.

"There are mice in the Coke machine," Franklin said.

The girl picked up a box of chocolate-covered raisins and
moved to the far side of the counter.

"Mice. Swimming in there," Franklin said.

"There are not," she said. She moved farther away.

*

Instead of going to work, Franklin went to the racetrack. He
stared at the horses, at their small heads, their straight ears, their
big bodies, their delicate legs. How could such animals do anything? He bet on number one in the first race, "Fine 'N' Fancy,"
and lost. In the next race he bet on number two, "Daddy's
Delight," and lost again. He won in the next race by betting on
number three, "Golden Gospel." He stuffed his winnings into his
trouser pockets and went out to the parking lot, where he had left
his car. The aerial had been bent into an arc. Franklin got into
the car and tried the radio. Static. Franklin got out, kicked the
side of the car below the aerial, got back in and drove away. He
drove until he got to the seamy part of town. He locked his doors
and drove slowly down the main street, looking for—or thinking
about looking for—a woman. At a McDonald's he double-parked
and got out. A young black woman was twisting a mulatto child's
arm behind its back, yelling, "Do you understand?"

"Sir?" the boy behind the counter said as Franklin approached.

"I don't want any of this awful shit," Franklin said and started away. He patted the head of the child whose arm was being twisted on the way out.

A Puerto Rican girl was sitting on the hood of his car, swinging her legs. She had on bright-blue platform shoes with blue plastic bows on the ankle straps.

"Your car?" she said, hopping down.

"Want to get inside?" Franklin asked, drawing the money out of his pocket.

"No," the girl said.

"Were you going to eat at McDonald's?"

"No," she said.

"Because if you were, I could take you someplace nicer for dinner."

"What for?" she laughed. She had a broken front tooth. She had on orange lipstick.

"Company," he said.

"You're not that bad," she said. "Don't you have a girlfriend?"

"You're right," Franklin said. "I'm not that bad. I just don't have my girlfriend with me at the moment, so I thought you might want to go to dinner with me."

The girl was laughing harder. Franklin looked in back of him and saw a policeman. The girl continued to laugh, walking away.

"Wait a minute," the cop called. "He bothering you?"

"No," the girl said.

"Wait a minute," the cop said to Franklin. "I've got a present for you, big spender." It was a ten-dollar ticket.

"Give me a break," Franklin said.

"If I heard you just then, I'd take you in for harassing an officer and creating a disturbance," the cop said. "Did I hear you say anything?"

Franklin shook his head.

"Am I watching you drive away?" the cop asked.

The cop waved as Franklin drove away, shaking.

*

"Hello, sonny," Franklin said. He was very drunk.

"Who's this?" Franklin Junior asked.

"Your daddy," Franklin said. Perhaps he was not as drunk as he thought; he was keeping up his end of the conversation pretty well.

"Pop?" Franklin Junior said.

"It is I," Franklin said.

"What's the matter with you, Pop?"

"It's what's the matter with your mother."

"What *is* wrong with her?" Franklin Junior asked quickly.

"It must remain a rhetorical question," Franklin said.

A muted conversation.

"Pop?"

"Yes, sonny?"

"Are you all right? Is Mom there?"

"Which question do you care most about?"

"Pop?"

"How are you doing in your new life?" Franklin asked.

"Let me speak to Mom, Pop."

"She's not here, sonny. You'll have to speak to me."

"Okay. What is it, Pop? Are you sick?"

"You didn't anwer my question," Franklin said.

"Three minutes. Please signal when through," the operator said.

"Operator?" Franklin Junior said. "Pop?"

Both were gone. Franklin had dropped the phone so he could pick up a glass he had dropped.

*

Beth Fisher did not know where Franklin was, and she didn't care. What a mess that man was! He had convinced her that they should marry because it was in the stars: they had been born on the same day of March. He mentioned that first when he introduced her to his friends. Even Franklin had not been able to see anything more in the relationship to talk about. All those wasted years! She had called her daughter-in-law, lamenting her marriage to Franklin. The girl had told her that there was nothing as exhilarating as driving a rig. It was all she could talk about. And Linny —he was so full of questions about Franklin that he wouldn't listen to her.

Beth got a job in the lingerie department of a store and prayed that Franklin wouldn't come back. Women came into the department all day, holding up fluffy nylon nightgowns and admiring themselves in the mirror, buying matching satin slippers, wanting to appear beautiful for their husbands. Beth thought they were silly. She believed that she was becoming a feminist. She joined N.O.W. She ate what she wanted and thought that she looked healthier when she was heavy. By December she was quite fat; she often spoke in favor of abortions to the ladies buying the frilliest nightgowns. In January she was moved to the drapery department.

She went out a few times with a salesman from the drapery department, who said that the other women were spiteful. They went to a bar and ate pizza and drank Bass ale, and after that he took her home and didn't kiss her. The salesman thought that she should file for legal separation. He said that men could be spiteful creatures. He gave her a kitten for Christmas. "This is Hildegaard," he said as he handed the small white kitten to her. When he wasn't there she called the cat Snowflake.

Shortly after Christmas, Beth came home and found Franklin in the living room. He was reading a novel. A shark, more teeth than body, lunged across the cover; to the side, a man was being slugged in the face, She had time to consider the book because Franklin didn't put it down when she came in. His shoes were by the chair. His toes had broken through the sock of the right foot; they protruded in a tiny fan.

"I'm not exactly clear on what happened between us," he said.

She went into the kitchen and got a beer. She came back to the living room.

"I realized that there was nothing I wanted to say to you and there was nothing I wanted to hear," she said.

Franklin nodded.

"The movie theater manager keeps calling," Beth says. "He sees great significance in the fact that you disappeared after seeing *Dirty Harry*."

"Maybe I could get the job back," Franklin said. The kitten hopped onto the footstool and bit at Franklin's toes.

"What have you been doing?" Franklin asked.

"Working. In a store."

"I've been living off a Puerto Rican woman I picked up outside a McDonald's. She was making plans to go to Puerto Rico. When she went to work today I left."

"I don't believe you," Beth said.

Franklin looked at the shark's teeth.

*

Franklin and Beth were snowed in. He had spent the night (the cliché would be "on the couch"; he was sprawled in the Eames chair with his feet on a pile of magazines on top of the telephone book), intending to leave in the morning, but by morning he couldn't have opened the front door if he had wanted to. Leave like Santa Claus? He looked up the chimney, full of soot, then made a fire and sat cross-legged, trying to think—he thought this was a position people got into to meditate—when Beth came downstairs, excited and surprised by the snow. They had celery and beans for lunch. Beth wore a thin blue bathrobe that made her hips look even more enormous. He thought of the horses, the racetrack . . . He wanted flan, he wanted his Puerto Rican lover back, to kiss her orange lips. The orange lipstick was flavored with oranges. His Puerto Rican lover wanted to go to Florida and eat oranges. More than that, she wanted to go to Puerto Rico: her sister the nun, her brother the blacksmith, the grave of her youngest sister, the other sister a cook for wealthy people, another brother—wasn't there another one, or was that the one who was born dead? Born with the measles. He told her that that wasn't possible. But a doctor had been there! Then he hadn't known what he was talking about. Those big bright lips. He tickled them with a feather once when she was asleep. He pulled it out of his pillow and brushed it across her lips and she drew them together, sat up scratching herself. She wanted to be Eric Clapton's lover. He had never heard of Eric Clapton. She said that Eric Clapton was addicted to heroin. She agreed with Franklin that his son was addicted to drugs; otherwise he would love his parents. She wanted him to call his son. What for? For reconciliation! But there had been no fight. Nothing ever came entirely apart.

He had had to hound her and hound her to be his lover. For almost a week after first seeing her he sat in his car, parked outside McDonald's, and waited, and then he hounded her, offered his car, which was all he had with him. She refused. She was not a whore, she was a clerk. He didn't want a whore, he wanted a clerk. This made her eyes big, like her mouth. She wore such high heels. She was as tall as he was in those shoes, and without them she was just a tiny woman. He offered his belt or shirt, if she would not take the money or the car. "Okay," she said. "Which?" he asked, "The belt or the shirt?", wondering where he would get a belt to keep his pants up late at night after she put him out. She had a girlfriend who walked into her apartment in the morning and beat his head with the pillow when she saw him sleeping there. What an odd person the friend was, and his lover—what a strange woman, comparing him to Eric Clapton, saying that she never had a chance in hell with Eric Clapton anyway.

Beth said that they would have to feed the birds. Feed the birds? He lived in suburbia. In the grocery stores there were little bells of suet and birdseed that women brought home and hung in trees. Beth didn't have one of those; she wanted him to tear up bread, put it in a pan, take it to the birds. He told her that he couldn't get out the front door because the snow had drifted. She said that the birds would die. He climbed out the bathroom window. The breadcrumbs were blown out of the pie tin, mixed with the snow, disappeared. He climbed back in through the window. He wrapped a towel around his head and sat in front of the fire.

"Being born on the same day seemed a very good thing to go on," he said.

He examined his wife. He thought the bathrobe peculiar, had no idea that she had gotten it very cheaply: marked down to seven dollars by the buyer after Beth jabbed a pen through the back of it. From forty-five dollars to twenty-five (small hole) to fifteen-fifty (large hole, two runs) to seven dollars (hole, runs, hem coming loose).

"It's hard to imagine that somewhere in the world it's warm today," Beth said, forehead against the foggy window. She was chewing celery, heavily sprinkled with chili powder.

Wolf Dreams

▪▪▪▪▪▪▪▪▪▪▪▪▪▪▪▪▪▪▪▪▪▪▪

■■■■■■■■■■■■■■■■■■■■■■

When Cynthia was seventeen she married Ewell W. G. Peterson. The initials stood for William Gordon; his family called him William, her parents called him W.G. (letting him know that they thought his initials were pretentious), and Cynthia called him Pete, which is what his Army buddies called him. Now she had been divorced from Ewell W. G. Peterson for nine years, and what he had been called was a neutral thing to remember about him. She didn't hate him. Except for his name, she hardly remembered him. At Christmas, he sent her a card signed "Pete," but only for a few years after the divorce, and then they stopped. Her second husband, whom she married when she was twenty-eight, was named Lincoln Divine. They were divorced when she was twenty-nine and a half. No Christmas cards. Now she was going to marry Charlie Pinehurst. Her family hated Charlie—or perhaps just the idea of a third marriage—but what she hated was the way Charlie's name got mixed up in her head with Pete's and Lincoln's. Ewell W. G. Peterson, Lincoln Divine, Charlie Pinehurst, she kept thinking, as if she needed to memorize them. In high school her English teacher had made her memorize poems that made no sense. There was no way you could remember what came next in those poems. She got Ds all through high school, and she didn't like the job she got after she graduated, so she was happy to marry Pete when he asked her, even if it did mean leaving her friends and her family to live on an Army base. She liked it there. Her parents had told her she would never be satisfied with anything; they were surprised when it turned out that she had no complaints about living on the base. She got to know all the wives, and they had a diet club, and she lost twenty pounds, so that she got down to what she weighed when she started high school. She also worked at the local radio station, recording stories and poems—she never knew why they were recorded—and found that she didn't mind literature if she could just read it and not have to think about it. Pete hung around with the men when he had time off; they never really saw much of each other. He accused her of losing weight so she could attract "a khaki lover." "One's not enough for you?" he asked. But when he was around, he didn't want to love her; he'd work out with the barbells in the spare bedroom. Cynthia liked having two bedrooms. She liked the whole house. It was a frame row house with shutters missing downstairs, but it was larger than her parents' house inside. When they moved in, all the Army wives said the same thing—that the bedroom wouldn't be spare for long. But it stayed empty, except for the barbells and some kind of trapeze that Pete hung from the ceiling. It was nice living on the base, though. Sometimes she missed it.

With Lincoln, Cynthia lived in an apartment in Columbus, Ohio. "It's a good thing you live halfway across the country," her father wrote her, "because your mother surely does not want to see that black man, who claims his father was a Cherappy Indian." She never met Lincoln's parents, so she wasn't sure herself about the Indian thing. One of Lincoln's friends, who was always trying to be her lover, told her that Lincoln Divine wasn't even his real name—he had made it up and got his old name legally changed when he was twenty-one. "It's like believing in Santa Claus," the friend told her. "There is no Lincoln Divine."

Charlie was different from Pete and Lincoln. Neither of them paid much attention to her, but Charlie was attentive. During the years, she had regained the twenty pounds she lost when she was first married and added twenty-five more on top of that. She was going to have to get in shape before she married Charlie, even though he wanted to marry her now. "I'll take it as is," Charlie said. "Ready-made can be altered." Charlie was a tailor. He wasn't really a tailor, but his brother had a shop, and to make extra money Charlie did alterations on the weekends. Once, when they were both a little drunk, Cynthia and Charlie vowed to tell each other a dark secret. Cynthia told Charlie she had had an abortion just before she and Pete got divorced. Charlie was really shocked by that. "That's why you got so fat, I guess," he said. "Happens when they fix animals, too." She didn't know what he was talking about, and she didn't want to ask. She'd almost forgotten it herself. Charlie's secret was that he knew how to run a sewing machine. He thought it was "woman's work." She thought that was crazy; she had told him something important, and he had just said he knew how to run a sewing machine.

"We're not going to live in any apartment," Charlie said. "We're going to live in a house." And "You're not going to have to go up and down stairs. We're going to find a split-level." And "It's not going to be any neighborhood that's getting worse. Our neighborhood is going to be getting better." And "You don't have to lose weight. Why don't you marry me now, and we can get a house and start a life together?"

But she wouldn't do it. She was going to lose twenty pounds and save enough money to buy a pretty wedding dress. She had already started using more makeup and letting her hair grow, as the beauty-parlor operator had suggested, so that she could have curls that fell to her shoulders on her wedding day. She'd been reading brides' magazines, and long curls were what she thought was pretty. Charlie hated the magazines. He thought the magazines had told her to lose twenty pounds—that the magazines were responsible for keeping him waiting.

She had nightmares. A recurring nightmare was one in which she stood at the altar with Charlie, wearing a beautiful long dress, but the dress wasn't quite long enough, and everyone could see that she was standing on a scale. What did the scale say? She would wake up peering into the dark and get out of bed and go to the kitchen.

This night, as she dipped potato chips into cheddar-cheese dip, she reread a letter from her mother: "You are not a bad girl, and so I do not know why you would get married three times. Your father does not count that black man as a marriage, but I have got to, and so it is three. That's too many marriages, Cynthia. You are a good girl and know enough now to come home and settle down with your family. We are willing to look out for you, even your dad, and warn you not to make another dreadful mistake." There was no greeting, no signature. The letter had probably been dashed off by her mother when she, too, had insomnia. Cynthia would have to answer the note, but she didn't think her mother would be convinced by anything she could say. If she thought her parents would be convinced she was making the right decision by seeing Charlie, she would have asked him to meet her parents. But her parents liked people who had a lot to say, or who could make them laugh ("break the monotony," her father called it), and Charlie didn't have a lot to say. Charlie was a very serious person. He was also forty years old, and he had never been married. Her parents would want to know why that was. You couldn't please them: they hated people who were divorced and they were suspicious of single people. So she had never suggested to Charlie that he meet her parents. Finally, he suggested it himself. Cynthia thought up excuses, but Charlie saw through them. He thought it was all because he had confessed to her that he sewed. She was ashamed of him—that was the real reason she was putting off the wedding, and why she wouldn't introduce him to her parents. "No," she said. "No, Charlie. No, no, no." And because she had said it so many times, she was convinced. "Then set a date for the wedding," he told her. "You've got to say when." She promised to do that the next time she saw him, but she couldn't think right, and that was because of the notes that her mother wrote her, and because she couldn't get any sleep, and because she got depressed by taking off weight and gaining it right back by eating at night.

As long as she couldn't sleep, and there were only a few potato chips left, which she might as well finish off, she decided to level with herself the same way she and Charlie had the night they told their secrets. She asked herself why she was getting married. Part of the answer was that she didn't like her job. She was a typer—a *typist*, the other girls always said, correcting her—and also she was thirty-two, and if she didn't get married soon she might not find anybody. She and Charlie would live in a house, and she could have a flower garden, and, although they had not discussed it, if she had a baby she wouldn't have to work. It was getting late if she intended to have a baby. There was no point in asking herself more questions. Her head hurt, and she had eaten too much and felt a little sick, and no matter what she thought she knew she was still going to marry Charlie.

Cynthia would marry Charlie on February the tenth. That was what she told Charlie, because she hadn't been able to think of a date and she had to say something, and that was what she would tell her boss, Mr. Greer, when she asked if she could be given her week's vacation then.

"We would like to be married the tenth of February, and, if I could, I'd like to have the next week off."

"I'm looking for that calendar."

"What?"

"Sit down and relax, Cynthia. You can have the week off if that isn't the week when—"

"Mr. Greer, I could change the date of the wedding."

"I'm not asking you to do that. Please sit down while I—"

"Thank you. I don't mind standing."

"Cynthia, let's just say that week is fine."

"Thank you."

"If you like standing, what about having a hot dog with me down at the corner?" he said to Cynthia.

That surprised her. Having lunch with her boss! She could feel the heat of her cheeks. A crazy thought went through her head: Cynthia Greer. It got mixed up right away with Peterson, Divine, and Pinehurst.

At the hot-dog place, they stood side by side, eating hot dogs and french fries.

"It's none of my business," Mr. Greer said to her, "but you don't seem like the most excited bride-to-be. I mean, you do seem excited, but . . ."

Cynthia continued to eat.

"Well?" he asked. "I was just being polite when I said it was none of my business."

"Oh, that's all right. Yes, I'm very happy. I'm going to come back to work after I'm married, if that's what you're thinking."

Mr. Greer was staring at her. She had said something wrong.

"I'm not sure that we'll go on a honeymoon. We're going to buy a house."

"Oh? Been looking at some houses?"

"No. We might look for houses."

"You're very hard to talk to," Mr. Greer said.

"I know. I'm not thinking quickly. I make so many mistakes typing."

A mistake to have told him that. He didn't pick it up.

"February will be a nice time to have off," he said pleasantly.

"I picked February because I'm dieting, and by then I'll have lost weight."

"Oh? My wife is always dieting. She's eating fourteen grapefruit a week on this new diet she's found."

"That's the grapefruit diet."

Mr. Greer laughed.

"What did I do that was funny?"

She sees Mr. Greer is embarrassed. A mistake to have embarrassed him.

"I don't think right when I haven't had eight hours' sleep, and I haven't even had close to that. And on this diet I'm always hungry."

"Are you hungry? Would you like another hot dog?"

"That would be nice," she says.

He orders another hot dog and talks more as she eats.

"Sometimes I think it's best to forget all this dieting," he says. "If so many people are fat, there must be something to it."

"But I'll get fatter and fatter."

"And then what?" he says. "What if you did? Does your fiancé like thin women?"

"He doesn't care if I lose weight or not. He probably wouldn't care."

"Then you've got the perfect man. Eat away."

When she finishes that hot dog, he orders another for her.

"A world full of food, and she eats fourteen grapefruit a week."

"Why don't you tell her not to diet, Mr. Greer?"

"She won't listen to me. She reads those magazines, and I can't do anything."

"Charlie hates those magazines, too. Why do men hate magazines?"

"I don't hate all magazines. I don't hate *Newsweek*."

She tells Charlie that her boss took her to lunch. At first he is impressed. Then he seems let down. Probably he is disappointed that his boss didn't take him to lunch.

"What did you talk about?" Charlie asks.

"Me. He told me I could get fat—that it didn't matter."

"What else did he say?"

"He said his wife is on the grapefruit diet."

"You aren't very talkative. Is everything all right?"

"He said not to marry you."

"What did he mean by that?"

"He said to go home and eat and eat and eat but not to get married."

"One of the girls said that before she got married he told her the same thing."

"What's that guy up to? He's got no right to say that."

"She got divorced, too."

"What are you trying to tell me?" Charlie says.

"Nothing. I'm just telling you about the lunch. You asked about it."

"Well, I don't understand all this. I'd like to know what's behind it."

Cynthia does not feel that she has understood, either. She feels sleep coming on, and hopes that she will drop off before long. Her second husband, Lincoln, felt that she was incapable of understanding anything. He had a string of Indian beads that he wore under his shirt, and on their wedding night he removed the beads before they went to bed and held them in front of her face and shook them and said, "What's this?" It was the inside of her head, Lincoln told her. She understood that she was being insulted. But why had he married her? She had not understood Lincoln, and, like Charlie, she didn't understand what Mr. Greer was up to. "Memorize," she heard her English teacher saying. "Anyone can memorize." Cynthia began to go over past events. I married Pete and Lincoln and I will marry Charlie. Today I had lunch with Mr. Greer. Mrs. Greer eats grapefruit.

"Well, what are you laughing about?" Charlie asked. "Some private joke with you and Greer, or something?"

Cynthia saw an ad in the newspaper. "Call Crisis Center," it said. "We Care." She thinks that a crisis center is a good idea, but she isn't having a crisis. She just can't sleep. But the idea of it is very good. If I were having a crisis, what would I do? she wonders. She has to answer her mother's note. Another note came today. Now her mother wants to meet Charlie: "As God is my witness, I tried to get through to you, but perhaps I did not say that you would really be welcome at home and do not have to do this foolish thing you are doing. Your dad feels you are never going to

find true happiness when you don't spend any time thinking between one husband and the next. I know that love makes us do
funny things, but your dad has said to tell you that he feels you
do not really love this man, and there is nothing worse than just
doing something funny with not even the reason of love driving
you. You probably don't want to listen to me, and so I keep these
short, but if you should come home alone we would be most glad.
If you bring this new man with you, we will also come to the station. Let us at least look him over before you do this thing. Your
dad has said that if he had met Lincoln it never would have
been."

Cynthia takes out a piece of paper. Instead of writing her
mother's name at the top, though, she writes, "If you are still at
that high school, I want you to know I am glad to be away from it
and you and I have forgotten all those lousy poems you had me
memorize for nothing. Sincerely, Cynthia Knight." On another
piece of paper she writes, "Are you still in love with me? Do you
want to see me again?" She gets another piece of paper and draws
two parallel vertical lines with a horizontal line joining them at
the bottom—Pete's trapeze. "APE MAN," she prints. She puts
the first into an envelope and addresses it to her teacher at the
high school. The second is for Lincoln. The next goes to Pete,
care of his parents. She doesn't know Lincoln's address, so she rips
up that piece of paper and throws it away. This makes her cry.
Why is she crying? One of the girls at work says it's the times they
are living in. The girl campaigned for George McGovern. Not
only that, but she wrote letters against Nixon. Cynthia takes another piece of paper from the box and writes a message to President Nixon: "Some girls in my office won't write you because they
say that's crank mail and their names will get put on a list. I don't
care if I'm on some list. You're the crank. You've got prices so
high I can't eat steak." Cynthia doesn't know what else to say to
the President. "Tell your wife she's a stone face," she writes. She
addresses the envelope and stamps it and takes the mail to the
mailbox before she goes to bed. She begins to think that it's
Nixon's fault—all of it. Whatever that means. She is still weeping. Damn you, Nixon, she thinks. Damn you.

Lately, throughout all of this, she hasn't been sleeping with Charlie. When he comes to her apartment, she unbuttons his shirt, rubs her hands across his chest, up and down his chest, and undoes his belt.

She writes more letters. One is to Jean Nidetch, of Weight Watchers. "What if you got fat again, if you couldn't stop eating?" she writes. "Then you'd lose all your money! You couldn't go out in public or they'd see you! I hope you get fatter and fatter and die." The second letter (a picture, really) is to Charlie—a heart with "Cynthia" in it. That's wrong. She draws another heart and writes "Charlie" in it. The last letter is to a woman she knew when she was married to Pete. "Dear Sandy," she writes. "Sorry I haven't written in so long. I am going to get married the tenth of February. I think I told you that Lincoln and I got divorced. I really wish I had you around to encourage me to lose weight before the wedding! I hope everything is well with your family. The baby must be walking now. Everything is fine with me. Well, got to go. Love, Cynthia."

They are on the train, on the way to visit her parents before the wedding. It is late January. Charlie has spilled some beer on his jacket and has gone to the men's room twice to wash it off, even though she told him he got it all out the first time. He has a tie folded in his jacket pocket. It is a red tie with white dogs on it that she bought for him. She has been buying him presents, to make up for the way she acts toward him sometimes. She has been taking sleeping pills, and now that she's more rested she isn't nervous all the time. That's all it was—no sleep. She even takes half a sleeping pill with her lunch, and that keeps her calm during the day.

"Honey, do you want to go to the other car, where we can have a drink?" Charlie asks her.

Cynthia didn't want Charlie to know she had been taking the pills, so when she had a chance she reached into her handbag and shook out a whole one and swallowed it when he wasn't looking. Now she is pretty groggy.

"I think I'll come down later," she says. She smiles at him.

As he walks down the aisle, she looks at his back. He could be anybody. Just some man on a train. The door closes behind him.

A young man sitting across the aisle from her catches her eye. He has long hair. "Paper?" he says.

He is offering her his paper. She feels her cheeks color, and she takes it, not wanting to offend him. Some people wouldn't mind offending somebody who looks like him, she thinks self-righteously, but you are always polite.

"How far you two headed?" he asks.

"Pavo, Georgia," she says.

"Gonna eat peaches in Georgia?" he asks.

She stares at him.

"I'm just kidding," he says. "My grandparents live in Georgia."

"Do they eat peaches all day?" she asks.

He laughs. She doesn't know what she's done right.

"Why, lordy lands, they do," he says with a thick drawl.

She flips through the paper. There is a comic strip of President Nixon. The President is leaning against a wall, being frisked by a policeman. He is confessing to various sins.

"Great, huh?" the man says, smiling, and leans across the aisle.

"I wrote Nixon a letter," Cynthia says quietly. "I don't know what they'll do. I said all kinds of things."

"You did? Wow. You wrote Nixon?"

"Did you ever write him?"

"Yeah, sure, I write him all the time. Send telegrams. It'll be a while before he's really up against that wall, though."

Cynthia continues to look through the paper. There are full-page ads for records by people she has never heard of, singers she will never hear. The singers look like the young man.

"Are you a musician?" she asks.

"Me? Well, sometimes. I play electric piano. I can play classical piano. I don't do much of it."

"No time?" she says.

"Right. Too many distractions."

He takes a flask out from under his sweater. "If you don't feel like the long walk to join your friend, have a drink with me."

Cynthia accepts the flask, quickly, so no one will see. Once it is in her hands, she doesn't know what else to do but drink from it.

"Where you coming from?" he asks.

"Buffalo."

"Seen the comet?" he asks.

"No. Have you?"

"No," he says. "Some days I don't think there is any comet. Propaganda, maybe."

"If Nixon said there was a comet, then we could be sure there wasn't," she says.

The sound of her own voice is strange to her. The man is smiling. He seems to like talk about Nixon.

"Right," he says. "Beautiful. President issues bulletin comet *will* appear. Then we can all relax and know we're not missing anything."

She doesn't understand what he has said, so she takes another drink. That way, she has no expression.

"I'll drink to that, too," he says, and the flask is back with him.

Because Charlie is apparently going to be in the drinking car for a while, the man, whose name is Peter, comes and sits next to her.

"My first husband was named Pete," she says. "He was in the Army. He didn't know what he was doing."

The man nods, affirming some connection.

He nods. She must have been right.

Peter tells her that he is on his way to see his grandfather, who is recovering from a stroke. "He can't talk. They think he will, but not yet."

"I'm scared to death of getting old," Cynthia says.

"Yeah," Peter says. "But you've got a way to go."

"And then other times I don't care what happens, I just don't care what happens at all."

He nods slowly. "There's plenty happening we're not going to be able to do anything about," he says.

He holds up a little book he has been looking through. It is called *Know What Your Dreams Mean*.

"Ever read these things?" he asks.

"No. Is it good?"

"You know what it is—right? A book that interprets dreams."

"I have a dream," she says, "about being at an altar in a wedding dress, only instead of standing on the floor I'm on a scale."

He laughs and shakes his head. "There's no weird stuff in here. It's all the usual Freudian stuff."

"What do you mean?" she asks.

"Oh—you dream about your teeth crumbling; it means castration. That sort of stuff."

"But what do you think my dream means?" she asks.

"I don't even know if I half believe what I read in the book," he says, tapping it on his knee. He knows he hasn't answered her question. "Maybe the scale means you're weighing the possibilities."

"Of what?"

"Well, you're in a wedding dress, right? You could be weighing the possibilities."

"What will I do?" she says.

He laughs. "I'm no seer. Let's look it up in your horoscope. What are you?"

"Virgo."

"Virgo," he says. "That would figure. Virgos are meticulous. They'd be susceptible to a dream like the one you were talking about."

Peter reads from the book: "Be generous to friends, but don't be taken advantage of. Unexpected windfall may prove less than you expected. Loved one causes problems. Take your time."

He shrugs. He passes her the flask.

It's too vague. She can't really understand it. She sees Lincoln shaking the beads, but it's not her fault this time—it's the horoscope's fault. It doesn't say enough.

"That man I'm with wants to marry me," she confides to Peter. "What should I do?"

He shakes his head and looks out the window. "Don't ask me," he says, a little nervously.

"Do you have any more books?"

"No," he says. "All out."

They ride in silence.

"You could go to a palmist," he says after a while. "They'll tell you what's up."

"A palmist? Really?"

"Well, I don't know. If you believe half they say . . ."

"You don't believe them?"

"Well, I fool around with stuff like this, but I sort of pay attention to what I like and forget what I don't like. The horoscope told me to delay travel yesterday, and I did."

"Why don't you believe them?" Cynthia asks.

"Oh, I think most of them don't know any more than you or me."

"Then let's do it as a game," she says. "I'll ask questions, and you give the answer."

Peter laughs. "O.K.," he says. He lifts her hand from her lap and stares hard at it. He turns it over and examines the other side, frowning.

"Should I marry Charlie?" she whispers.

"I see . . ." he begins. "I see a man. I see a man . . . in the drinking car."

"But what am I going to do?" she whispers. "Should I marry him?"

Peter gazes intently at her palm, then smooths his fingers down hers. "Maybe," he says gravely when he reaches her fingertips.

Delighted with his performance, he cracks up. A woman in the seat in front of them peers over the back of her chair to see what the noise is about. She sees a hippie holding a fat woman's hand and drinking from a flask.

"Coleridge," Peter is saying. "You know—Coleridge, the poet? Well, he says that we don't, for instance, dream about a wolf and then get scared. He says it's that we're scared to begin with, see, and therefore we dream about a wolf."

Cynthia begins to understand, but then she loses it. It is the fault of the sleeping pill and many drinks. In fact, when Charlie comes back, Cynthia is asleep on Peter's shoulder. There is a scene—or as much of a scene as a quiet man like Charlie can make. Charlie is also drunk, which makes him mellow instead of really angry. Eventually, brooding, he sits down across the aisle. Late that night, when the train slows down for the Georgia station, he gazes out the window as if he noticed nothing. Peter helps Cynthia get her bag down. The train has stopped at the station, and Charlie is still sitting, staring out the window at a few lights that shine along the tracks. Without looking at him, without knowing what will happen, Cynthia walks down the aisle. She is the last one off. She is the last one off before the train pulls out, with Charlie still on it.

Her parents watch the train go down the track, looking as if they are visitors from an earlier century, amazed by such a machine. They had expected Charlie, of course, but now they have Cynthia. They were not prepared to be pleasant, and there is a strained silence as the three watch the train disappear.

That night, lying in the bed she slept in as a child, Cynthia can't sleep. She gets up, finally, and sits in the kitchen at the table. What am I trying to think about, she wonders, closing her hands over her face for deeper concentration. It is cold in the kitchen, and she is not so much hungry as empty. Not in the head, she feels like shouting to Lincoln, but in the stomach—somewhere inside. She clasps her hands in front of her, over her stomach. Her eyes are closed. A picture comes to her—a high, white mountain. She isn't on it, or in the picture at all. When she opens her eyes she is looking at the shiny surface of the table. She closes her eyes and sees the snow-covered mountain again—high and white, no trees, just mountain—and she shivers with the coldness of it.

Wanda's

▪▪▪▪▪▪▪▪▪▪▪▪▪▪▪▪▪▪▪▪▪▪▪▪

■■■■■■■■■■■■■■■■■■■■■■■

When May's mother went to find her father, May was left with her Aunt Wanda. She wasn't really an aunt; she was a friend of her mother's who ran a boardinghouse. Wanda called it a boardinghouse, but she rarely accepted boarders. There was only one boarder, who had been there six years. May had stayed there twice before. The first time was when she was nine, and her mother left to find her father, Ray, who had gone to the West Coast and had vacationed too long in Laguna Beach. The second time was when her mother was hung over and had to have "a little rest," and she left May there for two days. The first time, she left her for almost two weeks, and May was so happy when her mother came back that she cried. "Where did you think Laguna Beach was?" her mother said. "A hop, skip, and a jump? Honey, Laguna Beach is practically across the world."

The only thing interesting about Wanda's is her boarder, Mrs. Wong. Mrs. Wong once gave May a little octagonal box full of pastel paper circles that spread out into flowers when they were dropped in water. Mrs. Wong let her drop them in her fishbowl. The only fish in the fishbowl is made of bright-orange plastic and is suspended in the middle of the bowl by a sinker. There are many brightly colored things in Mrs. Wong's room, and May is allowed to touch all of them. On her door Mrs. Wong has a little heart-shaped piece of paper with "Ms. Wong" printed on it.

Wanda is in the kitchen, talking to May. "Eggs don't have many calories, but if you eat eggs the cholesterol kills you," Wanda says. "If you eat sauerkraut there's not many calories, but there's a lot of sodium, and that's bad for the heart. Tuna fish is full of mercury—what's that going to do to a person? Who can live on chicken? You know enough, there's nothing for you to eat."

Wanda takes a hair clip out of her pants pocket and clips back her bangs. She puts May's lunch in front of her—a bowl of tomato soup and a slice of lemon meringue pie. She puts a glass of milk next to the soup bowl.

"They say that after a certain age milk is no good for you—you might as well drink poison," she says. "Then you read somewhere else that Americans don't have enough milk in their diet. I don't know. You decide what you want to do about your milk, May."

Wanda sits down, lights a cigarette, and drops the match on
the floor
"Your dad really picks swell times to disappear. The hot
months come, and men go mad. What do you think your dad's
doing in Denver, honey?"
May shrugs, blows on her soup.
"How do you know, huh?" Wanda says. "I ask dumb questions.
I'm not used to having kids around." She bends to pick up the
match. The tops of her arms are very fat. There are little bumps
all over them.
"I got married when I was fifteen," Wanda says. "Your mother
got married when she was eighteen—she had three years on me—
and what's she do but drive all around the country rounding up
your dad? I was twenty-one the second time I got married, and
that would have worked out fine if he hadn't died."
Wanda goes to the refrigerator and gets out the lemonade. She
swirls the container. "Shaking bruises it," she says, making a joke.
She pours some lemonade and tequila into a glass and takes a
long drink.
"You think I talk to you too much?" Wanda says. "I listen to
myself and it seems like I'm not really conversing with you—like
I'm a teacher or something."
May shakes her head sideways.
"Yeah, well, you're polite. You're a nice kid. Don't get married
until you're twenty-one. How old are you now?"
"Twelve," May says.
After lunch, May goes to the front porch and sits in the white
rocker. She looks at her watch—a present from her father—and
sees that one of the hands is straight up, the other straight down,
between the Road-Runner's legs. It is twelve-thirty. In four and a
half hours she and Wanda will eat again. At Wanda's they eat at
nine, twelve, and five. Wanda worries that May isn't getting
enough to eat. Actually, she is always full. She never feels like eating. Wanda eats almost constantly. She usually eats bananas and
Bit-O-Honey candy bars, which she carries in her shirt pocket.
The shirt belonged to her second husband, who drowned. May
found out about him a few days ago. At night, Wanda always
comes into her bedroom to tuck her in. Wanda calls it tucking in,

but actually she only walks around the room and then sits at the foot of the bed and talks. One of the stories she told was about her second husband, Frank. He and Wanda were on vacation, and late at night they sneaked onto a fishing pier. Wanda was looking at the lights of a boat far in the distance when she heard a splash. Frank had jumped into the water. "I'm cooling off!" Frank hollered. They had been drinking, so Wanda just stood there laughing. Then Frank started swimming. He swam out of sight, and Wanda stood there at the end of the pier waiting for him to swim back. Finally she started calling his name. She called him by his full name. "Frank Marshall!" she screamed at the top of her lungs. Wanda is sure that Frank never meant to drown. They had been very happy at dinner that night. He had bought her brandy after dinner, which he never did, because it was too expensive to drink anything but beer in restaurants.

May thinks that is very sad. She remembers the last time she saw her father. It was when her mother took the caps off her father's film containers and spit into them. He grabbed her mother's arm and pushed her out of the room. "The great artist!" her mother hollered, and her father's face went wild. He has a long, straight nose (May's is snubbed, like her mother's) and long, brown hair that he ties back with a rubber band when he rides his motorcycle. Her father is two years younger than her mother. They met in the park when he took a picture of her. He is a professional photographer.

May picks up the *National Enquirer* and begins to read an article about how Sophia Loren tried to save Richard Burton's marriage. In a picture, Sophia holds Carlo Ponti's hand and beams. Wanda subscribes to the *National Enquirer*. She cries over the stories about crippled children, and prays for them. She answers the ads offering little plants for a dollar. "I always get suckered in," she says. "I know they just die." She talks back to the articles and chastises Richard for ever leaving Liz, and Liz for ever having married Eddie, and Liz for running around with a used-car salesman, and all the doctors who think they have a cure for cancer.

After lunch, Wanda takes a nap and then a shower. Afterward, there is always bath powder all over the bathroom—even on the mirror. Then she drinks two shots of tequila in lemonade, and then she fixes dinner. Mrs. Wong comes back from the library punctually at four o'clock. May looks at Wanda's *National Enquirer*. She turns the page, and Paul Newman is swimming in water full of big chunks of ice.

Mrs. Wong's first name is Maria. Her name is written neatly on her notebooks. "Imagine having a student living under my roof!" Wanda says. Wanda went to a junior college with May's mother but dropped out after the first semester. Wanda and May's mother have often talked about Mrs. Wong. From them May learned that Mrs. Wong married a Chinese man and then left him, and she has a fifteen-year-old son. On top of that, she is studying to be a social worker. "That ought to give her an opportunity to marry a Negro," May's mother said to Wanda. "The Chinese man wasn't far out enough, I guess."

Mrs. Wong is back early today. As she comes up the sidewalk, she gives May the peace sign. May gives the peace sign, too.

"Your mama didn't write, I take it," Mrs. Wong says.

May shrugs.

"I write my son, and my husband rips up the letters," Mrs. Wong says. "At least when she does write you'll get it." Mrs. Wong sits down on the top step and takes off her sandals. She rubs her feet. "Get to the movies?" she asks.

"She always forgets."

"Remind her," Mrs. Wong says. "Honey, if you don't practice by asserting yourself with women, you'll never be able to assert yourself with men."

May wishes that Mrs. Wong were her mother. It would be nice if she could keep her father and have Mrs. Wong for a mother. But all the women he likes are thin and blond and young. That's one of the things her mother complains about. "Do you wish I strung *beads?*" her mother shouted at him once. May sometimes wishes that she could have been there when her parents first met. It was in the park, when her mother was riding a bicycle, and her father waved his arms for her to stop so he could take her picture. Her father has said that her mother was very beautiful that day—that he decided right then to marry her.

"How did you meet your husband?" May asks Mrs. Wong.

"I met him in an elevator."

"Did you go out with him for a long time before you got married?"

"For a year."

"That's a long time. My parents only went out together for two weeks."

"Time doesn't seem to be a factor," Mrs. Wong says with a sigh. She examines a blister on her big toe.

"Wanda says I shouldn't get married until I'm twenty-one."

"You shouldn't."

"I bet I'll never get married. Nobody has ever asked me out."

"They will," Mrs. Wong says. "Or you can ask them.

"Honey," Mrs. Wong says, "I wouldn't ever have a date now if I didn't ask them." She puts her sandals back on.

Wanda opens the screen door. "Would you like to have dinner with us?" she says to Mrs. Wong. "I could put in some extra chicken."

"Yes, I would. That's very nice of you, Mrs. Marshall."

"Chicken fricassee," Wanda says, and closes the door.

The tablecloth in the kitchen is covered with crumbs and cigarette ashes. The cloth is plastic, patterned with golden roosters. In the center is a large plastic hen (salt) and a plastic egg (pepper). The tequila bottle is lined up with the salt and pepper shakers.

At dinner, May watches Wanda serving the chicken. Will she put the spoon in the dish? She is waving the spoon; she looks as if she is conducting. She drops the spoon on the table.

"Ladies first," Wanda says.

Mrs. Wong takes over. She dishes up some chicken and hands the plate to May.

"Well," Wanda says, "here you are happy to be gone from your husband, and here I am miserable because my husband is gone, and May's mother is out chasing down her husband, who wants to run around the country taking pictures of hippies."

Wanda accepts a plate of chicken. She picks up her fork and puts it in her chicken. "Did I tell you, Mrs. Wong, that my husband drowned?"

"Yes, you did," Mrs. Wong says. "I'm very sorry."

"What would a social worker say if some woman was unhappy because her husband drowned?"

"I really don't know," Mrs. Wong says.

"You might just say, 'Buck up,' or something." Wanda takes a bite of the chicken. "Excuse me, Mrs. Wong," she says with her mouth full. "I want you to enjoy your dinner."

"It's very good," Mrs. Wong says. "Thank you for including me."

"Hell," Wanda says, "we're all on the same sinking ship."

"What are you thinking?" Wanda says to May when she is in bed. "You don't talk much."

"What do I think about what?"

"About your mother off after your father, and all. You don't cry in here at night, do you?"

"No," May says.

Wanda swirls the liquor in her glass. She gets up and goes to the window.

"Hello, coleus," Wanda says. "Should I pinch you back?" She stares at the plant, picks up the glass from the windowsill, and returns to the bed.

"If you were sixteen, you could get a license," Wanda says. "Then when your ma went after your father you could chase after the two of them. A regular caravan."

Wanda lights another cigarette. "What do you know about your friend Mrs. Wong? She's no more talkative than you, which isn't saying much."

"We just talk about things," May says. "She's rooting an avocado she's going to give me. It'll be a tree."

"You talk about avocados? I thought that, being a social worker, she might do you some good."

Wanda drops her match on the floor. "I wish if you had anything you wanted to talk about that you would," she says.

"How come my mother hasn't written? She's been gone a week."

Wanda shrugs. "Ask me something I can answer," she says.

In the middle of the following week a letter comes. "Dear May," it says, "I am hot as hell as I write this in a drugstore taking time out to have a Coke. Ray is nowhere to be found, so thank God you've still got me. I guess after another day of this I

am going to cash it in and get back to you. Don't feel bad about
this. After all, I did all the driving. Ha! Love, Mama."

Sitting on the porch after dinner, May rereads the letter. Her
mother's letters are always brief. Her mother has signed "Mama"
in big, block-printed letters to fill up the bottom of the page.

Mrs. Wong comes out of the house, prepared for rain. She has
on jeans and a yellow rain parka. She is going back to the library
to study, she says. She sits on the top step, next to May.

"See?" Mrs. Wong says. "I told you she'd write. My husband
would have ripped up the letter."

"Can't you call your son?" May asks.

"He got the number changed."

"Couldn't you go over there?"

"I suppose. It depresses me. Dirty magazines all over the house.
His father brings them back for them. Hamburger meat and
filth."

"Do you have a picture of him?" May asks.

Mrs. Wong takes out her wallet and removes a photo in a plastic case. There is a picture of a Chinese man sitting on a boat.
Next to him is a brown-haired boy, smiling. The Chinese man is
also smiling. One of his eyes has been poked out of the picture.

"My husband used to jump rope in the kitchen," Mrs. Wong
says. "I'm not kidding you. He said it was to tone his muscles. I'd
be cooking breakfast and he'd be jumping and panting. Reverting
to infancy."

May laughs.

"Wait till you get married," Mrs. Wong says.

Wanda opens the door and closes it again. She has been avoid-
ing Mrs. Wong since their last discussion, two days ago. When
Mrs. Wong was leaving for class, Wanda stood in front of the
door and said, "Why go to school? They don't have answers.
What's the answer to why my husband drowned himself in the
ocean after a good dinner? There aren't any answers. That's what
I've got against woman's liberation. Nothing personal."

Wanda had been drinking. She held the bottle in one hand and
the glass in the other.

"Why do you identify me with the women's movement, Mrs.
Marshall?" Mrs. Wong had asked.

"You left a perfectly good husband and son, didn't you?"

"My husband stayed out all night, and my son didn't care if I was there or not."

"He didn't *care?* What's happening to men? They're all turning queer, from the politicians down to the delivery boy. I was ashamed to have the delivery boy in my house today. What's gone wrong?"

Wanda's conversations usually end by her asking a question and then just walking away. That was something that always annoyed May's father. Almost everything about Wanda annoyed him. May wishes she could like Wanda more, but she agrees with her father. Wanda is nice, but she isn't very exciting.

Now Wanda comes out and sits on the porch. She picks up the *National Enquirer.* "Another doctor, another cure," Wanda says, and she sighs.

May is not listening to Wanda. She is watching a black Cadillac with a white top coming up the street. The black Cadillac looks just like the one that belongs to her father's friends Gus and Sugar. There is a woman in the passenger seat. The car comes by slowly, but then speeds up. May sits forward in her rocking chair to look. The woman did not look like Sugar. May sits back.

"Men on the moon, no cure for cancer," Wanda says. "Men on the moon, and they do something to the ground beef now so it won't cook. You saw me put that meat in the pan tonight. It just wouldn't cook, would it?"

They rock in silence. In a few minutes, the car coasts by again. The window is down, and music is playing loudly. The car stops in front of Wanda's. May's father gets out. It's her father, in a pair of shorts. A camera bounces against his chest.

"What the hell is this?" Wanda hollers as May runs toward her father.

"What the hell are you doing here?" Wanda yells again.

May's father is smiling. He has a beer can in one hand, but he hugs May to him, even though he can't pick her up. Looking past his arm, May sees that the woman in the car is Sugar.

"You're not taking her *anywhere!*" Wanda says. "You've got no right to put me in this position."

"Aw, Wanda, you know the world always dumps on you," Ray says. "You know I've got the right to put you in this position."

"You're drunk," Wanda says. "What's going on? Who's that in the car?"

"It's awful, Wanda," Ray says. "Here I am, and I'm drunk, and I'm taking May away."

"Daddy—were you in Colorado?" May says. "Is that where you were?"

"Colorado? I don't have the money to go West, sweetheart. I was out at Gus and Sugar's beach place, except that Gus has split, and Sugar is here with me to pick you up."

"She's not going with you," Wanda says. Wanda looks mean.

"Oh, Wanda, are we going to have a big fight? Am I going to have to grab her and run?"

He grabs May, and before Wanda can move they are at the car. The music is louder, the door is open, and May is in the car, crushing Sugar.

"Move over, Sugar," Ray says. "Lock the door. Lock the door!"

Sugar slides over behind the wheel. The door slams shut, the windows are rolled up, and as Wanda gets to the car May's father locks the door and makes a face at her.

"Poor Wanda!" he shouts through the glass. "Isn't this awful, Wanda?"

"Let her out! Give her to me!" Wanda shouts.

"Wanda," he says, "I'll give you this." He puckers his lips and blows a kiss, and Sugar, laughing, pulls away.

"Honey," Ray says to May, turning down the radio, "I don't know why I didn't have this idea sooner. I'm really sorry. I was talking to Sugar tonight, and I realized, My God, I can just go and get her. There's nothing Wanda can do."

"What about Mom, though?" May says. "I got a letter, and she's coming back from Colorado. She went to Denver."

"She didn't!"

"She did. She went looking for you."

"But I'm here," Ray says. "I'm right here with my Sugar and my May. Honey, we've made our own peanut butter, and we're going to have peanut butter and apple butter, and a beer, too, if you want it, and go walking in the surf. We've got boots—you can have my boots—and at night we can walk through the surf."

May looks at Sugar. Sugar's face is set in a wide smile. Her hair is white. She has dyed her hair white. She is smiling.

Ray hugs May. "I want to know every single thing that's happened," he says.

"I've just been, I've just been sitting around Wanda's."

"I *figured* that's where you were. At first I assumed you were with your mother, but I remembered the other time, and then it hit me that you had to be there. I told Sugar that—didn't I, Sugar?"

Sugar nods. Her hair has blown across her face, almost obscuring her vision. The traffic light in front of them changes from yellow to red, and May falls back against her father as the car speeds up.

Sugar says that she wants to be called by her real name. Her name is Martha Joanna Leigh, but Martha is fine with her. Ray always calls her all three names, or else just Sugar. He loves to tease.

It's a little scary at Sugar's house. For one thing, the seabirds don't always see that the front wall is glass, and sometimes a bird flies right into it. Sugar's two cats creep around the house, and at night they jump onto May's bed or get into fights. May has been here for three days. She and Ray and Sugar swim every day, and at night they play Scrabble or walk on the beach or take a drive. Sugar is a vegetarian. Everything she cooks is called "three"-something. Tonight, they had three-bean loaf; the night before, they had mushrooms with three-green stuffing. Dinner is usually at ten o'clock, which is when May used to go to bed at Wanda's.

Tonight, Ray is playing Gus's zither. It sounds like the music they play in horror movies. Ray has taken a lot of photographs of Sugar, and they are tacked up all over the house—Sugar cooking, Sugar getting out of the shower, Sugar asleep, Sugar waving at the camera, Sugar angry about so many pictures being taken. "And if Gus comes back, loook out," Ray says, strumming the zither.

"What if he does come back?" Sugar says.

"Listen to this," Ray says. "I've written a song that's about something I really feel. John Lennon couldn't have been more honest. Listen, Sugar."

"Martha," Sugar says.

"Coors beer," Ray sings, "there's none here. You have to go West to drink the best—Coooors beeeer."

May and Sugar laugh. May is holding a ball of yarn that Sugar is winding into smaller balls. One of the cats, which is going to have kittens, is licking its paws, with its head against the pillow Sugar is sitting on. Sugar has a box of rags in the kitchen closet. Every day she shows the box to the cat. She has to hold the cat's head straight to make it look at the box. The cat has always had kittens on the rug in the bathroom.

"And tuh-night Johnny's guests are . . ." Ray is imitating Ed McMahon again. All day he has been announcing Johnny Carson, or talking about Johnny's guests. "Ed McMahon," he says, shaking his head. "Out there in Burbank, Califoria, Ed has probably got a refrigerator full of Coors beer, and I've got to make do with Schlitz." Ray runs his fingers across the strings. "The hell with you, Ed. The hell with you." Ray closes the window above his head. "Wasn't there a talking horse named Ed?" He stretches out on the floor and crosses his feet, his arms behind his head. "What do you want to do?" he says.

"I'm fine," Sugar says. "You bored?"

"Yeah. I want Gus to show up and create a little action."

"He just might," Sugar says.

"Old Gus never can get it together. He's visiting his old mama way down in Macon, Georgia. He'll just be a rockin' and a talkin' with his poor old mother, and he won't be home for days and days."

"You're not making any sense, Ray."

"I'm Ed McMahon," Ray says, sitting up. "I'm standing out there with a mike in my hand, looking out on all those faces, and suddenly it looks like they're *sliding down on me*. Help!" Ray jumps up and waves his arms. "And I say to myself, 'Ed, what are you *doing* here, Ed?'"

"Let's go for a walk," Sugar says. "Do you want to take a walk?"

"I want to watch the damned Johnny Carson show. How come you don't have a television?"

Sugar pats the last ball of wool, drops it into the knitting basket. She looks at May. "We didn't have much for dinner. How about some cashew butter on toast, or some guacamole?"

"O.K.," May says. Sugar is very nice to her. It would be nice to have Sugar for a mother.

"Fix me some of that stuff, too," Ray says. He flips through a pile of records and picks one up, carefully removes it, his thumb in the center, another finger on the edge. He puts it on the record player and slowly lowers the needle to Rod Stewart, hoarsely singing "Mandolin Wind." "The way he sings 'No, no,'" Ray says, shaking his head.

In the kitchen, May takes a piece of toast out of the toaster, then takes out the other piece and puts it on her father's plate. Sugar pours each of them a glass of cranberry juice.

"You just love me, don't you, Sugar?" Ray says, and bites into his toast. "Because living with Gus is like living with a mummy—right?"

Sugar shrugs. She is smoking a cigarillo and drinking cranberry juice.

"I'm your Marvin Gardens," Ray says. "I'm your God-damned *Park Place*."

Sugar exhales, looks at some fixed point on the wall across from her.

"Oh, *metaphor*," Ray says, and cups his hand, as though he can catch something. "Everything is like everything else. Ray is like Gus. Sugar's getting tired of Ray."

"What the hell are you talking about, Ray?" Sugar says.

"Your one cat is like your other cat," Ray says. "All is one. Om, om."

Sugar drains her glass. Sugar and Ray are both smiling. May smiles, to join them, but she doesn't understand them.

Ray begins his James Taylor imitation. "Ev-ery-body, have you hoid, she's gonna buy me a mockin' boid . . ." he sings.

Ray used to sing to May's mother. He called it serenading. He'd sit at the table, waiting for breakfast, singing and keeping the beat with his knife against the table. As May got older, she was a little embarrassed when she had friends over and Ray began serenading. Her father is very energetic; at home, he used to sprawl out on the floor to arm-wrestle with his friends. He told May that he had been a Marine. Later, her mother told her that that wasn't true—he wasn't even in the Army, because he had too many allergies.

"Let's take a walk," Ray says now, hitting the table so hard that the plates shake.

"Get your coat, May," Sugar says. "We're going for a walk."

Sugar puts on a tan poncho with unicorns on the front and stars on the back. May's clothes are at Wanda's, so she wears Sugar's raincoat, tied around her waist with a red Moroccan belt. "We look like we're auditioning for Fellini," Sugar says.

Ray opens the sliding door. The small patio is covered with sand. They walk down two steps to the beach. There's a quarter-moon, and the water is dark. There is a wide expanse of sand between the house and the water. Ray skips down the beach, away from them, becoming a blur in the darkness.

"Your father's in a bad mood because another publisher turned down his book of photographs," Sugar says.

"Oh," May says.

"That raincoat falling off you?" Sugar says, tugging on one shoulder. "You look like some Biblical figure."

It's windy. The wind blows the sand against May's legs. She stops to rub some of it away.

"Ray?" Sugar calls. "Hey, Ray!"

"Where is he?" May asks.

"If he didn't want to walk with us, I don't know why he asked us to come," Sugar says.

They are close to the water now. A light spray blows into May's face.

"Ray!" Sugar calls down the beach.

"Boo!" Ray screams, in back of them. Sugar and May jump. May screams.

"I was crouching. Didn't you see me?" Ray says.

"Very funny," Sugar says.

Ray hoists May onto his shoulders. She doesn't like being up there. He scared her.

"Your legs are as long as flagpoles," Ray says to May. "How old are you now?"

"Twelve."

"Twelve years old. I've been married to your mother for thirteen years."

Some rocks appear in front of them. It is where the private beach ends and the public beach begins. In the daytime they often walk here and sit on the rocks. Ray takes pictures, and Sugar and May jump over the incoming waves or just sit looking at the water. They usually have a good time. Right now, riding on Ray's shoulders, May wants to know how much longer they are going to stay at the beach house. Maybe her mother is already back. If Wanda told her mother about the Cadillac, her mother would know it was Sugar's, wouldn't she? Her mother used to say nasty things about Sugar and Gus. "*College* people," her mother called them. Sugar teaches crafts at a high school; Gus is a piano teacher. At the beach house, Sugar has taught May how to play scales on Gus's piano. It is a huge black piano that takes up almost a whole room. There is a picture on top of a Doberman, with a blue ribbon stuck to the side of the frame. Gus used to raise dogs. Three of them bit him in one month, and he quit.

"Race you back," Ray says now, lowering May. But she is too tired to race. She and Sugar just keep walking when he runs off. They walk in silence most of the way back.

"Sugar," May says, "do you know how long we're going to be here?"

Sugar slows down. "I really don't know. No. Are you worried that your mother might be back?"

"She ought to be back by now."

Sugar's hair looks like snow in the moonlight. "Go to bed when we get back and I'll talk to him," Sugar says.

When they get to the house, the light is on, so it's easier to see where they're walking. As Sugar pushes open the sliding door, May sees her father standing in front of Gus in the living room. Gus does not turn around when Sugar says, "Gus. Hello."

Everyone looks at him. "I'm tired as hell," Gus says. "Is there any beer?"

184 Distortions

"I'll get you some," Sugar says. Almost in slow motion, she goes to the refrigerator.

Gus has been looking at Ray's pictures of Sugar, and suddenly he snatches one off the wall. "On *my* wall?" Gus says. "Who did that? Who hung them up?"

"Ray," Sugar says. She hands him the can of beer.

"Ray," Gus repeats. He shakes his head. He shakes the beer in the can lightly but doesn't drink it.

"May," Sugar says, "why don't you go upstairs and get ready for bed?"

"Go upstairs," Gus says. Gus's face is red, and he looks tired and wild.

May runs up the stairs and then sits down there and listens. No one is talking. Then she hears Gus say, "Do you intend to spend the night, Ray? Turn this into a little social occasion?"

"I would like to stay for a while to—" Ray begins.

Gus says something, but his voice is so low and angry that May can't make out the words.

Silence again.

"Gus—" Ray begins again.

"*What?*" Gus shouts. "What have you got to say to me, Ray? You don't have a damned thing to say to me. Will you get out of here now?"

Footsteps. May looks down and sees her father walk past the stairs. He does not look up. He did not see her. He has gone out the door, leaving her. In a minute she hears his motorcycle start and the noise the tires make riding through gravel. May runs downstairs to Sugar, who is picking up the pictures Gus has ripped off the walls.

"I'm going to take you home, May," Sugar says.

"I'm coming with you," Gus says. "If I let you go, you'll go after Ray."

"That's ridiculous," Sugar says.

"I'm going with you," Gus says.

"Let's go, then," Sugar says. May is the first one to the door.

Gus is barefoot. He stares at Sugar and walks as if he is drunk. He is still holding the can of beer.

Sugar gets into the driver's seat of the Cadillac. The key is in the ignition. She starts the car and then puts her head against the wheel and begins to cry.

"Get moving, will you?" Gus says. "Or move over." Gus gets out and walks around the car. "I knew you were going crazy when you dyed your hair," Gus says. "Shove over, will you?"

Sugar moves over. May is in the back seat, in one corner.

"For God's sake, stop crying," Gus says. "What am I doing to you?"

Gus drives slowly, then very fast. The radio is on, in a faint mumble. For half an hour they ride in silence, except for the sounds of the radio and Sugar blowing her nose.

"Your father's O.K.," Sugar says at last. "He was just upset, you know."

In the back seat, May nods, but Sugar does not see it.

At last the car slows, and May sits up and sees they are in the block where she lives. Ray's motorcycle is not in the driveway. All the lights are out in the house.

"It's empty," Sugar says. "Or else she's asleep in there. Do you want to knock on the door, May?"

"What do you mean, it's empty?" Gus says.

"She's in Colorado," Sugar says. "I thought she might be back."

May begins to cry. She tries to get out of the car, but she can't work the door handle.

"Come on," Gus says to her. "Come on, now. We can go back. I don't believe this."

May's legs are still sandy, and they itch. She rubs them, crying.

"You can take her back to Wanda's," Sugar says. "Is that O.K., May?"

"Wanda? Who's that?"

"Her mother's friend. It's not far from here. I'll show you."

"What am I even doing talking to you?" Gus says.

The radio drones. In another ten minutes they are at Wanda's.

"I suppose nobody's here, either," Gus says, looking at the dark house. He leans back and opens the door for May, who runs up the walk. "Please be here, Wanda," she whispers. She runs up to the door and knocks. No one answers. She knocks harder, and a light goes on in the hall. "Who is it?" Wanda calls.

"May," May says.

"May!" Wanda hollers. She fumbles with the door. The door opens. May hears the tires as Gus pulls the car away. She stands there in Sugar's raincoat, with the red belt hanging down the front.

"What did they do to you? What did they do?" Wanda says. Her eyes are swollen from sleep. Her hair has been clipped into rows of neat pin curls.

"You didn't even try to find me," May says.

"I called the house every hour!" Wanda says. "I called the police, and they wouldn't do anything—he was your father. I did too try to find you. Look, there's a letter from your mother. Tell me if you're all right. Your father is crazy. He'll never get you again after this, I know that. Are you all right, May? Talk to me." Wanda turns on the hall lamp. "Are you all right? You saw how he got you in the car. What could I do? The police told me there was nothing else I could do. Do you want your mother's letter? What have you got on?"

May takes the letter from Wanda and turns her back. She opens the envelope and reads: "Dear May, A last letter before I drive home. I looked up some friends of your father's here, and they asked me to stay for a couple of days to unwind, so here I am. At first I thought he might be in the closet—jump out at me for a joke! Tell Wanda that I've lost five pounds. Sweated it away, I guess. I've been thinking, honey, and when I come home I want us to get a dog. I think you should have a dog. There are some that hardly shed at all, and maybe some that just plain don't. It would be good to get a medium-size dog—maybe a terrier, or something like that. I meant to get you a dog years ago, but now I've been thinking that I should still do it. When I get back, first thing we'll go and get you a dog. Love, Mama."

It is the longest letter May has ever gotten from her mother. She stands in Wanda's hallway, amazed.

The
Parking Lot

▪▪▪▪▪▪▪▪▪▪▪▪▪▪▪▪▪▪▪▪▪▪▪▪▪

■■■■■■■■■■■■■■■■■■■■■■■

Walking across the parking lot, she becomes fascinated by the sameness of the surface: so black and regular. She rubs the tops of her arms—more to protest the cold than to warm herself. When she was a little girl her father rubbed her arms for her. She doesn't remember complaining about the cold, but her father often stopped, just the same, and rubbed her arms, which hung stiffly at her sides as she walked in a heavy winter coat, always one size too big. He rubbed so hard she was almost lifted off the ground. She gives another rub. Her shoulder bag swings forward and interrupts. She's awkward. Tired—the end of the day. She has been working here, in this gigantic building, for five months. She used to walk across the parking lot smelling the air, knowing it was almost spring. Now it is autumn. The surface of the parking lot, which she suddenly realizes she has been studying for five months, doesn't change.

At home, which is a four-room apartment (Do you count the bathroom? She always forgets), she collapses in her favorite chair. Collapse is no exaggeration. After she sits down it takes her at least an hour to get up. He has to bring her a drink, smooth her hair. He hovers over her. He's always lonesome without her. The other reason he hovers, she knows, is to make her nervous about all the fussing so she will get up. When she gets up she starts their dinner, and she is an excellent cook. He is a good cook too, and has offered to do the cooking, saying that she works hard enough during the day. Secretly, he wants her to continue. He is a good cook, but she is excellent. From her he learned to frequent gourmet shops, to sneer at frozen vegetables. In the morning before she leaves, she writes a note telling him what he needs to buy at the store. Tonight he watches as she squeezes lemon juice over chicken, picks parsley from the herb box and sprinkles it gently over the top. A dash of nutmeg. Her energy comes back to her as she prepares their dinner. She pats his hand, where it rests on the counter. His hand is in her way, but as she begins to feel less tired she becomes more tolerant.

As they eat she explains that tomorrow, Friday, she'll be late. She's taking care of Paula's children tomorrow night so she can have a night out—picking them up at nursery school after work. Paula is a girl she works with. He knows that. He nods vigorously to dismiss the explanation. Actually, he doesn't like conversation at dinner. The food she prepares is so delicious, so delicate. He doesn't want to be distracted.

She is always too tired to go out after the day of work, so they stay home at night. He stays in too much. She mentions it to him. Does she want to go out? He misunderstands. She meant that he should go out during the day. He does; he shops for food every day. Yes, but she didn't mean it so literally; she meant he should do something that wasn't an errand. It's such a beautiful time for the park. She is enthusiastic, but wouldn't want to be sitting in a park in autumn herself. Only work has seemed real to her since she began her job. She feels sorry for him—browsing in aisles of imported food, sitting on a bench by the fountain. The fluorescent lights in her office excite her. The wide, shining hallway gives her a sense of purpose.

By arrangement, they work alternate years. Last year he was a house painter. He was very good at it, and he made quite a bit of money. Before that, she was a waitress at a private club. She got good tips. She had nothing against that job. But this job—it amazes her that she could have been so wrong in thinking that working in an office would be depressing. She likes this even better than waitressing. She was more tired when she was a waitress, she thinks with satisfaction.

She finds herself in the parking lot, a whole day gone. What happened in the period between sitting at the dinner table and now, when she is walking across the parking lot? She's left work a little early, dutiful about picking up Paula's children. Usually she has to be alert walking through the parking lot, but tonight she's left earlier than the other drivers. Other people, already in their cars and as tired as her, back up without looking carefully. She would have been hit last week if she had not shrieked. She was nowhere near the man's car, but as he pulled out he swung backwards in an arc . . . she remembers putting her arms out, as though that would stop the car. The cry she gave stopped it.

She parks at the back of the lot because there's less chance of the car being hit there. They fight for places at the front. Let them. She wonders, as she puts the key in the lock to open the car

door, what people do about finding their car when they're color
blind. It's her car's color she rivets her eyes to. She moves toward
the bright, bright red. There are a lot of VW's in the lot that
look like hers. Sometimes there are three in a row, even back here.
They must look in the window, she thinks a little giddily. People
keep so much junk in their cars.

Paula's children are glad to see her. They've met her twice before. They're very glad to see her. Three- and four-year-old children
get nervous about any deviation from their routine, even when
they've been told what to expect. She feels sorry for them—particularly the three-year-old—and kids around with them. It's only
nervousness that makes them so glad she's there, but she's flattered
anyway.

He entertains the children while she fixes dinner. She makes a
formal meal for the four of them, as though they are honored
company: beef stroganoff, fresh lima beans, salade niçoise. The
children love it. They've never eaten by candlelight. The older
one is confused and wants to know if it's Halloween. She went a
little light on the burgundy in the sauce because of the children,
but compensated for it beautifully with a sprinkle of sage. He
looks at her across the table. She can tell by his smile that he's
grateful she didn't fix fried chicken, or something children supposedly like. The oldest child asks what the salad is. "Salade
niçoise," she tells her, and details the ingredients. He pays as close
attention as the child. Being a good cook himself, he appreciates
this.

It is Saturday, and his friend Sam is visiting. Sam has separated
from his wife and visits more often now. Jim and Sam always invite her to go out with them, but she doesn't feel like tagging
along. They don't make her feel that way, she makes herself feel
that way. By now they're so used to her staying that they don't expect an excuse. She's happy Jim is getting out of the apartment;
ever since he quit painting he's stayed close—just going out for
food and sometimes, but not often, a walk before bed. When they
leave the apartment it seems suddenly as though space is opening
up around her. It's still such a small apartment, though: you walk
into the living room, and if you turn right you're in the bedroom,

and if you turn left there's a small hallway with a bathroom and a kitchen at the end of it. The kitchen is really too small—the other rooms are an adequate size, except that she feels cramped when anyone besides the two of them are in the apartment. He thinks of moving, somewhere where there will be a larger kitchen, so she can work better. It's too much trouble to move, so she insists she can move freely in the kitchen. She takes a look at the kitchen; it's a bright, functional room, much too small. The living room is small, too. And the bedroom. She paces the apartment, then grabs a jacket and goes out, catches a bus and goes shopping. There's no sense in spending her day off feeling closed in. At the store she buys a little bottle of perfume that the salesgirl tells her smells autumn-y. The salesgirl has long fingernails painted pale orange. Her fingernail polish sparkles as she hands her the bag. Her smile is bright as well.

Sam comments on the perfume at dinner. She is glad that he doesn't say it smells like autumn, but only that it smells good. He takes her wrist in his hand for a second to sniff it. Sam has always been a little in love with her. She would like him anyway, because he is a nice person, but she likes him a little more because she knows about his secret love. They talk a little about his wife. She thinks he's secretly in love with his wife as well. She doesn't like his wife; she's the sort of woman who gives in to everything: she eats too much and is overweight, she thinks too hard and is always dissatisfied, turning all conversations to politics and the state of the country. She was never pleasant to have to dinner. A little embarrassed that he's talking about his wife again, Sam closes off with a bit of flattery: "And she wasn't as good a cook as you." They are eating a roast beef dinner. Baked stuffed potatoes. Very American—Sam's favorite kind of food. She likes to cook what people particularly like; it makes everything more pleasant. And sure enough, Sam isn't feeling blue any more when they've finished eating.

Late that night they go to a little restaurant for French pastry and espresso. She could have served that at home, but Sam likes to take them out—he feels a little guilty that he can't reciprocate any more. When Jim goes to the men's room Sam speaks hurriedly. She didn't expect that at all—was there an undercurrent all night she didn't catch? Sam says that he is worried about Jim. Jim doesn't go out much, and he seems at loose ends now that he isn't working. Sam laughs, a little embarrassed, sensing, no doubt, her surprise at all this hurried talk. "I don't want *everybody* to fall apart," he says. Then he asks outright if their arrangement is that Jim can't work when she works. No—he could if he wanted to. It's just that he doesn't have to. Sam seems confused by that. Or embarrassed. He says that it's all none of his business. But then he speaks again, a question she can't answer because Jim is walking toward them as he asks: "Wouldn't it be better if he went back to work?"

Sam's question nags at her. Back at work on Monday, she thinks about calling Jim. She's busy, though, and forgets to do it, or else when she remembers the phone is in use. By five o'clock she feels differently. Sam meant to be helpful, but he misunderstood. She regrets wasting so much of her day thinking about what he said. She regrets the weekend, too—Saturday was wasted; she had felt vaguely depressed all day, and now she realizes that Sam was responsible. Not only what he said about Jim—or what he insinuated, really—but his presence, a reminder of what can happen to a marriage, the distressing realization that two adults who care about each other, as Sam and his wife do, can't reach some agreement, have some arrangement that will make them both happy.

A car coasts along beside her. She recognizes the driver, a man she has spoken to several times in the elevator. "Parked all the way in the back?" he asks, and she tells him she is. She does what she knows is expected: she shrugs and looks a little perturbed about what everyone calls "the parking problem." She's sure that telling him she parks there deliberately would sound too preachy. So when he leans over and swings open the door on the passenger's side, she has to get in. They drive up alongside her car in a minute—too short a time to start a conversation, he says. She agrees. And instead of getting out she sits there. She smiles, which is something she hasn't done all weekend. During the next hour they have a conversation—in a bar. The conversation lasts about an hour, and then they go to a motel and go to bed. She thinks, then, of Jim—as she has most of the afternoon. She can't think of what to tell him, so she stays in the motel for another hour, thinking. Eventually they leave. He drives her back to her car. They smile again. This time there is no conversation, and she gets out.

He isn't in the apartment when she gets back. She knocks and he doesn't open the door. She imagines he's sulking, so she rummages through her purse until she finds the key and goes in, ready to defend herself. He isn't there. She looks for him like a dog searching for a missing bone, feeling foolish as she does it. Then she collapses in the chair. She falls asleep and is awakened by a key in the door. Jim looks terrible. Through the darkness of the room, and half asleep, she can tell that. He has a bag with him, which he sets on the floor by the chair. He smooths her hair. He tells her she looks tired. He has been out looking for shallots. It was his mistake to have slept away most of the afternoon, but who would think shallots would be impossible to find? He had to take the bus crosstown, and then he found them at that reliable specialty store next to the dry cleaner's.

Even with the shallots, the trout does not taste very good to her.

The next day she doesn't go to work. She gets up at seven-thirty, as usual, and dresses, but she parks at a downtown garage and goes shopping. For some reason, she's still tired. She would have preferred to stay at home, but she didn't want him to think anything was wrong, and she couldn't say that she didn't feel like going to work, because she had already told him how much she liked the job. She has no respect for women who say one thing one minute and another the next. She buys another bottle of perfume—a more expensive bottle—from the same salesgirl. She has been in the store several hours, going leisurely from department to department, when she realizes she hasn't left a list of instructions for Jim. Has he called her office? Does he already know she isn't there? In a panic, she asks a salesgirl where there is a telephone. She calls immediately. There's no answer! What does that mean? Then she hears his voice. He's been asleep. She's lucky, because it's late in the afternoon—two o'clock. She keeps her voice steady; she has called because she forgot to leave the list. "What did you want me to get?" he asks. Her mind goes blank. Finally she thinks

of something: lobster. And ground pork. Consomme. She will fix
lobster in lobster sauce. "We had fish last night," he says sleepily.
He's right; she's forgotten even eating last night. She never makes
a mistake in menu planning. He's just pointed out an error; he
knows she's slipping . . . "But that sounds good," he says. "Any
spices we don't have? Let me write this down."

It is a delicious dinner. They eat earlier than usual because she's
so hungry. She didn't want to eat lunch at the store, because it
was just a cafeteria; it was too much trouble to move the car to go
somewhere else. As she eats she concentrates, but still has no
memory of having eaten dinner the night before. He sighs with
contentment, spooning the rice onto his plate, ladling sauce over
top of it. It is a particularly good dinner. She prepared it very
slowly, with much care, fascinated herself by what she was doing.

She expects that he will be in her office waiting for her, but she
doesn't see him all that day. She walks up the stairs instead of taking the elevator. Eventually the fluorescent lights make her feel
warm, and with the warmth comes calm. She works with accuracy
and speed. The day is over before it begins. She feels real relief,
walking down the stairs, that she has not had to see him. She
knows men, and that is why she thought he would be standing in
her office, waiting for her when she came in in the morning, but
this time she has been wrong. As she starts her walk across the
parking lot she begins to think of dinner. Some of the ingredients
for this night's dinner are a little hard to find out of season, and
she hopes he has not had to take the crosstown bus again. She's
tired, and she knows what it is to exhaust yourself in a day.

Then she sees the car. Far in the distance, blocking her own car
from view, yet she knows with certainty that her car is behind it.
She walks more slowly. She tries to think, but nothing comes. Yes
—it's his car. She remembers the color. She remembers the make:
a Pontiac. She remembers him, too, sees his face as clearly as she
now sees the car, although he isn't looking in her direction, but in
front of him, down the lot. She's almost close enough to touch
him before he realizes she's there. In fact, her hand does touch
the glass. She stands there with her hand against his window until

he reaches across the seat and opens the door on her side. Then she gets into the car.

Tonight he has been unable to find fresh thyme. It is the first time he has ever failed. She makes the dinner without it, but it's flat, lacking a certain delicacy of flavor. And he knows it, too, his palate as fine as hers. Neither of them eats much. The wine they have with the meal is very good. He has selected wisely. But the main course is a disappointment. He looks sad—eats listlessly, says little. He has failed.

After dinner she goes into the bathroom. The two little bottles of perfume are on a shelf. She takes them down and smells them, both much the same. With her eyes closed, slowly breathing in the aroma, she remembers the motel room, the ride, the hamburger she ate with him at a roadside stand. She had been very nervous coming back to the apartment, late again, but once more he hadn't been there. He was hours late coming in, having searched everywhere for the thyme. And he was depressed not to have found it; he forgot to brush her hair. He sat in his own chair and said very little. Perhaps it is the memory of the hamburger— she never eats cheap food like that—or something about the strong smell of the perfume released in the small room that makes her sick. She is sick, vomiting in the bathroom for a long time before the sickness passes, and then she's all right. He'll say she has been pushing herself too hard, and that will start a whole discussion: moving to a larger apartment, his cooking dinners, everything. She goes into the living room to face it, but the room is empty. He has gone out for one of his infrequent walks.

Eventually she will be caught. She knows that. This night she is very late; she should have called with an excuse hours ago. She uses the telephone at the entrance to the parking lot, trying to keep her voice soft and regular, counting the white lines that divide the lot into the parking places until his voice comes on the line. Something happened to her car, she tells him. It did? His voice is strained. She doesn't say anything.

"There's a man," she says.

"Speak louder. You said the car broke down. Where?"

"In the parking lot. There's a man."

"Yes?"

"Who's going to fix it."

There is another silence.

"Will you call back if there's any real trouble?"

"Yes," she says.

He is waiting in the car. It's all right, she assures him. He rides her to her car at the back of the parking lot. She opens the door and gets in. She watches his car drive away in the rearview mirror, and then she gets out of the car and stands in the parking lot. Standing there, she thinks of her lover, gone in one direction, and of Jim, in another. She watches the leaves blow across the surface and sees that now the parking lot is mostly brown, instead of black. Autumn always makes her feel uneasy. Autumn, or the fact that she hasn't eaten all day. She gets in the car and drives home to make dinner.

Vermont

■■■■■■■■■■■■■■■■■■■■■■

Noel is in our living room shaking his head. He refused my offer and then David's offer of a drink, but he has had three glasses of water. It is absurd to wonder at such a time when he will get up to go to the bathroom, but I do. I would like to see Noel move; he seems so rigid that I forget to sympathize, forget that he is a real person. "That's not what I want," he said to David when David began sympathizing. Absurd, at such a time, to ask what he does want. I can't remember how it came about that David started bringing glasses of water.

Noel's wife, Susan, has told him that she's been seeing John Stillerman. We live on the first floor, Noel and Susan on the second, John on the eleventh. Interesting that John, on the eleventh, should steal Susan from the second floor. John proposes that they just rearrange—that Susan moved up to the eleventh, into the apartment John's wife only recently left, that they just . . . John's wife had a mastectomy last fall, and in the elevator she told Susan that if she was losing what she didn't want to lose, she might as well lose what she did want to lose. She lost John—left him the way popcorn flies out of the bag on the roller coaster. She is living somewhere in the city, but John doesn't know where. John is a museum curator, and last month, after John's picture appeared in a newsmagazine, showing him standing in front of an empty space where a stolen canvas had hung, he got a one-word note from his wife: "Good." He showed the note to David in the elevator. "It was tucked in the back of his wallet—the way all my friends used to carry rubbers in high school," David told me.

"Did you guys know?" Noel asks. A difficult one; of course we didn't *know*, but naturally we guessed. Is Noel able to handle such semantics? David answers vaguely. Noel shakes his head vaguely, accepting David's vague answer. What else will he accept? The move upstairs? For now, another glass of water.

David gives Noel a sweater, hoping, no doubt, to stop his shivering. Noel pulls on the sweater over pajamas patterned with small gray fish. David brings him a raincoat, too. A long white scarf hangs from the pocket. Noel swishes it back and forth listlessly. He gets up and goes to the bathroom.

"Why did she have to tell him when he was in his pajamas?" David whispers.

Noel comes back, looks out the window. "I don't know why I didn't know. I can tell you guys know."

Noel goes to our front door, opens it, and wanders off down the hallway.

"If he had stayed any longer, he would have said, 'Jeepers,'" David says.

David looks at his watch and sighs. Usually he opens Beth's door on his way to bed, and tiptoes in to admire her. Beth is our daughter. She is five. Some nights, David even leaves a note in her slippers, saying that he loves her. But tonight he's depressed. I follow him into the bedroom, undress, and get into bed. David looks at me sadly, lies down next to me, turns off the light. I want to say something but don't know what to say. I could say, "One of us should have gone with Noel. Do you know your socks are still on? You're going to do to me what Susan did to Noel, aren't you?"

"Did you see his poor miserable pajamas?" David whispers finally. He throws back the covers and gets up and goes back to the living room. I follow, half asleep. David sits in the chair, puts his arms on the armrests, presses his neck against the back of the chair, and moves his feet together. "Zzzz," he says, and his head falls forward.

Back in bed, I lie awake, remembering a day David and I spent in the park last August. David was sitting on the swing next to me, scraping the toes of his tennis shoes in the loose dirt.

"Don't you want to swing?" I said. We had been playing tennis. He had beaten me every game. He always beats me at everything—precision parking, three-dimensional ticktacktoe, soufflés. His soufflés rise as beautifully curved as the moon.

"I don't know how to swing," he said.

I tried to teach him, but he couldn't get his legs to move right. He stood the way I told him, with the board against his behind, gave a little jump to get on, but then he couldn't synchronize his legs. "Pump!" I called, but it didn't mean anything. I might as well have said, "Juggle dishes." I still find it hard to believe there's anything I can do that he can't do.

He got off the swing. "Why do you act like everything is a goddamn contest?" he said, and walked away.

"Because we're always having contests and you always win!" I
shouted.

I was still waiting by the swings when he showed up half an
hour later.

"Do you consider it a contest when we go scuba diving?" he
said.

He had me. It was stupid of me last summer to say how he always snatched the best shells, even when they were closer to me.
That made him laugh. He had chased me into a corner, then
laughed at me.

I lie in bed now, hating him for that. But don't leave me, I
think—don't do what Noel's wife did. I reach across the bed and
gently take hold of a little wrinkle in his pajama top. I don't know
if I want to yank his pajamas—do something violent—or smooth
them. Confused, I take my hand away and turn on the light.
David rolls over, throws his arm over his face, groans. I stare at
him. In a second he will lower his arm and demand an explanation. Trapped again. I get up and put on my slippers.

"I'm going to get a drink of water," I whisper apologetically.

Later in the month, it happens. I'm sitting on a cushion on the
floor, with newspapers spread in front of me, repotting plants. I'm
just moving the purple passion plant to a larger pot when David
comes in. It is late in the afternoon—late enough to be dark outside. David has been out with Beth. Before the two of them went
out, Beth, confused by the sight of soil indoors, crouched down
beside me to ask, "Are there ants, Mommy?" I laughed. David
never approved of my laughing at her. Later, that will be something he'll mention in court, hoping to get custody: I laugh at
her. And when that doesn't work, he'll tell the judge what I said
about his snatching all the best seashells.

David comes in, coat still buttoned, blue silk scarf still tied (a
Christmas present from Noel, with many apologies for losing the
white one), sits on the floor, and says that he's decided to leave.
He is speaking very reasonably and quietly. That alarms me. It

crosses my mind that he's mad. And Beth isn't with him. He has killed her!

No, no, of course not. I'm mad. Beth is upstairs in her friend's apartment. He ran into Beth's friend and her mother coming into the building. He asked if Beth could stay in their apartment for a few minutes. I'm not convinced: What friend? I'm foolish to feel reassured as soon as he names one—Louisa. I feel nothing but relief. It might be more accurate to say that I feel nothing. I would have felt pain if she were dead, but David says she isn't, so I feel nothing. I reach out and begin stroking the plant's leaves. Soft leaves, sharp points. The plant I'm repotting is a cutting from Noel's big plant that hangs in a silver ice bucket in his window (a wedding gift that he and Susan had never used). I helped him put it in the ice bucket. "What are you going to do with the top?" I asked. He put it on his head and danced around.

"I had an uncle who got drunk and danced with a lampshade on his head," Noel said. "That's an old joke, but how many people have actually *seen* a man dance with a lampshade on his head? My uncle did it every New Year's Eve."

"What the hell are you smiling about?" David says. "Are you listening to me?"

I nod and start to cry. It will be a long time before I realize that David makes me sad and Noel makes me happy.

Noel sympathizes with me. He tells me that David is a fool; he is better off without Susan, and I will be better off without David. Noel calls or visits me in my new apartment almost every night. Last night he suggested that I get a babysitter for tonight, so he could take me to dinner. He tries very hard to make me happy. He brings expensive wine when we eat in my apartment and offers to buy it in restaurants when we eat out. Beth prefers it when we eat in; that way, she can have both Noel and the toy that Noel inevitably brings. Her favorite toy, so far, is a handsome red tugboat pulling three barges, attached to one another by string. Noel bends over, almost doubled in half, to move them across the rug, whistling and calling orders to the imaginary crew. He does not just bring gifts to Beth and me. He has bought himself a new car,

and pretends that this is for Beth and me. ("Comfortable seats?"
he asks me. "That's a nice big window back there to wave out of,"
he says to Beth.) It is silly to pretend that he got the car for the
three of us. And if he did, why was he too cheap to have a radio
installed, when he knows I love music? Not only that but he's
bowlegged. I am ashamed of myself for thinking bad things about
Noel. He tries so hard to keep us cheerful. He can't help the odd
angle of his thighs. Feeling sorry for him, I decided that a cheap
dinner was good enough for tonight. I said that I wanted to go to
a Chinese restaurant.

At the restaurant I eat shrimp in black bean sauce and drink a
Heineken's and think that I've never tasted anything so delicious.
The waiter brings two fortune cookies. We open them; the fortunes make no sense. Noel summons the waiter for the bill. With
it come more fortune cookies—four this time. They are no good,
either: talk of travel and money. Noel says, "What bloody rot."
He is wearing a gray vest and a white shirt. I peek around the
table without his noticing and see that he's wearing gray wool
slacks. Lately it has been very important for me to be able to see
everything. Whenever Noel pulls the boats out of sight, into another room, I move as quickly as Beth to watch what's going on.

Standing behind Noel at the cash register, I see that it has
started to rain—a mixture of rain and snow.

"You know how you can tell a Chinese restaurant from any
other?" Noel asks, pushing open the door. "Even when it's raining, the cats still run for the street."

I shake my head in disgust.

Noel stretches the skin at the corners of his eyes. "Sorry for
honorable joke," he says.

We run for the car. He grabs the belt of my coat, catches me,
and half lifts me with one arm, running along with me dangling
at his side, giggling. Our wool coats stink. He opens my car door,
runs around, and pulls his open. He's done it again; he has made
me laugh.

We start home.

We are in heavy traffic, and Noel drives very slowly, protecting
his new car.

"How old are you?" I ask.

"Thirty-six," Noel says.
"I'm twenty seven," I say.
"So what?" he says. He says it pleasantly.
"I just didn't know how old you were."
"Mentally, I'm neck and neck with Beth," he says.
I'm soaking wet, and I want to get home to put on dry clothes. I look at him inching through traffic, and I remember the way his face looked that night he sat in the living room with David and me.
"Rain always puts you in a bad mood, doesn't it?" he says. He turns the windshield wipers on high. Rubber squeaks against glass.
"I see myself dead in it," I say.
"You see yourself dead in it?"
Noel does not read novels. He reads *Moneysworth*, the *Wall Street Journal*, *Commentary*. I reprimand myself; there must be fitting ironies in the *Wall Street Journal*.
"Are you kidding?" Noel says. "You seemed to be enjoying yourself at dinner. It was a good dinner, wasn't it?"
"I make you nervous, don't I?" I say.
"No. You don't make me nervous."
Rain splashes under the car, drums on the roof. We ride on for blocks and blocks. It is too quiet; I wish there were a radio. The rain on the roof is monotonous, the collar of my coat is wet and cold. At last we are home. Noel parks the car and comes around to my door and opens it. I get out. Noel pulls me close, squeezes me hard. When I was a little girl, I once squeezed a doll to my chest in an antique shop, and when I took it away the eyes had popped off. An unpleasant memory. With my arms around Noel, I feel the cold rain hitting my hands and wrists.
A man running down the sidewalk with a small dog in his arms and a big black umbrella over him calls, "Your lights are on!"

It is almost a year later—Christmas—and we are visiting Noel's crazy sister, Juliette. After going with Noel for so long, I am considered one of the family. Juliette phones before every occasion, saying, "You're one of the family. Of course you don't need an invitation." I should appreciate it, but she's always drunk when she calls, and usually she starts to cry and says she wishes Christmas

and Thanksgiving didn't exist. Jeanette, his other sister, is very
nice, but she lives in Colorado. Juliette lives in New Jersey. Here
we are in Bayonne, New Jersey, coming in through the front door
—Noel holding Beth, me carrying a pumpkin pie. I tried to sniff
the pie aroma on the way from Noel's apartment to his sister's
house, but it had no smell. Or else I'm getting another cold. I
sucked chewable vitamin C tablets in the car, and now I smell of
oranges. Noel's mother is in the living room, crocheting. Better, at
least, than David's mother, who was always discoursing about
Andrew Wyeth. I remember with satisfaction that the last time I
saw her I said, "It's a simple fact that Edward Hopper was better."

Juliette: long, whitish-blond hair tucked in back of her pink
ears, spike-heel shoes that she orders from Frederick's of Holly-
wood, dresses that show her cleavage. Noel and I are silently wondering if her husband will be here. At Thanksgiving he showed up
just as we were starting dinner, with a black-haired woman who
wore a dress with a plunging neckline. Juliette's breasts faced the
black-haired woman's breasts across the table (tablecloth
crocheted by Noel's mother). Noel doesn't like me to criticize
Juliette. He thinks positively. His other sister is a musician. She
has a husband and a weimaraner and two rare birds that live in a
birdcage built by her husband. They have a lot of money and they
ski. They have adopted a Korean boy. Once, they showed us a
film of the Korean boy learning to ski. Wham, wham, wham—
every few seconds he was groveling in the snow again.

Juliette is such a liberal that she gives us not only the same bedroom but a bedroom with only a single bed in it. Beth sleeps on
the couch.

Wedged beside Noel that night, I say, "This is ridiculous."

"She means to be nice," he says. "Where else would we sleep?"

"She could let us have her double bed and she could sleep in
here. After all, he's not coming back, Noel."

"Shh."

"Wouldn't that have been better?"

"What do you care?" Noel says. "You're nuts about me, right?"

He slides up against me and hugs my back.

"I don't know how people talk any more," he says. "I don't know any of the current lingo. What expression do people use for 'nuts about'?"

"I don't know."

"I just did it again! I said 'lingo.' "

"So what? Who do you want to sound like?"

"The way I talk sounds dated—like an old person."

"Why are you always worried about being old?"

He snuggles closer. "You didn't answer before when I said you were nuts about me. That doesn't mean that you don't like me, does it?"

"No."

"You're big on the one-word answers."

"I'm big on going to sleep."

" 'Big on.' See? There must be some expression to replace that now."

I sit in the car, waiting for Beth to come out of the building where the ballet school is. She has been taking lessons, but they haven't helped. She still slouches forward and sticks out her neck when she walks. Noel suggests that this might be analyzed psychologically; she sticks her neck out, you see, not only literally but . . . Noel thinks that Beth is waiting to get it. Beth feels guilty because her mother and father have just been divorced. She thinks that she played some part in it and therefore she deserves to get it. It is worth fifty dollars a month for ballet lessons to disprove Noel's theory. If it will only work.

I spend the day in the park, thinking over Noel's suggestion that I move in with him. We would have more money . . . We are together so much anyway . . . Or he could move in with me, if those big windows in my place are really so important. I always meet reasonable men.

"But I don't love you," I said to Noel. "Don't you want to live with somebody who loves you?"

"Nobody has ever loved me and nobody ever will," Noel said. "What have I got to lose?"

I am in the park to think about what I have to lose. Nothing. So why don't I leave the park, call him at work, say that I have decided it is a very sensible plan?

A chubby little boy wanders by, wearing a short jacket and pants that are slipping down. He is holding a yellow boat. He looks so damned pleased with everything that I think about accosting him and asking, "Should I move in with Noel? Why am I reluctant to do it?" The young have such wisdom—some of the best and worst thinkers have thought so: Wordsworth, the followers of the Guru Maharaj Ji . . . "Do the meditations, or I will beat you with a stick," the Guru tells his followers. Tell me the answer, kid, or I will take away your boat.

I sink down onto a bench. Next, Noel will ask me to marry him. He is trying to trap me. Worse, he is not trying to trap me but only wants me to move in so we can save money. He doesn't care about me. Since no one has ever loved him, he can't love anybody. Is that even true?

I find a phone booth and ·stand in front of it, waiting for a woman with a shopping bag to get out. She mouths something I don't understand. She has lips like a fish; they are painted bright orange. I do not have any lipstick on. I have on a raincoat, pulled over my nightgown, and sandals and Noel's socks.

"Noel," I say on the phone when I reach him, "were you serious when you said that no one ever loved you?"

"Jesus, it was embarrassing enough just to admit it," he says. "Do you have to question me about it?"

"I have to know."

"Well, I've told you about every woman I ever slept with. Which one do you suspect might have loved me?"

I have ruined his day. I hang up, rest my head against the phone. "Me," I mumble. "I do." I reach in the raincoat pocket. A Kleenex, two pennies, and a pink rubber spider put there by Beth to scare me. No more dimes. I push open the door. A young woman is standing there waiting for me. "Do you have a few moments?" she says.

"Why?"

"Do you have a moment? What do you think of this?" she says.

It is a small stick with the texture of salami. In her other hand she holds a clipboard and a pen.
"I don't have time," I say, and walk away. I stop and turn. "What is that, anyway?" I ask.
"Do you have a moment?" she asks.
"No. I just wanted to know what that thing was."
"A dog treat."
She is coming after me, clipboard outstretched.
"I don't have time," I say, and quickly walk away.
Something hits my back. "Take the time to stick it up your ass," she says.
I run for a block before I stop and lean on the park wall to rest. If Noel had been there, she wouldn't have done it. My protector. If I had a dime, I could call back and say, "Oh, Noel, I'll live with you always if you'll stay with me so people won't throw dog treats at me."
I finger the plastic spider. Maybe Beth put it there to cheer me up. Once, she put a picture of a young, beautiful girl in a bikini on my bedroom wall. I misunderstood, seeing the woman as all that I was not. Beth just thought it was a pretty picture. She didn't understand why I was so upset.
"Mommy's just upset because when you put things on the wall with Scotch Tape, the Scotch Tape leaves a mark when you remove it," Noel told her.
Noel is wonderful. I reach in my pocket, hoping a dime will suddenly appear.

Noel and I go to visit his friends Charles and Sol, in Vermont. Noel has taken time off from work; it is a vacation to celebrate our decision to live together. Now, on the third evening there, we are all crowded around the hearth—Noel and Beth and I, Charles and Sol and the women they live with, Lark and Margaret. We are smoking and listening to Sol's stereo. The hearth is a big one. It was laid by Sol, made out of slate he took from the side of a hill and bricks he found dumped by the side of the road. There is a mantel that was made by Charles from a section of an old carousel he picked up when a local amusement park closed down; a gargoyle's head protrudes from one side. Car keys have been draped over the beast's eyebrows. On top of the mantel there is an L. L. Bean catalogue, Margaret's hat, roaches and a roach clip, a can of peaches, and an incense burner that holds a small cone in a puddle of lavender ashes.

Noel used to work with Charles in the city. Charles quit when he heard about a big house in Vermont that needed to be fixed up. He was told that he could live in it for a hundred dollars a month, except in January and February, when skiers rented it. The skiers turned out to be nice people who didn't want to see anyone displaced. They suggested that the four stay on in the house, and they did, sleeping in a side room that Charles and Sol fixed up. Just now, the rest of the house is empty; it has been raining a lot, ruining the skiing.

Sol has put up some pictures he framed—old advertisements he found in a box in the attic (after Charles repaired the attic stairs). I study the pictures now, in the firelight. The Butter Lady —a healthy coquette with pearly skin and a mildewed bottom lip —extends a hand offering a package of butter. On the wall across from her, a man with oil-slick black hair holds a shoe that is the same color as his hair.

"When you're lost in the rain in Juarez and it's Eastertime, too," Dylan sings.

Margaret says to Beth, "Do you want to come take a bath with me?"

Beth is shy. The first night we were here, she covered her eyes when Sol walked naked from the bathroom to the bedroom.

"I don't have to take a bath while I'm here, do I?" she says to me.

"Where did you get that idea?"

"Why do I have to take a bath?"

But she decides to go with Margaret, and runs after her and grabs on to her wool sash. Margaret blows on the incense stick she has just lit, and fans it in the air, and Beth, enchanted, follows her out of the room. She already feels at ease in the house, and she likes us all and wanders off with anyone gladly, even though she's usually shy. Yesterday, Sol showed her how to punch down the bread before putting it on the baking sheet to rise once more.

He let her smear butter over the loaves with her fingers and then sprinkle cornmeal on the top.

Sol teaches at the state university. He is a poet, and he has been hired to teach a course in the modern novel. "Oh, well," he is saying now. "If I weren't a queer and I'd gone into the Army, I guess they would have made me a cook. That's usually what they do, isn't it?"

"Don't ask me," Charles says. "I'm queer, too." This seems to be an old routine.

Noel is admiring the picture frames. "This is such a beautiful place," he says. "I'd love to live here for good."

"Don't be a fool," Sol says. "With a lot of fairies?"

Sol is reading a student's paper. "This student says, 'Humbert is just like a million other Americans,' " he says.

"Humbert?" Noel says.

"You know—that guy who ran against Nixon."

"Come on," Noel says. "I know it's from some novel."

"*Lolita*," Lark says, all on the intake. She passes the joint to me.

"Why don't you quit that job?" Lark says. "You hate it."

"I can't be unemployed," Sol says. "I'm a faggot and a poet. I've already got two strikes against me." He puffs twice on the roach, lets it slip out of the clip to the hearth. "And a drug abuser," he says. "I'm as good as done for."

"I'm sorry you feel that way, dear," Charles says, putting his hand gently on Sol's shoulder. Sol jumps. Charles and Noel laugh.

It is time for dinner—moussaka, and bread, and wine that Noel brought.

"What's moussaka?" Beth asks. Her skin shines, and her hair has dried in small narrow ridges where Margaret combed it.

"Made with mice," Sol says.

Beth looks at Noel. Lately, she checks things out with him. He shakes his head no. Actually, she is not a dumb child; she probably looked at Noel because she knows it makes him happy.

Beth has her own room—the smallest bedroom, with a fur rug on the floor and a quilt to sleep under. As I talk to Lark after dinner, I hear Noel reading to Beth: "*The Trout Fishing Diary of Alonso Hagen*." Soon Beth is giggling.

I sit in Noel's lap, looking out the window at the fields, white and flat, and the mountains—a blur that I know is mountains. The radiator under the window makes the glass foggy. Noel leans forward to wipe it with a handkerchief. We are in winter now. We were going to leave Vermont after a week—then two, now three. Noel's hair is getting long. Beth has missed a month of school. What will the Board of Education do to me? "What do you think they're going to do?" Noel says. "Come after us with guns?"

Noel has just finished confiding in me another horrendous or mortifying thing he would never, never tell anyone and that I must swear not to repeat. The story is about something that happened when he was eighteen. There was a friend of his mother's whom he threatened to strangle if she didn't let him sleep with her. She let him. As soon as it was over, he was terrified that she would tell someone, and he threatened to strangle her if she did. But he realized that as soon as he left she could talk, and that he could be arrested, and he got so upset that he broke down and ran back to the bed where they had been, pulled the covers over his head, and shook and cried. Later, the woman told his mother that Noel seemed to be studying too hard at Princeton—perhaps he needed some time off. A second story was about how he tried to kill himself when his wife left him. The truth was that he couldn't give David his scarf back because it was stretched from being knotted so many times. But he had been too chicken to hang himself and he had swallowed a bottle of drugstore sleeping pills instead. Then he got frightened and went outside and hailed a cab. Another couple, huddled together in the wind, told him that they had claimed the cab first. The same couple was in the waiting room of the hospital when he came to.

"The poor guy put his card next to my hand on the stretcher," Noel says, shaking his head so hard that his beard scrapes my cheek. "He was a plumber. Eliot Raye. And his wife, Flora."

A warm afternoon. "Noel!" Beth cries, running across the soggy lawn toward him, her hand extended like a fisherman with his catch. But there's nothing in her hand—only a little spot of blood on the palm. Eventually he gets the story out of her: she fell. He will bandage it. He is squatting, his arm folding her close like some giant bird. A heron? An eagle? Will he take my child and fly away? They walk toward the house, his hand pressing Beth's head against his leg.

We are back in the city. Beth is asleep in the room that was once Noel's study. I am curled up in Noel's lap. He has just asked to hear the story of Michael again.

"Why do you want to hear that?" I ask.

Noel is fascinated by Michael, who pushed his furniture into the hall and threw his small possessions out the window into the back yard and then put up four large, connecting tents in his apartment. There was a hot plate in there, cans of Franco-American spaghetti, bottles of good wine, a flashlight for when it got dark . . .

Noel urges me to remember more details. What else was in the tent?

A rug, but that just happened to be on the floor. For some reason, he didn't throw the rug out the window. And there was a sleeping bag . . .

What else?

Comic books. I don't remember which ones. A lemon meringue pie. I remember how disgusting that was after two days, with the sugar oozing out of the meringue. A bottle of Seconal. There was a drinking glass, a container of warm juice . . . I don't remember.

We used to make love in the tent. I'd go over to see him, open the front door, and crawl in. That summer he collapsed the tents, threw them in his car, and left for Maine.

"Go on," Noel says.

I shrug. I've told this story twice before, and this is always my stopping place.

"That's it," I say to Noel.

He continues to wait expectantly, just as he did the two other times he heard the story.

One evening, we get a phone call from Lark. There is a house near them for sale—only thirty thousand dollars. What Noel can't fix, Charles and Sol can help with. There are ten acres of

land, a waterfall. Noel is wild to move there. But what are we
going to do for money, I ask him. He says we'll worry about that
in a year or so, when we run out. But we haven't even seen the
place, I point out. But this is a fabulous find, he says. We'll go see
it this weekend. Noel has Beth so excited that she wants to start
school in Vermont on Monday, not come back to the city at all.
We will just go to the house right this minute and live there forever.

But does he know how to do the wiring? Is he sure it can be
wired?

"Don't you have any faith in me?" he says. "David always
thought I was a chump, didn't he?"

"I'm only asking whether you can do such complicated things."

My lack of faith in Noel has made him unhappy. He leaves the
room without answering. He probably remembers—and knows
that I remember—the night he asked David if he could see what
was wrong with the socket of his floor lamp. David came back to
our apartment laughing. "The plug had come out of the outlet,"
he said.

In early April, David comes to visit us in Vermont for the weekend with his girlfriend, Patty. She wears blue jeans, and has kohl
around her eyes. She is twenty years old. Her clogs echo loudly on
the bare floorboards. She seems to feel awkward here. David
seems not to feel awkward, although he looked surprised when
Beth called him David. She led him through the woods, running
ahead of Noel and me, to show him the waterfall. When she got
too far ahead, I called her back, afraid, for some reason, that she
might die. If I lost sight of her, she might die. I suppose I had always thought that if David and I spent time together again it
would be over the hospital bed of our dying daughter—something
like that.

Patty has trouble walking in the woods; the clogs flop off her
feet in the brush. I tried to give her a pair of my sneakers, but she
wears size 8½ and I am a 7. Another thing to make her feel awkward.

David breathes in dramatically. "Quite a change from the high
rise we used to live in," he says to Noel.

Calculated to make us feel rotten?

"You used to live in a high rise?" Patty asks

He must have just met her. She pays careful attention to everything he says, watches with interest when he snaps off a twig and
breaks it in little pieces. She is having trouble keeping up. David
finally notices her difficulty in keeping up with us, and takes her
hand. They're city people; they don't even have hiking boots.

"It seems as if that was in another life," David says. He snaps
off a small branch and flicks one end of it against his thumb.

"There's somebody who says that every time we sleep we die;
we come back another person, to another life," Patty says.

"Kafka as realist," Noel says.

Noel has been reading all winter. He has read Brautigan, a lot
of Borges, and has gone from Dante to García Márquez to Hilma
Wolitzer to Kafka. Sometimes I ask him why he is going about it
this way. He had me make him a list—this writer before that one,
which poems are early, which late, which famous. Well, it doesn't
matter. Noel is happy in Vermont. Being in Vermont means that
he can do what he wants to do. Freedom, you know. Why should
I make fun of it? He loves his books, loves roaming around in the
woods outside the house, and he buys more birdseed than all the
birds in the North could eat. He took a Polaroid picture of our
salt lick for the deer when he put it in, and admired both the salt
lick ("They've been here!") and his picture. Inside the house
there are Polaroids of the woods, the waterfall, some rabbits—
he tacks them up with pride, the way Beth hangs up the pictures
she draws in school. "You know," Noel said to me one night,
"when Gatsby is talking to Nick Carraway and he says, 'In any
case, it was just personal'—what does that mean?"

"When did you read *Gatsby*?" I asked.

"Last night, in the bathtub."

As we turn to walk back, Noel points out the astonishing number of squirrels in the trees around us. By David's expression, he
thinks Noel is pathetic.

I look at Noel. He is taller than David but more stooped; thin-
ner than David, but his slouch disguises it. Noel has big hands
and feet and a sharp nose. His scarf is gray, with frayed edges.
David's is bright red, just bought. Poor Noel. When David called

to say he and Patty were coming for a visit, Noel never thought of saying no. And he asked me how he could compete with David. He thought David was coming to his house to win me away. After he reads more literature he'll realize that is too easy. There will have to be complexities. The complexities will protect him forever. Hours after David's call, he said (to himself, really—not to me) that David was bringing a woman with him. Surely that meant he wouldn't try anything.

Charles and Margaret come over just as we are finishing dinner, bringing a mattress we are borrowing for David and Patty to sleep on. They are both stoned, and are dragging the mattress on the ground, which is white with a late snow. They are too stoned to hoist it.

"Eventide," Charles says. A circular black barrette holds his hair out of his face. Margaret lost her hat to Lark some time ago and never got around to borrowing another one. Her hair is dusted with snow. "We have to go," Charles says, weighing her hair in his hands, "before the snow woman melts."

Sitting at the kitchen table late that night, I turn to David. "How are you doing?" I whisper.

"A lot of things haven't been going the way I figured," he whispers.

I nod. We are drinking white wine and eating cheddar-cheese soup. The soup is scalding. Clouds of steam rise from the bowl, and I keep my face away from it, worrying that the steam will make my eyes water, and that David will misinterpret.

"Not really things. People," David whispers, bobbing an ice cube up and down in his wineglass with his index finger.

"What people?"

"It's better not to talk about it. They're not really people you know."

That hurts, and he knew it would hurt. But climbing the stairs to go to bed I realize that, in spite of that, it's a very reasonable approach.

Tonight, as I do most nights, I sleep with long johns under my nightgown. I roll over on top of Noel for more warmth and lie there, as he has said, like a dead man, like a man in the Wild West, gunned down in the dirt. Noel jokes about this. "Pow,

pow," he whispers sleepily as I lower myself on him. "Poor critter's deader 'n a doornail." I lie there warming myself. What does he want with me?

"What do you want for your birthday?" I ask.

He recites a little list of things he wants. He whispers: a bookcase, an aquarium, a blender to make milkshakes in.

"That sounds like what a ten-year-old would want," I say.

He is quiet too long; I have hurt his feelings.

"Not the bookcase," he says finally.

I am falling asleep. It's not fair to fall asleep on top of him. He doesn't have the heart to wake me and has to lie there with me sprawled on top of him until I fall off. Move, I tell myself, but I don't.

"Do you remember this afternoon, when Patty and I sat on the rock to wait for you and David and Beth?"

I remember. We were on top of the hill, Beth pulling David by his hand, David not very interested in what she was going to show him, Beth ignoring his lack of interest and pulling him along. I ran to catch up, because she was pulling him so hard, and I caught Beth's free arm and hung on, so that we formed a chain.

"I knew I'd seen that before," Noel says. "I just realized where —when the actor wakes up after the storm and sees Death leading those people winding across the hilltop in *The Seventh Seal.*"

Six years ago. Seven. David and I were in the Village, in the winter, looking in a bookstore window. Tires began to squeal, and we turned around and were staring straight at a car, a ratty old blue car that had lifted a woman from the street into the air. The fall took much too long; she fell the way snow drifts—the big flakes that float down, no hurry at all. By the time she hit, though, David had pushed my face against his coat, and while everyone was screaming—it seemed as if a whole chorus had suddenly assembled to scream—he had his arms around my shoulders, pressing me so close that I could hardly breathe and saying, "If anything happened to you . . . If anything happened to you . . ."

When they leave, it is a clear, cold day. I give Patty a paper bag with half a bottle of wine, two sandwiches, and some peanuts to eat on the way back. The wine is probably not a good idea; David had three glasses of vodka and orange juice for breakfast. He began telling jokes to Noel—dogs in bars outsmarting their owners, constipated whores, talking fleas. David does not like Noel; Noel does not know what to make of David.

Now David rolls down the car window. Last-minute news. He tells me that his sister has been staying in his apartment. She aborted herself and has been very sick. "Abortions are legal," David says. "Why did she do that?" I ask how long ago it happened. A month ago, he says. His hands drum on the steering wheel. Last week, Beth got a box of wooden whistles carved in the shape of peasants from David's sister. Noel opened the kitchen window and blew softly to some birds on the feeder. They all flew away.

Patty leans across David. "There are so many animals here, even in the winter," she says. "Don't they hibernate any more?"

She is making nervous, polite conversation. She wants to leave. Noel walks away from me to Patty's side of the car, and tells her about the deer who come right up to the house. Beth is sitting on Noel's shoulders. Not wanting to talk to David, I wave at her stupidly. She waves back.

David looks at me out the window. I must look as stiff as one of those wooden whistles, all carved out of one piece, in my old blue ski jacket and blue wool hat pulled down to my eyes and my baggy jeans.

"*Ciao*," David says. "Thanks."

"Yes," Patty says. "It was nice of you to do this." She holds up the bag.

It's a steep driveway, and rocky. David backs down cautiously— the way someone pulls a zipper after it's been caught. We wave, they disappear. That was easy.

Gaps

Wesley has gaps between his teeth. When Wesley doesn't have anything to do, he pokes things in the spaces to see what will fit: stems, pennies, things. Or he takes a walk to the train station, swivels the seat down in the photo-matic, and deposits a quarter. Last winter Wesley took a lot of pictures before he ran out of money. By the time he got more money, his bowler hat, which photographed well, had blown away in the wind.

In one of today's pictures Wesley has pulled up his lip to expose the gaps between his teeth. The picture pleases him, and he studies it. That's how he happens to have the picture in his hand to show Bob Nails.

*

Jeannie Regis' hair is all different colors. In the sunshine it's one color. At night, when he lights up her hair with the flashlight, it's like . . . copper. He shines the flashlight down the back of her hair. In the half-dark she looks like a painting his father used to have in his bedroom. He aims the beam down her spine. Fuzz. Red fuzz when he holds the light close to the skin. She keeps the flashlight on the night table because, when the babies call for her, the bright hall light frightens them. They wake up in the middle of the night, wanting water. Bob Nails thinks about filling the baby bath and putting it on the floor, maybe sailing little plastic boats in the water, putting glasses on the floor beside it.

There are two glasses on the night table. He drinks the last quarter inch of Bourbon and clicks off the flashlight.

*

When you say "the idiot," everybody knows you mean Wesley. Wesley acted like an idiot long before the tests confirmed it, so Wesley's mother tells everyone there was no point in the tests. Wesley is "the idiot," Thomas is "the normal one," and of course Mrs. Dutton has always been "the poor woman." She sends him in to shower and finds him sitting on the toilet, afraid to get into the water. She has to throw back the shower curtain and get all wet herself, soaping and rinsing him, turning the water off and on, off and on so that Wesley will stay in the bathtub.

When Wesley's brother, Thomas, was eighteen, the minister took him aside and told him he should volunteer to wash his brother. Thomas enlisted in the Army instead. He was Bob Nails's best friend, so Bob Nails thought about joining the Army too. Bob Nails's father wouldn't sign the papers, and he told him that if he found a way around it he'd shoot him in the back. Bob Nails told him he didn't care—he was in love with Jeannie Parater and he didn't really want to leave. Mr. Nails told him he'd shoot him in the back if he got married. When school was over, Bob Nails went to work in the gas station. At the end of summer, Jeannie Parater left town, and when they tried to draft Bob Nails he was rejected because he couldn't hear in one ear.

*

"Well, I guess I'm just going to have to scream at you like you was the idiot," Sam Siddell, Junior, says to Bob Nails. "Army says you can't hear, I guess that means you don't have fit hearing. Same thing with a fairy being rejected," Sam continues, biting off the end of a Chesterfield and tapping tobacco onto his tongue.

"What's that supposed to mean?"

"Only thing it means," Sam Siddell, Junior, says, lighting the cigarette, "is that the Army says a man's got something wrong with him, a man's got something wrong with him." He smiles at Bob Nails. Sam Siddell, Junior, has two yellow circles of tobacco stain on his front teeth.

"Well, can I have my job back or can't I?" Bob Nails says.

Sam Siddell rocks back in the green metal chair behind his desk. "If you can hear," he says.

"When did you notice anything wrong with my hearing?"

"I didn't bring it up—the Army did. Army brings up things for a reason—only wants fit men. It don't take people who lost an arm, or people who couldn't tell when there was orders to follow, or a fairy that wasn't like other men."

Bob Nails doesn't say anything. A man Sam intended to hire to replace Bob Nails keeps looking from the garage into Sam's office.

"Knew about my brother, didn't you?" Sam asks.

"What about him?"

"Army sent him home."

With the toe of his boot, Sam Siddell strokes the calendar girl's bare legs.

"Sometimes, when you know something about other people's misfortunes, you're willing to give them a minute," Sam says.

Bob Nails goes home and asks his father about Sam's brother, who works for him at the grocery store.

"That boy got sent home after he lost half his leg when he done something wrong with explosives," Bob Nails's father says. "I don't know what Sam's excuse is for losing half his mind. He ever talks to you that way, you let me know and I'll shoot him in the back."

*

A woman is found dead, on a deserted farm off the highway. Two hunters discover her. First they see the car, a black Chevrolet, sitting in some brambles. It might have hit the tree to one side. The car looks okay—it doesn't seem to have hit anything. A woman is sitting in the driver's seat. Such a strange look frozen on her face; running toward her, they both think she's frightened of them, of the guns. The doors aren't locked; they open easily—but the police find that out. The men look in but don't touch the door. One of the hunters has begun to sweat; he's afraid he might pass out, so he begins to list facts in his mind: the upholstery is red, the car black, there is a woman. The other hunter makes the telephone call and tells these things to the police.

*

Jeannie? No. She's home, but she's unbuttoning one of the babies' coats and can't answer the phone. What's wrong with Bob Nails? What's he doing here in the middle of the afternoon? He's talking so loudly that the babies wake up and cry. What's wrong with him? He tells her all he knows: a woman is dead in a Chevrolet. But her Chevrolet is parked outside—didn't he notice? Bob Nails looks out the kitchen window.

"If you'd miss me so much, why don't you marry me?" she says.

Late in the afternoon he's still there. He doesn't want to frighten her by telling her that more people might be dead. He doesn't want to know himself, so he doesn't turn on the radio. He stays for dinner, and as they eat she says it again. He thinks about it. Jeannie? No.

*

On the day of the murder, Wesley Dutton walks to the train station. The people coming into town don't know there's been a murder, and Wesley doesn't either because no one has told him. He goes into the photo-matic as usual and sits, waiting for his pictures to develop. He sits there too long. There are girls waiting. He knows it, but he doesn't move. One of the girls giggles and tells her friend to open the curtain, that maybe it's just a pair of legs in there and they can toss them out. Wesley thinks that's funny. When he laughs, the girls get quiet. A little while later a man who works in the train station pulls open the curtain.

"Come on out now, Wesley," he says.

The girls are standing in back of the man. Wesley smiles and stands, reaches into the metal slot for the pictures, nods, and walks away. But his heart is racing. How did the man know his name? The pictures are too dark. Only the last one is any good. He tears it off to study, but something else attracts his attention. It's Bob Nails, running toward him. Bob Nails is out of breath. He slows down and raises a hand. Wesley raises his hand too, to give Bob Nails the picture. Bob Nails nods, returns the picture, and goes on running.

If Wesley keeps it, he'll leave it in a pocket and his mother will ruin it when she does the wash. She's told him she isn't going through his pockets any more; she'll wash what he gives her. Tissues get washed and dried, pennies brighten from wash to wash. Today Mrs. Dutton found a dollar bill she'd washed and said she wouldn't give Wesley any more money. She screamed. That's why he went to the train station.

*

Sam Siddell is speaking to Bob Nails. He speaks normally to the other men, but backs off from Bob Nails and speaks in a whisper. At first Bob Nails was convinced that Sam was looking for an excuse to fire him, but Sam gives him the most interesting jobs and never criticizes his work. He stands under the lift, across the shop from Bob Nails, and whispers—Bob Nails thinks it's something about a woman who's come in with an old Chevy. But what would that have to do with Sam's brother going hunting? Bob Nails finally has to stop work and ask Sam what he's said.

"I said a girl got killed," Sam shouts.

"Not somebody from town?"

"Might of been," Sam hollers.

Bob Nails goes into the office to call Jeannie.

"Young woman," Sam murmurs as he walks in behind him. "Young woman," he repeats loudly, nodding in agreement with himself.

She doesn't answer. Bob Nails tells Sam he's going to check, he'll be right back.

"It ain't his faulty hearing that disturbs me," Sam Siddell says to the other men. "It's his faulty ideas of who's good women and who ain't."

Sam walks up to a car that's being repaired and spits on the hood.

"Not that it ain't a tragedy he's got failed hearing."

*

It's 1966 and Bob Nails is at Jeannie Parater's house and she's showing him pictures of paintings in a book. Bob Nails is going to ask her to marry him before she goes away to college. He's going to join the Army so they'll leave town, which is what she always talks about. Tom Dutton likes the Army; he says he's never getting out. Bob Nails's father has told him that if he gets married and joins the Army he'll shoot him in the back, no matter what country they send him to. When Bob Nails's father isn't going to shoot someone in the back, then he's going to get an incurable cancer, and when he gets that, then he's going to wire everybody's car and all the people in the business world who've cheated him will be blown sky high; or he'll get two heart attacks and hang the loan shark he's into before he gets the third.

"Why do you always want to be talking violence?" Bob Nails's mother says to his father. "If you talked nicer it would be nicer for Bobby to be home."

Before that, Bob Nails couldn't really give her a reason for being at the Paraters' all the time. Now he had one, so when his mother asked why he couldn't spend more time at home, he said his father was always talking about killing people and blowing things up and he didn't want to hear it. His mother nodded sadly. She only got mad once, when Bob Nails and Jeannie drove to another town and spent the weekend.

"Do you think your father talks violence in his sleep? At ten o'clock he goes to bed. At ten o'clock you can come home," Bob Nails's mother says.

He's not sure why he never asked Jeannie to marry him. There was something crazy about her—the way she kept showing him pictures: lines and dots and landscapes, all drawn by different men. She said the idea to spend the weekend with him just came to her when they were sitting in the diner. On Monday she didn't want to leave, but he made her get in the car, convinced now that she wouldn't want to marry him, that she'd shown him all those pictures just to smart off. He didn't say anything on the way back. He began to feel the way his father did—that he could kill, strangle, blow things up. But he loved her and didn't know why. He stayed home at night and thought about it. After a while he went back to see her, but it was only for two weeks because she left in September. Later that month Bob Nails's father had his first heart attack.

*

She's giggling, driving too fast on purpose to confuse him. He hates her when she's this way.

"And do you know what she told my mother? She said the day the Apollo spacecraft landed on the moon Wesley wouldn't leave the television, even to eat."

"What's so funny about that?"

She's steering with her left hand, and she's right-handed. There's a yellow warning sign, but she's going too fast to notice.

"Some people don't laugh in the face of progress," he adds, gripping the dashboard.

"Wait! Let me tell it."

She's looking at him instead of the road.

"So later that afternoon Mrs. Dutton heard Wesley pacing. She looked in his bedroom and there he was walking around with two big squares of foam rubber tied under his shoes. He'd cut up the pillows!"

Why did he agree to this ride? Every time the car cuts around a curve he's sure he's going to die. Now they're on a road he's not familiar with. Neither is she. She throws the gearshift into reverse and they're back on the main road.

"Where was the accident? I'm confused now."

"What accident?"

"Sam might make fun of you for going deaf, but he should know you've gone stupid too. The murdered woman."

They're going around another curve. A car approaching clicks its high beam on and off.

"Is it one of the roads over top of that hill?"

They're at the top before he has time to answer. Bob Nails is sure she's going to kill them. "Yeah," he agrees immediately. "That road, I think."

She turns and slows down. "This can't be it. There'd be some markings."

"Why are you looking for it? What do you care?"

"I just want to know," she says.

"Know *what?*" Bob Nails says.

"Listen," Jeannie says, slamming on the brakes. "You always were after me because I wanted to find out about things. You hate books. You're glad I came back. You don't want me to find out about anything. You don't want me to find out about you."

"Me?" he says. "What are you talking about?"

They're sitting in the dark and the car has come to a stop, not quite in the middle of the road. She's stretched her neck toward him so she can scream in his face. There's a surprised look on her face.

"What?" he asks.

She looks away, through the wheel. "I just wanted to see it. I'll bet lots of people are driving there to look."

"Sure," he says, relieved that she's talking quietly. "We just found the wrong road is all."

She smiles at him and starts to drive again, carefully. Bob Nails begins to feel better, thinks about suggesting a drink. Which way is she headed . . . what's closest?

"But we'll find it," she says evenly. "Is it this road?"

Bob Nails and Jeannie leave the bar. It's almost midnight—Jeannie's mother won't stay awake any later with the babies, and she refuses to sleep in the spare bed. Bob Nails never liked Jeannie's mother. She's been at his mother's house almost constantly since the funeral, when his father died after his second heart attack. Bob Nails drives the car because Jeannie's drunk.

"Would you be mad if I still wanted to see where the accident was?"

"Why do you keep calling it an accident? She was murdered," Bob Nails says.

"What's the big deal about being so precise?"

"You're the one who always thought you had to understand everything in detail," Bob Nails says.

"You're drunk. You always want to fight when you're drunk."

"I don't know what I want. I'm sorry you're having a bad time. I should of planned something."

He looks over to see if she agrees, but she's just smiling prettily. Her face is pretty even if her hair is messed up.

"Then if you don't have anything planned why don't we do what I want to do?"

"Hell," he says, accelerating, "I'll find the goddamn place."

He makes a turn and drives a few miles. This is all familiar ground—where he and Tom Dutton used to hunt pheasants when they were young. He tries to remember what he read in the newspaper. Peterson's old farm, he guesses. Around the corner he coasts to a stop.

"Okay," he says.

"Where?" she asks, sitting forward.

"Must of been here somewhere . . ."

He turns the car onto the shoulder and the headlights illuminate a patch of field.

"Quiet," she whispers, sliding close.

"Quiet? What for?"

Jeannie lights a cigarette and tosses the match into the ashtray. "How do they think it happened?"

"I don't know. They figured she picked up a hitchhiker and he shot her."

"She was riding along the road," Jeannie says, before she hears his explanation, "and she picked up a man who stabbed her in the neck."

"I thought he shot her."

"Bang!"

Bob Nails's hands tighten on the wheel. "What the hell was that for?"

"If you were her you'd be dead."

What's she doing now? What's she starting to laugh about? But she isn't laughing. She's just the way she was. He shivers, feeling her finger on the back of his neck. She shivers too. Something is moving—an animal, trying to get away from the headlights. He's not sure this is where it happened, because it could have been the other side of Peterson's farm. He thought there would be a NO TRESPASSING sign, but there isn't. He thought it was an animal, but it isn't. It's Wesley Dutton.

"Wesley?" Jeannie whispers. "What's Wesley doing here?"

Bob Nails opens the car door. "Hi," he says.

"Hi," Wesley says.

It's cold outside. Hunching his shoulders against the wind, Bob Nails walks into the field. Wesley has on his winter coat, a hat, and a scarf double-knotted at the throat. His hands are dirty and he's holding something out to Bob Nails. Pictures. He's been putting them in the ground, he tells Bob Nails. Why? Wesley tells him about a man in a movie who misses a dead lady and goes to her grave to put his picture in the ground there. Wesley's eyes fill with tears. He sits and rubs his hands over the dirt. He says he just found out from people talking at the train station. They said it was Peterson's farm.

Bob Nails gives Wesley a hand and tells him he'll take him home. Wesley squats to pick up the remaining pictures.

"Hello, Wesley," Jeannie says when he climbs into the back seat.

"Good evening," Wesley says.

"Why were you out there?" she asks.

Wesley smiles politely. In a moment his expression changes. He remembers. He hitched a ride. He smiles triumphantly.

They ride the rest of the way to Wesley's house in silence. When they pull up, it's dark inside.

"Don't worry, Wesley," Bob Nails says, opening the car door. So Wesley's mother won't hear the door slam and wake up, Bob Nails drives off holding it shut. At the end of the block, closing the door, he notices his watch and sees that it's two in the morning.

"She'll stay with them. She just tells me to come back to bluff," Jeannie says.

He passes her house and keeps driving. After a while he realizes that he's driving in circles. He's tired, there's something wrong, and he's not sure what. He drives fifteen more miles to a hotel and gets a room for the night. Once in the room, they talk. Even though they stay awake for hours, they can't understand, can't agree on anything for sure.

He oversleeps and goes to work hours late, leaving Jeannie at the hotel. She said she was going home in the morning, but when they woke up they both knew she wouldn't. Bob Nails is exhausted. He begins to explain why he's late to Sam. When he tells Sam about finding Wesley Dutton on Peterson's farm, and what Jeannie thinks, Sam's mouth drops open. His mouth drops open even before he hears what Jeannie thinks. He tells Bob Nails to get the hell out in the garage to fix the car on the lift before the customer shows up and the job isn't done.

Bob Nails is surprised when the police show up at the garage. Later, Sam tells him that he was too dead tired to know right from wrong, so he decided to take care of it for him.

*

Bob Nails's mother tells him on the telephone that Wesley was sent to the state hospital. According to Mrs. Dutton, when they were taking him away, Wesley just smiled politely and tried to help the detective into his coat, and the detective misunderstood and thought Wesley was trying to take it. The detectives exchanged looks. Bob Nails says he'll listen to the rest of it when he comes home for his things. He hangs up and paces around the room, remembering the story his mother told him years ago about what Wesley did when he heard a TV newscaster say that Mrs. Kennedy put her wedding ring in her husband's casket. He went to the graveyard the next day, and someone asked him what he was doing there. Wesley said he had his mother's diamond ring and that he had to give it to someone who was dead. The man took the ring away and called Mrs. Dutton, but Wesley tried to fight, so the man held it on his tongue until Mrs. Dutton arrived.

Jeannie wants Bob Nails to buy her an engagement ring. That's always on his mind, and Wesley Dutton is always on his mind. It's quiet out on the street, quiet in the room. Jeannie's sulking because he won't drive to Peterson's farm. She said it would be exciting, like criminals returning to the scene of the crime. They aren't criminals; can't she understand that?

He looks out the window. He's started to hate the cheap room, the lousy furniture, the plastic lampshades. It will be better when they move to an apartment. The room is too cold. Jeannie sits wrapped in her coat, reading the same magazines again. His father died reading a magazine; when his mother came into the room his face was all red and he was staring at the page, but his mother knew he didn't look that way from anything he read in *Consumer Reports*.

"Let's get a drink," he says.

"You know," she says slowly, "there never was any such movie."

"I don't want to talk about Wesley Dutton."

He wants to talk about what's going on, but he doesn't know how to do it. She's going to get the babies when they move. Is that when he's supposed to marry her? She looks so pretty. Her hair shines. He thinks about asking why her hair shines. When she stands, her hair covers her shoulders. Her coat is wrinkled because it's been bunched up underneath her. In high school the girls used to call her "Queen Jean" because her clothes were wrinkled and her sweaters never had enough buttons. It makes him angry to remember her being ridiculed.

"If you don't want to talk, you don't have to," she says, turning and walking across the room. He gets his jacket and follows her down the stairs. When he pushes open the door a wind hits them. She bows her head and starts across the street.

"Not that bar," he says. "Someplace nice."

Doesn't she hear him? He catches up with her, grabs the back of her scarf.

"I don't notice that that bar smells any particular way," she says.

"I didn't say anything about that."

"You said that was why you wouldn't go there last night, didn't you?"

What should he say? He drives past several bars, hoping she'll be in a better mood when they stop, but she hasn't spoken since they got in the car. They pass a row of bars, and later another bar pointed to by a red neon arrow shooting through a blue neon waterfall. He can't tell if she likes any of the bars, because she's looking at her hands in her lap. At the next bar he pulls in.

All the booths are taken, so they sit at a little wooden table covered by place mats soaking in puddles. They serve food here. He orders two cheeseburgers. Jeannie just looks at hers, so he eats that too. They sit in silence, pouring from a pitcher of beer. There's a clock advertising Schlitz above the bar. A foam of tiny lights constantly overflows the beer mug. Every so often a man sitting at the bar below the light looks at them—at him, or at Jeannie? Bob Nails decides the man must be looking at her.

They leave the bar at midnight. Tomorrow she starts her job with the telephone company. What's she going to do with the babies if she gets a job? What makes her hair shine? Couldn't Wesley have gone to the farm to see what it looked like, the way they did?

"Well?" Bob Nails says.

He's holding the car door open, but she hasn't gotten in. She's looking over his shoulder.

"What do you think that says?"

Jeannie's looking at a sign across the street. He squints, trying to focus. Jeannie squints too, but walks down the gravel driveway toward it. He wants to call after her to find out if she's that unsteady from drinking, or if it's because the driveway is so full of holes. Instead, he follows her.

The sign is in the window of a little house. A light glows in one of the rooms, but the sign has been turned off.

"She's a *fortune* teller!" Jeannie says.

"Come on," Bob Nails says.

"There's a light inside."

"Jeannie, it's late at night."

But she's already knocked on the door and is knocking again, harder. He grabs her hand and holds it at his side. Inside the house a dog barks, then is quiet.

"Satisfied?" he says, leaning against the door.

He stumbles for balance when the door is opened. In the corner of his eye he sees an old man with a rifle, but the next second he isn't sure there was any old man. A young girl is facing them, wearing a quilted robe, her hair rolled in curlers. Her face is very pink. Bob Nails smells incense, or musk perfume. The girl cocks her head.

"Is it too late to have our fortunes told?" Jeannie asks.

The girl's mouth moves oddly, as if she might be chewing gum. Very softly, very precisely, she says, "You are going to die," and closes the door.

It's Just
Another Day
in Big Bear City,
California

||||||||||||||||||||||

Spaceship, flying saucer, an hallucination . . . they don't know
yet. They don't even notice it until it is almost over their car. Estelle, who has recently gone back to college, is studying Mortuary
Science. Her husband, Alvin William "Big Bear" Benton, is so
drunk from the party they have just left that he wouldn't notice if
it were Estelle, risen from the passenger seat, up in the sky.
Maybe that's where she'd like to be—floating in the sky. Or in the
morgue with bodies. Big Bear Benton thinks she is completely
nuts, and people who are nuts can do anything. *Will* do anything.
Will go back to school after ten years and study Mortuary Science. It's enough to make him get drunk at parties. They used to
ask his wife about the children at these parties, but now they ask,
subtly, about the bodies. They are more interested in dead bodies
than his two children. So is Estelle. He is not interested in anything, according to his wife, except going to parties and getting
drunk.

Spaceship, flying saucer, an hallucination . . . Big Bear concentrates on the object and tells himself that he is just hallucinating.
There is a pinpoint of light, actually a spot of light about the size
of a tennis ball, dropping through space. Then it is the size of a
football . . . he is trying to think it is a real object, no matter
what it is doing up there . . . but maybe it's a flying saucer. Or a
spaceship. He looks at Estelle, who is also drunk. She is staring at
her hands, neatly folded on her lap. Those hands roam around in
dead bodies the way coyotes roam around the desert—just for
something to do. This is the first time he has ever been glad to
concentrate on Mortuary Science. Like reading the stock pages in
the bathroom.

"What is that?" Big Bear says, fighting to stay calm.

"Well, you know what it looks like," Estelle says. "It looks like
a spaceship."

"Yeah, I know. But what is it really?"

Now that Estelle is becoming educated and urbane, he has become more childish. He is always asking questions.

"I don't know. It's a spaceship come to take us to Mars."

Big Bear begins to worry about the car being blown over. The
car is a 1965 Peugeot, a real piece of crap that Big Bear would
have gotten rid of long ago if it had not belonged to his wife's

brother, who died in Viet Nam. His wife won't hear of getting rid of the car. She has some of her brother's underwear that she won't take out of the drawer. It's in Big Bear's drawer, in fact—not hers—and her reason for that is that it's men's underwear. But her brother's car is done for now, because the wind is going to blow it over and mash the roof.

"What's going on?" Big Bear yells to Estelle. It comes out a whisper. It occurs to Big Bear that this is some kind of joke. He would discuss with Estelle the possibility of the people at the party pulling a joke on them, but it's too noisy to converse. Through the windstorm he hears, "Earthlings! We are visitors from a friendly planet" and wets his pants.

*

Big Bear hears Estelle in the kitchen, memorizing: "The heart is a hollow muscular pump surrounded by the pericardium. . . ." Just by the tone of her voice, he understands that there is no hope for the human body. His two children, Sammy and David, stand around the kitchen eating cookies and listening to their mother. They like it better than talking to Big Bear, which makes him brood. His children are interested in intestines, the liver, bones, tissue, the optic nerve. It makes Big Bear sick just to think about it. If he could think of an excuse to stop giving Sammy and David an allowance, he would.

Big Bear tilts back his La-Z-Boy reclining chair and examines his feet, which block his view of the television.

*

Big Bear gives his wife a valentine, shyly. He thinks that the saleswoman might have been making a fool of him when she told him that the huge card with the quilted taffeta heart and embossed cupids would get across his message best. The card cost two dollars and fifty cents. The woman was young and had aviator glasses and an ironic smile. He prides himself in knowing women, but lately he doesn't trust any of them. Imagine Estelle enrolling in college, signing up for Mortuary Science. "Oh, this is lovely," she said when Big Bear gave her the valentine. He didn't want to mess it up in case there was something she could do with the card, so he just wrote his name on a little piece of paper and tucked it in the card. It falls out when Estelle opens it. He is standing right in front of her—she knows who it's from—why did he even put the piece of paper in? She picks it up. "Love, Bear," it says. "Oh, this is lovely," she says. Valentine's Day is not one of Big Bear's favorite occasions. He always feels like a fool. His wife did not give him a valentine. She forgot, she says. But she doesn't forget about the pericardium that surrounds that hollow muscular pump that no longer beats with love for him.

*

"Roll up your window," Big Bear says. Estelle is rolling down her window. She is rolling it down to throw her cigarette away. A spaceship has landed in front of their Peugeot and she is rolling down her window.

"Earthlings! Like you, we have ears, but they are very sensitive. We can hear what you are saying and do not want you to be afraid."

Big Bear stares. A round dome that seems to be made of something soft—foam rubber?—bobs slightly in front of them. The thing covers the whole road.

"We also read minds. There are three of us, and two of us speak English."

"Oh, holy shit!" Big Bear says. "Estelle?"

She has rolled the window down and is letting the smoke from another cigarette she just lit blow out of the car.

"We will leave our spaceship, Bill and Estelle. Please do not worry."

"God almighty," Big Bear says. "Roll it up, Estelle."

"What does it matter?" Estelle says. Big Bear reaches across her lap and rolls up the window. The car is still running, his foot is still on the brake. He thinks about trying to get around the spaceship. There is no way to get around it without driving into a marsh. Big Bear throws the car into reverse and starts backward, but when he does that a wind stops the car and slowly pulls it forward again.

"Please get out of your car," the voice says.

There is a man standing in the road. He has on a shirt and a pair of slacks. His face is red. He waves.

"Come on," Estelle says.

"Stay in the car, Estelle."

"We need pictures of both of you," the voice says.

Big Bear's pants are wet. He cringes. Estelle has left the car and is walking toward the red-faced man. He thinks about stepping on the gas and crushing her, running into her from behind, not letting her have her way.

"Estelle?" he says to the empty seat.

"Please get out," the voice says.

"I'm not getting out," Big Bear says.

"We must have pictures. There are twenty exposures on the roll."

"What do you need pictures for?"

"To take back, Bill. They sent us for pictures."

"What are they going to do with the pictures?"

"I don't know. I just take the pictures."

Big Bear rubs his hand over his face. "I will never drink again," he says. "Estelle?" he says.

"This is a random landing. We'll never see you again. We need twenty pictures, and we would like to be your friends before we leave. Please get out of the car."

Estelle is talking to the man. He rolls down his window and puts his head out. It smells damp. There is a lot of fog. The lights have been turned out on the spaceship, and it is hard to tell just how large it is. It looked huge in the sky over the car, but it doesn't look that big now. Just big enough to block the road. Big Bear puts the car in reverse again. Just as before, a stream of air draws him forward.

"We found you by accident. You'll do fine for the pictures, though. If you'll please get out."

Big Bear wants to go home and go to sleep. Big Bear wants to go home to throw away all his liquor. He wants his children. His children!

"What are you going to do to me?" he asks again.

"Take your picture," the man says.

Disgusted, Big Bear opens the door and gets out. He walks forward. The man shakes his hand and introduces himself as Bobby. Estelle smiles at him.

"You're drunk," Big Bear says to Estelle.

"That's okay," the man says. "If you two could stand by your car?"

Big Bear doesn't want to turn his back on the man.

"The other ones?" Big Bear asks.

"Donald is playing a game inside. He's tired of coming to Earth."

"What game?" Big Bear asks suspiciously, not sure why he's suspicious.

"Scrabble. He was worried about using the word 'toque.' That's a foreign word, isn't it?"

"Toe?"

"Toque."

"I'm drunk as a skunk," Big Bear says.

*

"Bear, you'll never make it."

"We'll make it."

"Why should you even try to make it?" Laura says. Laura is the wife of the man whose party Big Bear and Estelle have attended.

"Big Bear can make it!" Big Bear yells.

"You're a big oaf," Laura says, and walks away. That leaves her husband to get their coats.

"If we don't make it, I'll end up the same place I'd be working tomorrow anyway," Estelle says. Estelle is more drunk than Big Bear, and Big Bear is focusing on his feet to stay alert.

"What are you ashamed of?" Estelle asks Big Bear.

"Nothing. What are you talking about?" He fears that another one of her honesty sessions is coming on—a talk about how she wishes she had never married him or had children.

"You're staring at the floor, Bear. What's the matter with you?"

"He's drunk," their host says good-naturedly. Big Bear and Paul, their host, were in the service together. It was Paul's idea to keep calling him Big Bear when they got back to America. In

Japan, a geisha came up with the name. Laura will have no part of it. She calls him Alvin. Big Bear holds Estelle's coat, happy to get away from the party.

The Peugeot is parked in Paul's driveway. Death. Death everywhere. Japan, Viet Nam, Mortuary Science.

"What's the matter with you, Bear?" Estelle asks. "You're not really too drunk to drive, are you?"

*

"Daddy! Did you know that there was a Big Bear City in California?"

"No."

"I found out in geography. My teacher said to ask if it was named for you."

"I've never met your teacher. How did she know I was called Big Bear?"

"I told her."

"Well, stop telling everybody. That's just a joke, you know."

"But that's what everybody calls you."

"Go watch TV or something."

"What are you two talking about?" Estelle calls from the kitchen.

"Geography," Big Bear answers.

"Mom, there's a place called Big Bear City in California."

"I don't want to hear any more about it," Big Bear says.

"What are you so grumpy about?" Estelle asks, standing in the kitchen doorway. "You're as grumpy as a bear."

"Oh, come off it. You two leave me alone."

"Why is that always what you want? Why can't anybody talk to you?" Estelle says.

"Leave me alone," Big Bear says, and tilts himself out of view in his La-Z-Boy reclining chair.

*

"I thought jumping rope with the intestine was a joke," Estelle says. "That's not what you're doing, is it? It's not really an intestine?"

*

"No, there are no cows on Mars, so we consider your milk a delicacy. We have alcohol. Juniper berries grow in profusion. It's really very pretty, all the bushes, in addition to the gin it produces."

"Are they coming out?" Big Bear asks, nodding toward the spaceship.

"We've been on so many missions that they just don't care any more."

"What do they come for, then?"

"There has to be a certain number aboard."

"What for?"

"I never asked. We keep busy, though."

"What do you do?"

"Well, Donald likes to play games. He got some jigsaw puzzles the last time we were here, and he never tires of that, particularly a round puzzle that's a pizza."

"He just plays games?"

"They drink milk if we stop for it. We have to stop in the woods, of course, and there usually aren't any stores. They loved Maine. There were stores in the middle of nowhere."

"We love Maine," Estelle says.

"It's awfully nice," the spaceman says.

"Are you going to take more pictures?" Big Bear asks.

"I'm just trying to think . . . where would be a good spot?"

"Can't we just stand by the car?"

"I think they'll want variety."

Estelle smiles. "Would you like me to take off my clothes?" she asks.

"She's kidding," Big Bear says.

"I thought we'd take those later," the spaceman says.

"We're not taking our clothes off," Big Bear says.

"I'll put you under a spell, Bill," the spaceman says.

"You can't put me under any spell."

"Please try not to be hostile. I personally have no interest in taking nude photographs."

"Then let's leave that crap out."

"I can't leave it out. They said to get some."

"Tell them it was foggy and it didn't turn out."

"I'll undrooo," Eotollo oayo.

"Don't you think it's a little cold for nude posing?" Big Bear says.

"Yes," the spaceman says. "Maybe we should go to your place."

*

Sleep soundly, sweet ones. Don't wake up and want water, or you might see the spacemen in the kitchen. You don't like it when your brother plays with your special toys . . . how would you like it if a spaceman was tapping pegs through holes and squares through squares? You wouldn't like it. It's good you're a sound sleeper. One of the spacemen is in the bathroom. Imagine walking into the bathroom and seeing a spaceman urinating.

*

"I said I'm not too drunk to drive, and I'm not."

"You're no judge. Laura is probably right."

"Side with me. I'm your husband."

"In effect I *am* siding with you. If you had an accident . . ."

"Big Bear doesn't have accidents."

"Like John Wayne?"

"What are you taunting me for? You want to get home or don't you?"

"It might be better if I drove."

"It might be better, but you're not going to do it."

"All right. But drive slowly. There's so much fog."

"This piece of crap car isn't helping us any. The thing's so light, a wind would blow it over. When are you going to give up and let me turn it in for another one?"

"I thought flashy cars didn't matter to you."

"What did I say about flash? I just said a car—a decent car."

"This is a decent car. It was driven by my brother before he died in that horrible war."

"Where did you get his underwear from in the first place?"

"I don't want to talk about my brother."

"I don't want that underwear in my drawer. Where the hell did you get your brother's underwear?"

"Where do you think? From his drawer."

"Well, why did you take that, if it isn't prying?"

"It's not as though I just took that."

"What else did you take?"

"I took his things. I don't want to talk about my brother, Bear."

"What things? Tell me or I'm not going to pull out of the driveway, and Laura can wave and scowl all night."

"I took shirts and sweaters. Satisfied?"

The car pulls out of the driveway. Big Bear despises the car.

"Why haven't I ever seen them?"

"I put them away for the boys."

"They don't want your brother's stuff. By the time it fits them they wouldn't wear anything that unfashionable."

"I am not aware of radical style changes in men's sweaters."

"I want the underwear to go! You keep the shirts, I'll throw out the underwear."

"You keep your hands off my brother's things."

"You put it in my drawer and order me not to touch it. Why didn't you put it in your own damn drawer?"

"It makes me sad."

"Then get rid of it."

"Can we please talk about something else? I thought you liked my brother."

"I didn't have anything against your brother, but I don't want his underwear in my drawer."

"If you keep driving this fast, you'll die before it can be removed."

"Don't change the subject. The subject is underwear. You can keep it under your pillow if you want, but get it out of my drawer."

"Yes, sir."

"I don't feel guilty," Big Bear says. "Nobody would put up with that."

In front of their car something hovers in the sky, but it's too close to be a plane. It's shapeless, which is funny, because it's close enough to figure out a shape. A mound. A mound?

"What's that?" Big Bear asks.

*

"Maybe we should get the uncomfortable pictures over with, and then we could take a few more by the car, or over there."

"Oh, cut it out," Big Bear says. "No nudie shots."

"I'm a family man, too, Bill. I'd like to just simplify matters and get home to my family. Could you drop your pants?"

"No."

Estelle is unbuttoning her coat.

"No," Big Bear says to her, and grabs her hand. She tries to get it away from him.

Estelle is shrugging her dress down, smiling at the spaceman. The camera clicks.

"How old are your children?" she asks.

"That's enough!" Big Bear says. "Can we go home?"

"I'd like the others, and then you can go on your way."

"It's too God damn cold," Big Bear says.

"Let's take them to our place, Bear. We could give them milk and they could take the other pictures."

"That would be fine," the spaceman says.

"You're not invited," Big Bear says.

"I was just invited." The spaceman smiles politely. "I'll get the others."

"I thought they had to stay with the ship."

"I'm doing you a favor, Bill. Would you rather stay here longer?"

Big Bear shivers. What if Sammy and David drank the last of the milk.

*

The other spacemen are named Donald and Fred. There is something wrong with Fred; his wrists are bent funny, and his mouth wrinkles when he tries to smile, which is all of the time. "He's retarded," Donald says. Good God, Big Bear thinks. Won't Fred hear Donald?

"We've been stuck with him on the last seven missions," Donald says.

They are walking up Big Bear's front walk. They are inside the house. The babysitter has gone to sleep in the spare bedroom. She turned off all the lights. Big Bear can't see. Donald has a flashlight. He turns it on.

"Thanks," Big Bear says.

He heads for the light switch. Fred, it seems, is not only retarded, but violent. He struggles with Donald and wins. Fred has the flashlight. He pokes it into his mouth. His cheeks light up. No one tries to take the flashlight away from Fred. "I've had it up to here with him," Donald says, but no one tries to get the flashlight. Big Bear has located the light switch, so it's okay. Sort of okay. Fred's cheeks are orange.

*

"Did you know that this was called mooning in the sixties? College kids did it."

The spaceman snaps away. Estelle is making a fool of herself.

*

"What are you going to bring me, Daddy?" the spaceman's son asks.

"You're greedy."

"What are you going to bring me?"

"What do you want?"

"More goldfish."

"The damn things die. I bring them all the way back and they're dead in a week."

"I told you. That's because I need a real aquarium with a pump and a filter."

"It's too much trouble to bring the things back. Isn't there something else I could bring you?"

"No. I want that."

"I'll do it if I have time. You can't just buy goldfish everywhere."

"Go where you can get them."

"This is my mission, kid. Okay?"

"When are you going to take me with you?"

"When you grow up."

"I *am* grown up."

"Grownups don't want goldfish."

*

"How did it go in the morgue, Estelle?"

"Fine," Estelle says.

"Did you cut up dead bodies?"

Estelle comes into the living room. She can hardly wait to see if Big Bear is drunk. Estelle stares at Big Bear, who is reclining in his La-Z-Boy reclining chair. She sees that he is reclining because he is drunk.

"I thought you were going to Pete's party tonight."

"We were *both* going."

"That's what I said," Estelle says.

"But now we're *not* both going," Big Bear grins. "We're not going anywhere."

"I know!" Estelle cries. She doubles over, as though somebody just passed her a football.

"Jesus Christ," Big Bear says. "I didn't know you wanted to go to Pete's. I'm not so drunk we can't go. Stand up, for Christ's sake. What's the matter with you, Estelle?"

*

"I hate not to be the perfect host," Big Bear says to the spacemen. "But tomorrow is another day and . . ."

They seem not to have understood. If they smoked, Big Bear could empty the ashtrays.

"To be honest with you," Big Bear says, although none of the spacemen seem interested, "we've had a big night and it's about time for you to go."

"The disgusting thing," Donald says. "Blowing bubbles in his milk."

"We're all out of milk, now, Bobby. It's about time for you to go," Big Bear says.

"I hope he falls over and we can just leave him," Donald says.

Fred has thrown a glass of milk against the wall. The glass was soft plastic, so it just bounced. The sound wasn't loud enough to awaken Sammy and David. Estelle finds herself looking on the bright side of the spaceman's little *faux pas*.

*

At a gas station in Big Bear City, California, a little boy gets out of his mother's car to buy a soft drink.

*

Laura takes Big Bear's coat. She turns to look at Big Bear as he walks away. I hope he picks the hors d'oeuvres that have liver hidden inside them, she thinks.

*

"Mommy!" the little boy says. "I put the money in and nothing happened."
"Push the coin release."
"What's that?"
"Can I help?" the service attendant asks.
"That's all right," the little boy's mother says. "I'll take care of it." She goes to the machine and pushes the coin-release lever. Nothing happens.

*

Lying in a field in Viet Nam, in the second before he dies, Estelle's brother wonders what will happen to his Peugeot. He wonders why he's thinking of his Peugeot instead of Estelle or his mother or father. Rather, he starts to wonder, but dies before the thought is fully formulated.

*

"Maybe I could get a picture of the two of you by the door. Could you get together and pretend that you're going grocery shopping?"
"We don't have to pretend we're going grocery shopping. We'll just stand by the door, as if we're going out."
"Pretend you're going grocery shopping," the spaceman says.
"We look the same way whether we're going to the P.T.A. meeting, or going to get groceries, or to visit her parents."

"Then, just stand by the door as though you were doing one of those things, please, Bill."

"Wake up, Estelle," Big Bear says. "Wake up. Come on, Estelle," Big Bear says. "This is the last picture. Are you going to wake up?"

*

"The machine doesn't work," the little boy's mother says to the service-station attendant. Just one more problem on grocery day in Big Bear City, California.

*

"You had quite a night," the babysitter says cheerfully. The babysitter and Sammy are awake. David is still sleeping. Big Bear envies David.

"I didn't know I left the milk bottle out," the babysitter says apologetically.

"Actually, we came home a while ago and some friends had milk."

The babysitter looks at the milk glasses. She also sees the one that has been thrown against the dining-room wall.

"Good-night," Big Bear says, and climbs the stairs. Since they did not smoke, Estelle will have no ashtrays to empty and will join him soon. Not that he really cares. He is so tired he'd sleep with the spacemen. Except Fred . . . Jesus, it sure is good they loaded him out of the house, Big Bear thinks. If I had irritated them, they might have left him. Big Bear is glad that he only has Sammy and David. If they had tried for a girl, like Estelle wanted, it might have been retarded.

Big Bear falls into bed, with visions of Fred. It rhymes: bed, Fred. Big Bear falls asleep.

*

There has been a spaceship sighting in Reno, Nevada, and that's where Estelle wants to go.

"Estelle, you heard them say that there are a lot of other spacemen. Any of them could have flown over Reno, Nevada."

"We haven't taken a trip in years. The boys should see some of the country."

"Aren't you going to summer school? What happened to your plans?"

"I don't want to talk about it."

"I paid a year's tuition. I'd like to have a talk about why you're quitting."

"Something disgusting happened."

"What?"

"I want to go to Reno," Estelle says. "Will you take me or won't you?"

"The spaceship won't still be there."

"There have been sightings all around Reno."

"We're going to take the boys to Reno and sit in a motel waiting to hear rumors of spaceships?"

"It's my birthday," Estelle says. "You have to please me on my birthday, and I want to take a trip."

"What do you mean, I have to please you on your birthday?"

"I suppose you don't have to be nice to me if you don't want to, Bear. Excuse my presumption."

"I already am nice to you. That night with the spacemen I let you act like a jackass. Anybody else would have straightened you out."

"How gallant of you not to criticize me in front of my friends."

"Friends? You met them once."

"Of course no one would want to be my friend," Estelle says. "Excuse me."

"I didn't say they weren't your friends. I did say that. I don't know. Let's forget this, okay?"

"Let's go to Reno, Nevada."

"Oh, leave me alone," Big Bear says.

*

Big Bear meant to avoid this card shop, but it's so convenient, and he doesn't have the time to look all around for another place to get Estelle's birthday card. The woman will probably not be there anyway.

The woman is there. She finds Big Bear as he stands browsing through the Relative Birthday group of cards. She asks if she can help him.

"No, thanks," Big Bear says.

"This is a nice one," the saleswoman says, taking a big pink card down.

Big Bear looks. There is a plastic window, in the shape of a heart, through which a blond lady is visible. "My Darling" it says across the top of the card.

"I don't like that one," Big Bear says.

"Then look at this one." She hands Big Bear a blue card with bluer velvet bluebirds on it. The bluebirds trail a ribbon that spells "Happy Birthday, Darling" as it unrolls.

"Okay," Big Bear says. "Fine."

The card costs one dollar and fifty cents. For a card! It takes the woman a long time to slip it carefully into the bag. It takes her a long time to count out his change. He is never going to come to this card shop again.

"Thank you, sir," the saleswoman says, with her usual ironic smile.

Big Bear holds the bag tightly and makes the mistake of crushing the velvet bird.

*

"You're wrecked. You going to work like that?"

"I couldn't work there if I wasn't wrecked."

"You should avoid getting wrecked sometime and try it."

"You try it if you're so curious. You can have my job."

"I don't want a job."

"Then that means I have to have one. So don't criticize me for getting wrecked."

"You're wrecked." The saleswoman's boyfriend laughs. He is also wrecked.

*

"Look at this one, look at this," Bobby says.

His friend's face turns red. "Put the things away," his friend says.

"Look, look, this one was Estelle's idea."

"I'm sure."

"No, I swear. She said this was a craze on campus in the sixties."

"*This* was something they did at college?"

"And look at this one. This is Bill pretending he's going to work. Look at it!"

"I've seen these things a dozen times already. Put those disgusting things away," his friend says.

"I'll put them away, but you've got to see the expression on her face in this one."

"I'm not likely to see her face in this series."

The spaceman's friend has just made a witty remark. Bobby appreciates it and starts laughing uncontrollably. He'd be doing that even if his friend weren't there, though. These pictures really kill him.

*

"Now the Air Force is even admitting that it's tied up with them," Big Bear says from his La-Z-Boy reclining chair.

"What do they say?"

"I just told you. All those sightings over Nebraska. The Air Force is coming out and admitting it."

"What do they *say*, Bear?"

"You love this subject, don't you? You love to talk about the spacemen."

"Who brought it up?" Estelle says.

"I did. I know you love the subject," Big Bear says.

*

"These bluebirds sing a happy tune. They say that you are mine . . ."

She is convulsed with laughter, that crazy, wiped-out laughter with no tears accompanying it. The eyes get wider and wider—wide enough to pour tears, but the laughter is all that comes.

"Why don't you stop memorizing the cards? Just take your shoes off and relax."

"It had velvet bluebirds on the front with a blue ribbon and a blue background, and it said 'These bluebirds sing . . .'"

"You're going to lose your job the first time you do a wiped-out thing like this with a customer."

"The bluebirds! The fucking bluebirds!"

*

"What the hell was that?"

"Probably hit ducks again. Remember the time we took off through a whole flock of them?" Bobby says.

"Disgusting," Donald says, but he is looking at Fred and not thinking about possible dead ducks.

*

"What are you mad at me for?" the little boy asks. "What did I do?"

"You didn't do anything. You got your soft drink. Drink it."

"You couldn't make the machine work either," the little boy says.

"It was broken," his mother says.

"Then what are you mad about?"

"I'm mad because you just add to the confusion. I want to get the groceries and go home and put them away. All right? Sit back and finish your drink."

It is just another day in Big Bear City, California.

Victor Blue

■■■■■■■■■■■■■■■■■■■■■■

Took monthly leaf cuttings to send to her friends in the violet association. Other than that, all routine: turning on fluorescent light, usual watering from dish beneath the pot. Store delivered decorative pots. Now the inside pots must be carefully lifted so that none of the delicate leaves snap. A tricky business. My fingers must not touch the leaves. The clay pots must be centered exactly in the decorative pots, then misted from a distance of two feet. Mrs. Edway has inspected them carefully to be certain there are no bruised leaves. After unjust complaint yesterday, put ice water on the violets today to get even. Wilted a little. Shook my head with her as she called the violets "temperamental." Annoyed me by talking about too many articles she'd read in the violet association publication. Made note to discard next issue of the magazine in post office when I pick up the mail. She calls the mails "unreliable." She has been crankier than usual. I suspect her pain is worse, but after years of marriage I know better than to ask. Mrs. Edway has always had her secrets.

Yesterday I began reading *Confessions of Z.* Next to be read are *The Red and the Black* and *The Charterhouse of Parma.* It sounds as though we are literate people. Also in the pile are *The Silver Chalice, French Science-fiction Stories,* and *Man Meets Dog.* Every time I read to her she reminds me how lucky we are that the librarian's mother is her personal friend, so the librarian sends us books by messenger every Saturday at noon, when the library closes. I am not sure whether the books are selected by the librarian or by the messenger, who is a young schoolgirl of racially mixed parentage. Sometimes, as Mrs. Edway called to my attention, we receive a selection of books from authors whose names follow alphabetically: Faulkner, Fitzgerald, Flaubert. Other times there seems to be little method in the selection. Mrs. Edway and I agree, however, that we should be grateful for the service, which began when Mrs. Edway (who had donated half a dozen specimen violets to the reading room of the library) wrote a note to the librarian saying that she would no longer be able to make a weekly inspection of the violets because of her poor health; in fact, she would no longer be able to use the library at all. Our service began the week the note was delivered. On that occasion the librarian came herself, dropping off several anthologies of

English and American literature. She declined to stay, although she did wait long enough to be given several Food'N'Bloom pellets.

Something interesting happened: after careful consideration as to whether we wanted a dog or a cat or nothing, we voted secretly, on separate pieces of paper, which we held up at the same time, so that one couldn't change his mind after seeing what the other had written. Each of us had written "cat." Next Saturday I will ask the messenger if any of her schoolmates have kittens they want to give away.

Mrs. Edway sees me writing and asks who I think is going to read all this. She is jealous for two reasons: I am using Xerox paper that Bernie brings me (he brings his father Xerox paper, while he brings his mother nothing), and because I have not begun the afternoon reading yet. I am not much interested in *Confessions of Z* and may call for a vote as to whether we should continue with it. She is cranky today because she did not have a good night, and if she suspects that I am not calling for the vote just out of routine, she is sure to answer, "Yes."

She is looking through a magazine now, holding it close to her face. I suspect she is studying ads for cat food. The pictures show so clearly which brand contains more liver that it will not be necessary to vote when it comes time. What a coincidence that she received a free coupon for creamy liver dinner in the mail this morning. Is it the same brand pictured in the magazine?

Bernie just called to check on things. Xerox has developed an improved reproduction-machine paper. He is going to a convention to describe the new product to clients. He tells me his mind will be at rest if I persuade her to see a doctor before he leaves town.

The messenger has come and gone. *Romeo and Juliet* was not accounted for when she returned the books we had finished to the library today. She told me the book had to be in this house, because it was not in her house. She described putting the pile on her bureau and removing the pile this morning to return on her way to school. She carried them in a book bag, so she could not have dropped the book. I tried to treat the subject lightly and asked, "Wherefore art thou, book?" as she sprawled to look under the bed. Wanted to ask about the kitten, but she seemed very agitated. Decided to wait until Saturday. She made a thorough search of all but one room, and did not have time to do that because it was her lunch hour, and she had to return to school.

I raised what I thought might be a touchy subject: a charcoal filter for the spigot. She agreed.

Abandoned *Confessions of Z* for *The Red and the Black*. Listened to Brahms. Dinner of crab-stuffed flounder, lima beans and corn. She went to bed an hour earlier than usual, not feeling well again.

Tuesday

Arose early, prepared pancake batter for breakfast. Wrote two notes: one to the mail-order house for a charcoal filter, the other to Dr. Yeusa. The messenger arrived just as I finished writing. She was distraught and said she must find *Romeo and Juliet*. The search ended in vain at eight-thirty when she had to leave for school.

Must call Mrs. Edway's attention to "High Hopes"—two withering leaves.

She slept through the phone call from Bernie, allowing me to tell him that I had contacted the doctor, asking him to stop by unannounced. He thanked me, promised a supply of the new Xerox paper.

When she awakens we will have breakfast and take the Tuesday stroll.

Radio bulletin about a missing two-engine plane.

Walked by the frozen pond, where children were ice-skating. One child recognized us, a girl about eleven, and asked if she could stop by with a selection of Girl Scout cookies. A nice little girl—remembered her from last year. Mrs. Edway knew her name, I think, but wouldn't say it in front of me. She points up my deficiencies, such as forgetting names, by not helping out. She knows the messenger's name, too, but won't use it. Am waiting to ask the favor about the kitten because things are still strained between us. Looked for *Romeo and Juliet* myself. No luck. Told the messenger it had to be either here or there. She is convinced it is here and has arranged to stop by with a friend after school. I think her job may be in jeopardy and will suggest to Mrs. Edway that she offer to repay the library for the loss and to assume responsibility.

Mrs. Edway's cousin from San Francisco mailed her a belated birthday gift: an embroidered picture of the Eiffel Tower, *La Tour Eiffel* in black cross-stitch at the bottom. Took a secret vote to see if it should be hung: "Yes." We decided on the dining room without having to vote. Mrs. Edway wrote a note to the librarian offering to replace the book before I suggested it. She leaves the envelopes for me to lick and seal because she doesn't like the taste. Peeked before I mailed it, but the note didn't mention the messenger's name.

Fell asleep in the afternoon after the episode in which Julien wishes he had died in M. de Renal's garden. Dinner was late, and I didn't concentrate as much as usual on the preparation because I was trying to piece together the nightmare I'd had about a plane circling a garden. Someone had asked questions of me, and the correct answer would allow the plane to land. If Mrs. Edway slept when I did, she didn't say. I awoke to see her examining a magazine close to her face. She always looks over the top of her magazine to let me know she is aware I'm dozing. When she dozes, I ignore it.

She makes a shopping list for Wednesday. I have my own little private joke about the list: she can't see well and lists toothpaste every week, although she has over a hundred tubes in reserve, and I keep buying them, stacking them up so if her vision improves and she sees them we will have something to argue about. We can well afford the toothpaste—no harm done. We spend some time, while the food cooks, making lists of vegetables and meats we will both eat, then buy seven dinners of items we have both agreed upon. She has added a few things to the list when she gives it to me: a hairnet, vitamins, toothpaste (I laugh to myself).

Chicken casserole and tossed salad for dinner. She asks me if it is iceberg lettuce. I chopped it small on purpose, knowing she'd ask. I answer that it is romaine. No argument.

Search parties have gone out for the plane.

Mrs. Edway answers the phone. It is the messenger, who says she was kept after school and hopes we weren't inconvenienced waiting for her. Sensing that things have turned around a bit, I ask her for the phone and tell the messenger that we are replacing the book. I inquire about the kitten. She thinks she knows where she can get one and promises to call back.

Pushing the grocery cart back from the store, I see a car parked in front of the house. Dr. Yeusa received my note in the morning mail. He is a thin man with curly, bushy hair and small silver-rimmed glasses. Mrs. Edway and the doctor look at each other over the tops of their glasses. She refuses to stand when asked, and asks him to join her on the couch. I will fix them tea. She is angry with me for what I have done, so surely I will at least fix tea. She allows the doctor to question her. It is a pain in the stomach that usually comes only at night. He takes her blood pressure; she turns her head to avoid looking. She sees the bad leaves on the violet, the ones I forgot to mention, and gets up, the device still wrapped around her arm. On her way back from the violets, the doctor blocks her way and examines her abdomen. He takes a blood sample and puts it out of sight in his bag at tea-drinking time. Before he leaves he phones in a prescription for sedatives.

She will not speak to me.

There is a knock at the door. Mrs. Edway says, "I like the mint and the assorted." But it isn't the Girl Scout. It's another girl, and she's brought a basket of kittens—all six weeks old, she says. She takes the blanket off. Mrs. Edway and I study the contents. We each write on a slip of paper which one we like. Her slip reads: gray and white, all gray, the largest kitten. Mine: gray, multicolored, orange-ish one. We confer; yes, by "the largest kitten" she meant the multicolored one. So it is narrowed down to that one or the gray one. I tell her that either is all right with me. She chooses the multicolored kitten. The girl stares, even after we have chosen. No, she says, they're free, and leaves the house.

I offer the kitten a can of liver, but it seems uninterested and walks off to explore the kitchen.

Dinner: liver and onions, succotash, pound cake. Lately we have been arguing about the necessity of both a green and a yellow vegetable daily, now that vitamin pills are so fashionable. I fix dinner, so she gets both, but the idea of having to eat them for good health gives us something to talk about. To annoy me, she used to finish her vegetables *and* take a vitamin pill. Now, since I shop, I ignore vitamin pills when they are on the list.

On one of my pieces of paper she has begun a thank-you note. I see "Merci, Celeste," but she shades the note with her hand when she sees me looking.

Two cowboys die, shot by another cowboy on horseback. The rest of the movie shows the cowboy's dog walking home without his master, and the wife of one of the dead cowboys standing on the front porch staring curiously at the dog, who slinks under the porch. The wife goes down the stairs to look at the dog. Program interrupted by delivery boy from drugstore. Embarrassed to say I nearly tipped him a nickel instead of a quarter. Usually keep that nickel separate from my other change because it's an Indian head. Mrs. Edway sits stirring the batter for carrot bread. The movie depresses her and she speaks bitterly against Bernie for not calling, wonders what will happen to the inn across the street when it's sold. She asks how many years we've lived in the house, and I tell her fifty. She gets confused when she's tired. She tosses the kitten a ball of yarn that is nearly as big as the animal itself. The kitten circles it. She asks what we decided to name the kitten. No use lying, telling her the name I like; if it doesn't ring a bell, she won't believe me. "Rainbow," I tell her all the same. She nods. I suspect she's not tired, but in pain.

She feels better later and says she doesn't remember discussing the kitten's name. Where is the piece of paper on which we agreed? The pieces of paper are piled next to the Xerox paper in boxes I bring back from the food store. Of course I can't produce the evidence. She wins her point and goes to bed.

The weather forecast is for snow.

Thursday

Bernie came in the afternoon, brought her a pumpkin pie Mary Louise made and a package of the new paper for me.

Bad news, but Bernie says they won't know how bad until more tests are made.

No snow yet. No decision about name.

Friday

She couldn't see the small illustrations in *Man Meets Dog*, so I copied them on large sheets of paper. Copied four of them. We've enjoyed the book more than *The Red and the Black*. Secret vote revealed that neither was sorry we had a kitten instead of a puppy.

The news has gotten around. She can't blame me because I didn't go out yesterday or today. She had two phone calls, both of them from women offering encouragement. She was polite and didn't talk long, but long enough to find out that it was Mary Louise who told them.

She won't eat the pie Bernie brought. She looked through her cookbooks today and found the recipe for apple, and has made an early store list, including the ingredients she'll need. She doesn't criticize Mary Louise for telling people what the doctor said, but she talks about Mary Louise's Catholicism and complains that she's more narrow-minded than the Pope. How foolish she is to think she'll go to purgatory because she's sterile!

She asks me if I remember the night she tried to talk Bernie out of marrying Mary Louise. I do. We talk about it, careful not to overestimate the extent to which Bernie lost his temper. Bernie never would listen to advice.

An uncomfortable moment when Mary Louise cried on the phone and said she had been to church to pray.

Two new violets have taken root.

Watched the sunset. Sky was very bright before the storm began. The colors disappeared in a second and were replaced by fast-rolling clouds and then the snow. Tried to take a picture with the Polaroid, but the sky darkened too fast. Very windy. Didn't stay out long because of the flu epidemic. She watched me from inside the house—face looked like a ghost's because of the fluorescent light shining around her. Used to read ghost stories to each other. For years she hasn't wanted to hear them. She used to get frightened and dive for cover, under the afghan, into the pillows, even though the plots were familiar. Finally cleaned, got rid of the old books last summer. She laughed when she found *The Lives of the Angels* that Mary Louise gave her for Christmas: a whole book filled with drawings of the angelic hierarchy, faint lines made with a thin pen point, pastel colors swirling behind them like the sky before the snow.

Trying not to think about it.

I do all the reading now because the years have proved that I'm the better reader. I cook better too, although she still fixes a few specialties. I'm not responsible for the flourishing violets—only do what she tells me. Keep track of what was done when by making notes on a calendar hanging above the plants, with pictures of specimen violets on it—a bonus from her violet association for subscribing for ten years.

Trivia.

Kitten's ripped up pieces of wool all over the rug.

Maybe it would cheer her up if I told her about the toothpaste.

Glanced at *The Charterhouse of Parma* and am thinking of putting it in the pile to be returned, pretending we've finished the week's reading.

A television special tonight on the astronauts.

Who's supposed to arrange for the tests?

Saturday

When I got back, Bernie's car was parked outside. They were standing in the doorway in their coats, ready to drive her for the tests. Mary Louise must have seen the pie in the kitchen, untouched. I had arrived home either a minute too soon or a minute too late. Had a nervous conversation with Bernie about paper and the flu epidemic. She left without a word to me. Don't know if she gave them trouble or not. Fat Mary Louise helped her down the walk. Bernie kept looking back at them, pretending to look at me, waving twice.

Wish I had started keeping this book long ago, so I wouldn't look back through it and read only about familiar routines.

Could do something different today, talk to neighbors, take a bus to the zoo, but that would seem disrespectful while Mrs. Edway is being tested.

Could get rid of the book and all the Xerox paper inserts, but I'd miss it, and she'd miss having cause to dislike me because I'm always writing in secret, refusing to show it to her. Would she be disappointed? She probably remembers what the last few years

have been like. There aren't any fantasies. I could go back and
write endearments in the margins, or at the end of the pages. Ink
wouldn't match. She couldn't read the small writing anyway.
Calling her Mrs. Edway is a form of endearment, I suppose.

Afternoon: rolled pastry crust for the meat pies. Almost forgot
book delivery. The messenger came in spite of the snow, carrying
two history books and three novels. She stopped long enough to
stroke the kitten. Kitten won't use its box, uses the corners of the
dining room. House smells a little bad. Went for some air, dressed
very warmly. Nobody at the pond today. Sign still up at the inn.
One two three four. We used to keep track of the nuumber of
steps it was from one place to another: between the pond and
inn, for instance, or from the house to the field on top of the hill.
She'd try to confuse me by counting out loud, and she took two
steps for every one of mine.

When she was pregnant I stuffed a pillow under my shirt and
walked around, colliding with her. Maybe that's why Bernie got
dizzy when he was a child.

Evening: mealybug discovered on "Victor Blue" during a routine check. Leave it there? Let all the plants be contaminated? Go
out in the snowstorm and catch the flu? Stop answering the door
when the messenger comes? Get no grocery list Tuesday night?
Do no shopping Wednesday? Take the kitten to the Humane Society? Feeling sorry for myself. Mrs. Edway tells me to spray the
plant with malathion. She wants to save "Victor Blue" even
though she says she will d–.

Night: bad television reception because of the storm. A secret
vote to see if we want to listen to the radio, if possible. Two No's.
She calls for a vote about what she said earlier. Hers, Yes, mine,
No.

Sunday

Discovered some of her old samplers: "Into Each Life Some
Rain Must Fall/Jesus Loves Us One and All." Another: "In
Heaven There Is Work and Play/Half of Each Makes Up Our
Day."

A notice in the mail this morning, signed "Suzie Duncan, Your
Girl Scout Representative," informing us that cookies had been

reordered, but there would be a two-to-three-week delay. A depressing thought: the posthumous delivery of Girl Scout mints.

Mystery of *Romeo and Juliet* solved. Book found in old box of signed agreements that had been carried upstairs. Called the messenger, apologized. Mrs. Edway got the number for me. Still don't know the messenger's name. Good she answered and not her parents.

She calls for another vote. Still a tie, of course. Now I have an advantage on my side, though. She came right out and asked if she could read the book I'd been keeping before k—— herself. I told her I'd discovered the old samplers. She was angry and accused me of spying on her because I know she can't climb stairs. I think she wants to read this to find out whether I've secretly loved or hated her all these years. It wouldn't be fair for her to get all this when I'd only have three incidents or facts imparted to me, written on sheets of Xerox paper not large enough to hold much information. It's the best she can do, she says. We take a secret vote on whether we should keep arguing: one Yes, one No. More talk about d— later in the afternoon. She asks if I resist the idea because I want to see her suffer, smug in her assumption that that's what the book says.

Night. *Petite marmite.*

A phone call from Mary Louise's priest, who identifies himself as Father Donnelly and explains that he knows we are not Catholic, but that Mary Louise has been very upset and he felt he might offer words of consolation. The words he offers are references to books of the Bible: numbers, suggested Psalms. Told him that "In Heaven There Is Work and Play/Half of Each Makes Up Our Day." He had no ready answer.

Keep thinking of what I'd do. Wouldn't want to stay in the house—not just because I'd have bad memories, but because I'm tired of the house. Violets are too much trouble. I complain to her about the problem it would create, and she suggests we d– together.

Tea and bed.

Monday

Took care of violets. A little worried about "Pledge of Pink," but no signs of mealybugs. Mrs. Edway inspected with a magnifying glass to prove me wrong, but after careful examination no argument resulted.

On the phone, she refused both further testing and interim treatment. Her doctor or Bernie?

Finished *petite marmite*.

Gave her the book when she went to bed. She flipped through, held it close to read passages but was too drowsy to concentrate. Bottle of sedatives three-quarters empty.

Just got the book back. Put the light out over the violets and have been watching the sky change color, from pale to dark. Radio says more snow, but there's a ring around the moon. Does that only mean rain?

*   *   *

One officer to another officer: "The old man says he killed a Mrs. Edway. Waited to come in because Tuesday is his day for a stroll."

The authorities are such young people.

Phone call: Bernie and Mary Louise come to the police station. Mary Louise cries and says I'm innocent. Just like his mother, Bernie is wild to get his hands on the book, but two policemen are reading it in another room. I am allowed to go into the room with Bernie and Mary Louise because they hope I'll talk more. Mary Louise does most of the talking, explaining that her mother-in-law had a terminal illness. Bernie hears a report from another policeman who's just arrived. Suicide. The policemen in the room doubt it and pore over the book. Bernie looks with them. Mary Louise looks all around, crying. They want to find something written down.

"What does this mean?" an officer asks, looking at a page near the end of the book.

Another officer looks over his shoulder, brings the book to me.

I won't do anything more, including talk.

An officer makes a phone call, spells the words to someone on the other end. "It's French," he says. "A vegetable soup cooked with a turkey carcass."

Mary Louise's fat hand patting my shoulder. Remember the

day Bernie first brought her home. He was going to marry her. Mary Louise sensed Mrs. Edway's depression, told Mrs. Edway she wasn't losing a son but gaining a daughter. When they left, Mrs. Edway said it looked like she'd be losing twice.

When Bernie was a little boy, we hid Easter eggs and Mrs. Edway directed him: "Warm, warmer, cooler . . ." Bernie loved it. Days later we had to turn the living room inside out, looking for an unfound Easter egg. Turned out to be the one Mrs. Edway had spent the most time decorating. She was upset, said she wished she was d—.

Don't cry, Mary Louise. Accidents happen. A ring around the moon last night, and today no rain, no snow.

The Lifeguard

■■■■■■■■■■■■■■■■■■■■■■■

■■■■■■■■■■■■■■■■■■■■■

"When was the last time your eyes were checked?"
"They've never been checked. They've always been blue."

*

When David Warner was five or six years old there was an ant
war one day, on the sidewalk outside his house. His mother boiled
a pan of water and poured it on the ants. But it wasn't enough
water—there were so many ants. So she boiled another pan of
water, and that was enough to kill them—kill them and wash
them away, so you couldn't really tell they had been killed. David
stayed on the sidewalk, looking at the ripples of black washed to
the edge of the sidewalk. "Why do you keep staring?" his mother
scolded. "I got rid of them." Her attention had been drawn to the
ant war by David, who had squatted on the sidewalk for a long
time. And then the next summer there was another ant war—he
was six or seven then, or maybe he was five—and she killed them
again, with two separate pots of boiling water. A cloud of steam
and whoosh. That was what David told them at the induction
center. It was spring, and he was thinking of the ant wars, and although he had rehearsed another story, the story about the ants
just came out. "What of it?" the psychiatrist said when David
finally got to see him. "I might do that. Just turn on the men and
do the same thing." "Kill them, do you mean?" "Yes, of course,
kill them, that's what I'm saying." "What do you suggest I write
in this space about the ant wars?" the psychiatrist asked. "I have
to explain this, you know. Why don't you tell me what you think
it would be good to put down." Fearing a trap, David said nothing—went into a crouch, part of the original plan. "I'm giving
you a break. Why don't you give me one?" the psychiatrist asked.
David, knowing it was a trap, crouched and rocked back and
forth.

*

He has been feeling lately that something good is going to happen. There is a visual distortion that accompanies the feeling; he
sees, imagines he sees, sunsets when there could not possibly be
sunsets. He sees them at midnight, when the moon shines over
the water, then burns sun-bright, and the birds sing. Even the

seagulls are quiet at midnight, so he is not just imagining that one thing is another. He is just plain inventing. Why is he doing that?

He goes to the beach every night, and about every third night he sees a sunset, hears music or singing . . .

He has just celebrated his thirty-first birthday by drinking a bottle of Ringnes beer and going down to the beach to bury the bottle in the sand, waiting for the sunset. It would be too much to expect that the sunset would herald something, that it would all make sense, that all the sunsets would have been foreshadowings of this great, bright dawn of his thirty-first birthday. There is no sunset. Seagulls squawk. They are looking for garbage. Naturally.

*

Andrew and Penelope and Randy. The neighborhood children pronounce it "Ranny." An annoyance—especially because it does not annoy his son. "Kill them!" he wants to say to Randy. "Make them call you by your right name!" Killing—just what the psychiatrist would expect of him. To pick up a newspaper one day and read about a little boy who was urged to kill another little boy by his deranged father, who babbled incoherently, who cried when the police came to take him away. The psychiatrist would consult that sheet of paper—was that loony '65 or '64?—and aha! of course! Lookit, honey! This man made an absolute fool of himself in my office, very sick stuff . . .

David has always been curious. What did the psychiatrist come up with?

He is losing touch, and it is appropriate that he does most of his walking in the sand, which he sinks into. He went into town, saw the doctor and had his eyes examined, explaining the sunsets as "bright flashes." The doctor asked when he last had his eyes checked, and David made a little witticism. The doctor said that there did not seem to be anything wrong with his eyes. "I know not seems," David muttered. The doctor laughed, suspecting another witticism. These schoolteachers are all mad.

*

Andrew and Penelope and Randy. Andrew and Penelope are twins, eight years old. Before they were born, the doctor took an

X ray and told them they would have triplets. He kept thinking that the doctor had done something with the other one, that he was selling it. He even told his wife that, and she went wild. The doctor assured them that he had interpreted the X ray wrong, and when that did not silence them he let them look at the X ray. "What's that shadow? What's that?" "I thought that might be a third." "It might be! Isn't that a leg?" "There were only two," the doctor said, and walked out of the room. The bill was exorbitant. And when she was pregnant with Randy he refused to treat her, sent her to his partner. He does not really believe there was a third child any more. It seems silly to him that they were so upset. No doubt the sunsets will someday seem silly too.

*

She complains that in the city there is dust; at the beach there is sand. Anyone would expect that. Why does it drive her crazy? The sand creeps in, gets swept out, gets dusted away, comes again. She can feel her heart beating as she opens the door and sweeps the sand out the door, into the rest of the sand. Sand to sand. Ashes to ashes. She is thinking about dying again. Why? Why the hell is she thinking about that? She is thirty years old.

In the bed at night, she feels a grain or two of sand between her fingers. She gets up and takes a shower. There is a circle of sand around the drain. Why doesn't the water wash it away? Everybody knows that water washes sand away.

*

Penelope gets the measles. Her eyes and her cheeks get puffy and pale. He consults a medical book and finds that nothing is said about the face bloating. He calls the doctor again. The doctor says that it is nothing; he examined Penelope the day before. She is just a little girl with the measles. David thinks that the man is indifferent—the way he speaks of her as just another itchy kid. They should see a specialist. He calls the doctor back—Penelope is in awe of all the confusion she has created—and asks for the name of a specialist. The doctor hangs up on him! He finds his wife in the kitchen, tells her about what the doctor did.

"You just can't get along with doctors," she says. The adjective would be *wistfully*. "She says wistfully." What is she wistful for? On the table is an open book. There is a photograph: "Seated man in a bra and stockings, N.Y.C. 1967."

"I want to leave the beach," she says.

"But I rented this place for the whole summer."

"I am attracted to the lifeguard."

"You're kidding me."

"I walk up and down the beach. I parade in front of him. I've bought two new bathing suits. Something is going to happen."

"What the hell are you talking about?"

No answer. The young man in bra and stockings has an enigmatic expression. Perhaps someone just said something that astounded him, then took his picture. Perhaps he was just walking around in his bra and stockings, and then he got tired and sat down, and then someone said something astounding and snapped his picture.

Where did she get that sick book? Is she serious about the lifeguard? You'd never leave me for a lifeguard, he wants to say to her, because I am a loving husband and father. Witness the fact that I've spent nine hundred dollars to rent this place at the beach to delight my wife and children, and that at this very moment I am trying to find a specialist for my ill child.

"You pick the perfect moment to bring this up," he says.

"What do you care when I bring it up? It had to be said."

She is sitting in her bathing suit, fingers lightly on the photograph, as if it might be a ouija board, as though her fingers might begin to move, as though the fingers might direct her somewhere . . . to the lifeguard? He decides to take a walk down to the beach and look more carefully at the lifeguard.

"How do you feel, Andrew?" he asks his son. His son is playing with a dump truck in front of the house.

"Fine," Andrew says.

"Where's Randy?" David asks.

"He's at the beach with the Collinses."

Andrew pushes the back of the dump truck down. Sand spills on top of five sticks, all neatly in a row.

"What are the sticks?" David asks.

"What do you mean?" Andrew asks.

"What kind of game are you playing?"

"I'm just using my dump truck."

Andrew seems very defensive. He has seemed that way all summer. Eight is a bad age. Penelope, on the other hand, is quite cheerful when she is well. Now she is sick. He should call a specialist. But first he wants to go look at the lifeguard.

*

The lifeguard is wearing glasses that can't be seen into, so his eyes show no expression. His mouth is covered with zinc oxide, smeared on so thickly that it's hard to tell if his bottom lip has curled into a faint smile or if it's just the guck. The lifeguard wears bright-blue swimming trunks. There is a chain around his neck with a whistle dangling from it. David would like to blow the whistle into the lifeguard's ear, make him show some emotion. The lifeguard looks remarkably fit. He would slug him, then grind him into the sand with one of those large, perfect feet. Then he would stand on top of him, the way people stand on top of sand dunes, and wait for him to die.

"Hi," he says to the lifeguard.

The lifeguard raises his hand. His palm is very white.

"Been in the water?" David asks.

"No," the lifeguard says. "Not yet, sir."

By the lifeguard's foot (large, perfect) is a sweatshirt. Dartmouth.

"You don't have to call me sir," David says. "I'm not much older than you."

The lifeguard smiles. The zinc oxide cracks.

"How old are you?" David asks.

"Twenty-two," the lifeguard says. He takes off his sunglasses and squints at the water. He puts them back on.

"Do you know my wife?" David asks.

"No," the lifeguard says.

"A tall, blond woman. She usually wears a red swimsuit."

"No," the lifeguard says.

"She also has a green swimsuit. Very tall. As tall as me."

"Does she come to the beach very early?"

"Yes. She likes it when it's deserted."

"I think so," the lifeguard says. "What about her?"

David had not prepared himself for that question. He smiles foolishly.

*

"You know, honey, you forgot my birthday," David says.
She shrugs.
"Have I done something?"
"No," she says.
"You just feel like giving me some shit," he says.
"I don't even feel like doing that. I'd just like to be alone. I think about the lifeguard all day."
"That might be like the sunsets I've been imagining. I've been seeing the sky at night as rosy and bright and pearly . . . I've been seeing flashes of light across the sky, hearing birds, I think . . ."
"I don't see the similarity," she says.
"We're both obsessed by something that isn't real."
"He's real. He's standing on the beach right now."
"But you're imagining he's better than he is."
"I see what you're saying," she says. "I think that maybe after living with you for ten years I'm going crazy too."
"What do you mean 'too'?"
"You're crazy. The way you're always arguing with doctors, the sunsets you were talking about."
"If I can't talk to you, who can I talk to?" David asks.
"Bea Collins said she saw you talking to the lifeguard."

*

The lifeguard awoke several times: once because he was sleeping on his arm, another time when there was a noise, either in the house or in his dream, and again when the bright light shone into the room. The third time he woke up, the lifeguard made a mental note to change the position of the bed so that the light wouldn't shine in his eyes every morning. Finally, he got up. He remembered awakening only once; the light, the bed . . .

He put on his blue swimming trunks and walked to the bathroom. It made no sense to have put them on, because he had to pull them down to urinate. He flushed the toilet—his pig room-

mate, a former waiter who had worked himself up to maitre d'
at the Cliff House this summer—couldn't even be bothered to
flush the toilet. The lifeguard felt himself getting angry. He went
to the kitchen and took a peach out of a bag on the counter. He
rolled the peach back and forth on the counter, but didn't eat it.

In the bedroom, the lifeguard examined himself in the mirror.
His lips were puffy from too much sun. As awful as it felt, he
should put zinc oxide on his mouth. There was a half-full glass of
water on the dresser, and the lifeguard dipped his comb in the
glass and combed his hair back. He had seen pictures of men in
the thirties and forties who slicked their hair back that way. It
didn't matter what the lifeguard did to his hair; the early-morning
mist and the hot sun would make it fall into his eyes.

A thought came to the lifeguard on his way out of the bedroom: you might also have looked at that glass as half empty.

He put on his sandals and went out. It was a steamy morning.
The cloudy sky might mean rain, or it could just be overcast all
day. Half the summer was gone. It was the fifteenth of July, and
at the end of August the lifeguard would return to Dartmouth to
begin his senior year as a mathematics major. Before becoming a
mathematics major, he had been a political-science major, and before that a psychology major. His girlfriend, who was a waitress at
the Cliff House—who associated with his pig roommate every day
and who thought he was a "nice guy"—was studying art and
thinking about becoming an interior decorator. She was a
Lutheran, and on Sunday she always went to church. The lifeguard felt himself getting angry.

He walked through the parking lot and across the wooden
planks leading to the beach. There was a woman sitting on a blanket on the sand, with a child sleeping beside her. It was windy,
and the woman held the edge of the blanket up so that sand
wouldn't blow in her child's face.

Later, her name, Toby Warner, would be as familiar to him as
his own, but today he didn't know, or care, who she was. It was
the fifteenth of July. The ocean was slate-gray. The seagulls flew
over the shoreline as unpredictably as rolled dice. He took a little
tube of zinc oxide out of the pocket of his blue shirt—a button-
down, wouldn't be seen dead in it anywhere but on the beach—

and smoothed it over his lips. He took the chain with the whistle
on it out of the same pocket and put it around his neck.

A seagull swooped low over the empty trash can, and the lifeguard blew his whistle at it. A shrill noise—quite a contrast to the
slow, regular slush of the waves. The woman laughed. She giggled
like a girl. Her little boy stirred, but continued to sleep. The lifeguard felt awkward; it was foolish to have blown it, awakened the
child. He took off his blue shirt and dropped it in the sand and
sat on it. He looked at his feet stretched in front of him, and
thought that his toenails never grew in the summer. Toenails continued to grow after death, so why would his stop growing in the
summer? The sand probably wore them down. All day the lifeguard sat or stood, but when he was off duty he always ran three
miles down to the main beach, where he met his girlfriend. Her
name was Laura. They must have eaten almost a hundred pizzas
together, at the stand by the main beach. Laura got the pizza all
over herself. The lifeguard was not in a very good mood. He was
displeased with Laura because of the way she ate pizza, for God's
sake, and he loved Laura. It also bothered him, though, that she
liked sausage on the pizza and he liked it plain—mozzarella only.
They could have compromised, but Laura pouted, so they always
ordered pizza with sausage. Tonight he would insist that they eat
it the way he liked. Maybe she would even be nice about it. That
made him feel better. He looked to his right and saw an old man
in a golf cap walking in the surf. The woman on the blanket had
her head on her knees, but he thought that she had been looking
at him the second before and that she did that to cover it up. The
little boy looked comfortable, and he was sleeping soundly. The
lifeguard suspected, as he often suspected when he contemplated
a child for a long time, that he was a father. Maybe he was in hell
and the punishment fit the crime—he was a lifeguard to watch
over little children, and one of them might be his. But his would
be only . . . two years old now? It couldn't possibly be the child
on the blanket. And this child had a mother. And he had never
seen the woman before. That made him feel better. He was proud
of his ability to think things through.

The sun was not shining brightly yet. That meant that it would
be overcast all day. The lifeguard put his shirt on so that he

wouldn't be burned. He had very tender skin for a lifeguard, and this year he wasn't tanning well. He tanned, then peeled, then didn't seem to tan again. His day would be spent sitting in the lifeguard's chair until noon, when the old man who collected fifty cents from cars entering the parking lot would replace him for an hour so that the lifeguard could eat lunch. He couldn't imagine what good the old man would be if anybody got into trouble, but who knew about the old man's abilities, and why would anybody get into trouble? The water was too cold to swim in. The people just stood around the shore. He liked the beach, but it got boring halfway through the summer. He dreamed about the damned seagulls, got tired of seeing people's flesh. He was bored, and when he was bored he squinted a lot; that made him take off his sunglasses to rub his eyes. He usually washed the sand off them twice a day in the water, dipping them gently into the surf and rubbing them against his bathing trunks. He was a careful person. He was careful to flush the toilet, for example. He thought about his roommate, and about eating pizza with Laura, the letter he should write home . . .

The lifeguard sighed. The beach was beginning to fill up. There was a middle-aged man who hung around his chair sometimes, saying, "Nothing ever happens, does it?" He called the lifeguard "kid." The lifeguard didn't like that, but he was undemonstrative." His previous girlfriend had left him because of that. When the lifeguard was a psychology major he had tried to figure out why he didn't show his emotions easily. He couldn't figure it out. It could have been for a million reasons. Everything in psychology can have a million answers. He switched majors.

The lifeguard had intended to have an introspective period during the summer—to get a case of beer and drink it and think all day to see what he came up with. His roommate was always figuring out his life, announcing that he was making a mistake about this or doing the wrong thing not to follow through with that. The roommate thought so much about himself that he forgot to feed his goldfish and it died. And of course he didn't flush the toilet. The lifeguard was pretty depressed. Introspection while he was depressed would probably not be valuable, so he would put it off. If he put it off for six weeks he would be back at Dartmouth, and he never had time to do anything but work then.

As he walked along the beach, the lifeguard passed a little boy with red hair who was sifting sand through a fish-shaped sifter. He was probably five or six, a cute little boy that the lifeguard thought about for a second, then forgot. Later, the lifeguard would remember him vividly, know more about him than he knew about his own son . . . if there was a son . . . but the lifeguard was busy trying to think positively. The little boy didn't enter into his thoughts.

The lifeguard climbed to the top of his chair.

*

On July the twenty-second, Toby and David Warner quarreled. He told her that she should not have allowed Penelope to go to the beach; she said that he was overly protective. Penelope's measles had been a slight case, and she had been completely well for two days. He said that Penelope had been weepy the night before; she said that was because he always hovered around her. Before the argument began, Toby had been sitting at the kitchen table, looking at the book of photographs. She had attempted to converse with him before they got into the argument; she talked about Diane Arbus's being influenced by the Chinese belief that people pass through boredom to fascination. It seemed to David that Toby was neither bored nor fascinated; she seemed to be in a fog. He had taken the clothes to the laundromat because it looked like Toby was going to smoke cigarettes and stare at the book all day. There had been several young men in the laundromat. They all looked like the lifeguard to him. Why was she interested in the lifeguard? Why would she be so blunt about it? What could he do about it? He had put too much detergent into one of the machines and it foamed over. The owner had given him a mop—pleasantly, considering the mess he had made. "If you was a hippie I'd feel differently," the owner had said. David had always been "a nice young man." Except for dodging the Army, which shocked his parents, he had never even let anyone down. Except Toby. He must have let her down. He folded the clothes crookedly, took some out of the dryer too soon.

"Would you like to go out for dinner?" David asked after the argument.

"Yes," she said. "That would be nice." Formal, forced pleasantness.

"Where did you get that book?" he asked.

"At the bookstore."

"What's your fascination with it?"

"You still want to fight, don't you?" she asked.

"I can't believe you let Penelope go to the beach."

"Andrew and Randy are with her. They'd bring her back if she felt sick."

"Randy's always playing with the Collins' kids. He'd never notice. What's his fascination with those little beasts?"

"Tom's a nice kid."

"The older one isn't."

"The older one's twelve. He has another set of friends."

"He got put out of the drugstore today. I was standing there reading a magazine while the clothes were drying, and he and some of his friends lit a pile of napkins on the counter."

"What happened?"

"The counter girl threw water on it and put it out. The manager put them all out of the store."

"I don't know. I can't forbid Randy to play with Tom because Tom's brother is screwed up."

"I didn't ask you to do that."

"Then what were you getting at?"

"I was just telling you what happened."

"You want to be argumentative," she said. "I told you that before."

David sighed—a very theatrical sigh—and walked out the kitchen door. He stumbled on the dump truck and twisted his ankle. He sat down and rubbed it, waiting for the bleeding to begin. It didn't bleed; it just hurt.

"Let's take a walk down to the beach," he called to Toby.

In a minute the kitchen door opened and she came out. No lover of the sun, she was quite pale. She was smoking. She had on a red T-shirt and cut-off jeans. She looked very maternal—not for any reason he could name. He was tempted to whine to her that he had hurt himself. Maybe that was what was wrong; the children were always complaining to her. He thought about asking how she felt about the children, but there were three of them. What was he going to do about it? He stepped on something and got a splinter in his foot.

"Stop and take it out," she said.

He sat in the sand on the side of the road, the tall grass tickling his arms, a dragonfly buzzing around him. He held out his foot to her and she removed the splinter. She had long fingernails. They were painted bright red, and because he only looked at what she was doing to his foot for a second, he thought that it was blood on his foot. He thought about how brave he was, back in the road walking on his bleeding foot, until he realized that the flash of red had been Toby's fingernail.

"We'll see that lifeguard any second," he said to her, squeezing her hand.

"You make beeg joke, hah? I love him . . ."

He suspected a literary allusion; it was either that or a line from some favorite movie of hers, and considering the kind of movies she liked, all hazy and European, he didn't really think it was a movie. An allusion to what? She read all the time—no way he could keep up with her. And such funny things stuck in her mind. He was always saying, "What's that from?"

The questions David and Toby would ask in the future would not have to do with how it was best to care for the children, or what book was being alluded to. All that would seem trivial, and they wouldn't do it. In fact, for a long period they would hardly communicate at all. They didn't know that, though. They expected to walk along the beach—pick up a few shells?—eat dinner, perhaps at the Cliff House, which all the natives said was very good, get their feet wet. They held hands, going up the path to the beach. He whistled softly. "When we leave here I'd like to get a puppy," Toby said. He was surprised—her idea just came out of the blue, like the rest of the events that day.

*

The tragedy was the fault of "the mad boy." The natives, slow-moving, quick-thinking people, understood the situation in the correct perspective. "The mad boy," Duncan Collins, twelve, took his brother Tom (the natives' eyes lit up for a second—you understand that the family named their son Tom Collins?) and two other children, Penelope and her twin Andrew, out in a boat he had made—he had been forbidden to go out in the boat by his father after an incident at the drugstore, but Duncan got it out of the garage without his father noticing that Duncan had even left his room, where he was being punished—and set fire to the boat. Duncan, Tom and Andrew died in the water. Penelope lived for a few minutes. The diver who was called to search the area (what for? There had been four children, and all were accounted for) brought a life jacket ashore. Duncan, who did not know how to swim, always wore a life jacket. What was he doing without it? Reasonably, the natives assumed that it was intentional. Suicide. Penelope was an excellent swimmer, but she was weak from a recent illness. Half her body was badly burned. Why didn't she get out of the boat before she got so badly burned? It was anybody's guess (the natives differed). Andrew was hardly burned at all, but the coroner said that he was the first to die. Tom died second. (Why did they compare the times of death? Just to have the facts? To have more to talk about?) The specifics of the incident were well-known, but nobody could really account for them. What did the other children think when Duncan Collins put a can of gasoline in the boat with them?

The lifeguard whistled for the boat to come in a little later than he should have, perhaps, but when he really started to go crazy at the police station later that night, they backed down about that. But to be honest—and the lifeguard always thought he was honest with himself—he should have whistled about two minutes before he did. He kept thinking for two minutes that the people in the boat would see that it was going out too far and come in. Two minutes, for Christ's sake—not too long to wait, expecting they'd see their error. He blew the whistle and thought he saw the boat edge in a little. He waited. Then the boat began to go out to sea quickly. He realized that the people were deliberately taunting him. The world was full of them—people who want the lifeguard to get wet. He blew the whistle and looked through his binoculars. They were kids! He felt very uneasy when he saw that, and he blew the whistle loudly, one long blow, scrambling down from the chair. He was untying the boat, so he did not see the exact moment the boat burst into flames. He did see a child jump overboard. He was totally confused when he saw the fire. But yes—one did jump overboard. The waves were very rough, and although he was an excellent rower, he had trouble getting up speed. Some man from the beach ran into the water just behind the rowboat—everyone else just stood there—and jumped in before the lifeguard could tell him to get lost. Later he was glad he had let the man in, because with each of them working an oar, the rowboat moved quickly. It was that man who pulled Penelope out of the water and rowed her to shore—almost pushed the lifeguard out of the boat, because of course someone had to get the others, and rowed into shore with Penelope. The man's name was Eugene Anderson. He was thirty-nine years old. He lived in Bangor, Maine. When Eugene Anderson disappeared with the boat, the lifeguard, in the icy water, swam around the fire. He saw no one inside the fire, which was by now dying out. He was extremely confused. He dived under about ten times . . . well, maybe fifteen . . . and heard a roar in the water that confused and frightened him more. Later, he realized that it was the sound of his heart. He found Andrew and Tom, and a diver who arrived, much to the lifeguard's surprise, from the main beach, got Duncan. Eugene Anderson and the diver tried to get Duncan to breathe on the beach, but he was dead. He was naked. His chest was charred. What in the hell was happening? the lifeguard kept thinking. He was exhausted from all the diving and couldn't do anything but support himself on one arm. He stared into the crowd. He was dizzy; it seemed like the people were standing at an odd angle. He reached toward them—he didn't know why he was doing it—and a woman rushed forward and grabbed his hand. She's breaking it, he thought, but couldn't do anything about it. By the time his breath started to come back, he saw that his leg was cut. He never figured out how he cut it—a cut about four inches long, down his shin. The police were there. The diver, when it was clear that Duncan was dead, picked up heaps of sand and threw them into the crowd, into the lifeguard's eyes, the policemen's eyes. The diver did not even act as well as the lifeguard, and the lifeguard was given Thorazine at the police station. They did something with the diver—took him somewhere. Eugene Anderson was a big help to the police. He was an accountant and a Boy Scout leader. The lifeguard kept interrupting his story, asking questions that he already knew the answers to. "That was a hell of a fire. But it went out so quickly, didn't it?" Eugene Anderson answered calmly. His bottom lip kept jerking, though. "They set it on fire deliberately. Boats don't just explode in the middle of the ocean," the lifeguard said to Eugene Anderson, and Eugene Anderson answered him as if it had been a question.

They were at the police station for a long time. There were reporters. Then they took them to the hospital. What for? They were all dead. The police didn't ask them to look at the bodies. They just drove them around. It was chaos. At ten o'clock the police called the lifeguard's house. His roommate answered. He went to the police station to pick up the lifeguard and drive him home.

*

David believed it was happening, but he thought it would turn out all right. He was usually negative in his thinking, and after that day he was more negative than ever, but at the time he kept thinking that it was going to turn out okay. He held Randy's hand. Toby held Randy's arm, and when David realized that they were pulling him, he let go . . . let her have him. He wanted to run up, be certain that they were his children, but stupidly he kept thinking *Randy is my child*, and he held onto Randy and didn't move. He fainted, and imagined, while he was passed out, that he was scrambling along the ground, a crab, an ant, moving very fast, whatever he was. He tried to figure out if he was being pursued, or if he was pursuing something, but it never came clear. When he regained consciousness he saw lines in the sand, made by his fingers, he supposed. He thought of his mother pouring the boiling water over the ants, then the long wait until the next pot boiled and she poured that. He counted: Penelope, Andrew.

Someone—it turned out to be a policeman—was slapping his face. It hurt to have sand slapped into your face. He saw the policeman as a shaky, pale figure, because he had just opened his eyes. The policeman, slapping him, had made his eyes open. Everything vibrated. He literally saw stars or spots of some kind, bright spots, interspersed with the sunset that glowed palely in the distance.

*

Toby was staring at the naked body of Duncan Collins, and the young boy's body was beautiful, smooth and golden. She was transfixed by him, stretched in the sand, his back gleaming wet. Then she saw the lifeguard—she blocked out the pile of bodies, the actual heap of them, looking only long enough to think that they were like a picture in *Life* of a Nazi concentration camp, thinking that this was some such remote tragedy, they were not her children. She did move forward, but it was to take the lifeguard's hand. She closed her eyes and pressed his hand hard, imagined that they were holding each other, that the breeze blowing through her hair made her beautiful, that the lifeguard was pressing her hand, that the pressure she felt was the lifeguard . . . she opened her eyes and saw, giddily, that it *was* the lifeguard. She was conscious of her breathing. It was hard because she was exerting so much energy squeezing the lifeguard's hand, but she didn't realize it and thought she was breathing shallowly, that she wasn't getting enough air. Air, breeze, the cool sand. The erotic fantasy she was having about the lifeguard lasted about two minutes, but she remembered them so vividly. The rest was a blur and stayed a blur, but the sedatives that she would later take, the psychiatrist, none of it shook those minutes out of her head. They were more real than anything, and they stayed that way.

*

In his senior year at Dartmouth, the lifeguard broke up with Laura and got back together with his old girlfriend, Michelle. She said that he seemed more . . . human. She came every weekend from Manchester, where she worked, and stayed with him in his apartment. He got drunk and introspected once or twice a week instead of once a year. She didn't drink, or at least she didn't get drunk, but she didn't say anything about his drinking, and she listened to him tell the story of what happened on the twenty-second of July over and over and over. She gave him a Mickey Mouse night light, and Mickey glowed and smiled through the night. He drank tequila and orange juice. Tequila. Mexico. Maybe he should get out of New Hampshire, go to . . . Mexico. What for? What's in Mexico? Sometimes he felt panicky, as though he had to get away. Michelle talked about her work at the clinic. They were sick people, physically sick. As opposed to me, he thought, they are sick. That made him feel hopeful.

It took him longer than it had in the past to do the mathematics problems, because he found himself tracing over numbers. His eights were one black circle on top of another. Michelle told him not to drink so much, and he gave it up, quit entirely. Some people couldn't give up alcohol that way, but he gave it up and wouldn't go back to it. He told Michelle these things earnestly, the way a convict would talk to the parole board. He thought of himself as a convict. The police station had scared him to death.

In the spring, Michelle picked flowers and put them in a vase on the dresser. They opened the window and slept with the fresh air, two blankets over them and a quilt, wanting to hurry the spring into summer. The Warners, although he was no longer in touch with them, were also anxious for the summer. When it was June and Randy was out of school, they were going to Europe. The lifeguard had no plans for the summer. He wondered what would happen between Michelle and him. Mickey Mouse glowed and smiled.

David and Toby Warner usually stayed awake for some time after they went to bed. There was no night light in their room. They preferred the uninterrupted darkness. They stared into it. Randy Warner, who had just celebrated his seventh birthday, slept easily. He took his dump truck to bed with him. Toby hated to see the thing, hated to see anything she associated with the previous summer, but she was very solicitous of Randy, and she didn't say anything. Sometimes when David was asleep and Toby was not, she would look at his blank face and know that he was dreaming sunsets. She half hated him for it and half admired him. David usually studied Toby in the early morning, when she slept deeply. It was the lifeguard, he knew, but the lifeguard wasn't a threat to him any more—he only felt slightly dismayed. In June, when they left for Europe, Randy did not take his dump truck along. He took, instead, a Captain Magic slate. He liked to write on it and draw pictures, then zip up the top part and watch it all disappear.

ABOUT THE AUTHOR

Ann Beattie lives in Charlottesville, Virginia with her husband, the painter Lincoln Perry.

Printed in the United States
by Baker & Taylor Publisher Services